Contents

12

Great Classics of
SCIENCE FICTION

edited by Groff Conklin

A FAWCETT GOLD MEDAL BOOK

Fawcett Publications, Inc., Greenwich, Conn.
Member of American Book Publishers Council, Inc.

George Sumner Albee, THE TOP. Copyright 1953 by Story Magazine. Reprinted by permission of the author and Whit Burnett from **The Magazine of Fantasy and Science Fiction**, August, 1962.

Poul Anderson, MY OBJECT ALL SUBLIME. Copyright © 1961 by Galaxy Publishing Corporation. Reprinted by permission of Scott Meredith, Inc., from **Galaxy**, June, 1961.

J. F. Bone, ON THE FOURTH PLANET. Copyright © 1963 by Galaxy Publishing Corporation. Reprinted by permission of the author and Harry Altshuler, Authors' Agent, from **Galaxy**, April, 1963.

Fredric Brown, EARTHMEN BEARING GIFTS. Copyright © 1960 by Galaxy Publishing Corporation. Reprinted by permission of Scott Meredith, Inc., from **Galaxy**, June, 1960.

Algis Budrys, DUE PROCESS. Copyright © 1960 by Street and Smith Publications, Inc. Reprinted by permission of Russell and Volkening, Inc., from **Astounding Science Fiction**, December, 1960.

A. Bertram Chandler, THE CAGE. Copyright © 1957 by Mercury Press, Inc. Reprinted by permission of Scott Meredith, Inc., from **The Magazine of Fantasy and Science Fiction**, June, 1957.

Zenna Henderson, THINGS. Copyright © 1960 by Mercury Press. Reprinted by permission of Willis Kingsley Wing from **The Magazine of Fantasy and Science Fiction**, July, 1960.

J. T. McIntosh, IMMORTALITY . . . FOR SOME. Copyright © 1960 by Street and Smith Publications, Inc. Reprinted by permission of James Macgregor from **Astounding Science Fiction**, March, 1960.

Robert Sheckley, HUMAN MAN'S BURDEN. Copyright © 1956 by Galaxy Publishing Corporation; copyright © 1957 by Bantam Books, Inc. Reprinted by permission of the author from **Galaxy**, September, 1956.

Cordwainer Smith, BALLAD OF LOST C'MELL. Copyright © 1962 by Galaxy Publishing Corporation. Reprinted by permission of Harry Altshuler from **Galaxy**, October, 1962.

William W. Stuart, STAR-CROSSED LOVER. Copyright © 1962 by Galaxy Publishing Corporation. Reprinted by permission of the author from **Galaxy**, April, 1962.

Robert F. Young, THIRTY DAYS HAD SEPTEMBER. Copyright © 1957 by Mercury Press. Reprinted by permission of the author and Theron Raines from **The Magazine of Fantasy and Science Fiction**, October, 1957.

Introduction

At the time of writing this introduction (early in October, 1963), there is a new flare-up in the perennial controversy concerning the place of scientists in modern society. The well-known British scientist-novelist Sir Charles P. Snow (better known to American readers as "C. P. Snow," I suppose) was under attack from various Deep Thinkers for his belief that scientists—because of their training, their knowledge of our increasingly technological world, and their belief in adherence to facts rather than in appeals to emotion or self-interest—should play a more important part in the political, economic, and social affairs of the world.

Even though several of the stories in this volume discuss the problems of ethics and social responsibility in the lives of human beings (and of non-humans as well), they do so in almost-dream terms. These are the terms of tomorrows, distant or otherwise, the terms of "Just suppose!" The purpose of the present collection is to give you several hours' escape from the persistent frustrations, irrelevancies, and irritations of your own daily life and general human folly.

Of course, if it happens to enlighten you about some of the problems facing you and the world at large, it will do so mainly by indirection. Many of these stories make their points by means of vivid, exciting, imaginative extrapolations: which means, to quote in part a dictionary definition of the word, "extending the variables" of today's scientific, technological, and social problems "beyond their established ranges." And therein lies much of the pleasure to be found in this book.

Like all good science fiction anthologies, the present one ranges the cosmos in both space and time. In time it operates in at least three different ways: First, in one tale it takes a grim look ahead at times yet to come, as reported by a citizen from that future era who has "time-traveled" back to contemporary Evanston, Illinois. Second, in several stories it thrusts us forward into some of those future times, and gives us first-hand views of the often rather gruesome results of the extrapolation of certain tendencies in our own society. And third, in a most individual sort of way, one story presents an almost frightening view of what too much time can mean to someone who has achieved quasi-immortality. Perhaps the Biblical span —three-score-and-ten—is just about the proper length of life for people!

In space, the tales in this book cover everything from life with some robots on a nearby asteroid, to a couple of stories about far-distant worlds where human voyagers find various unpredictable and not always desirable life forms. Thus it always was, in science fiction, and thus it always shall be— until mankind actually gets there and finds out whether such "Things" and events can be or not.

Finally, we explore some amusing—and some not-so-amusing—ideas about our own world in its multitudinously possible tomorrows. I have already mentioned this type of story under the rubric of "time tales"—but several of those included are deserving of a separate heading, since they are so fascinatingly real as not to partake of the notion of displacement in time at all. These range from the extraordinary description of the genetic invention of "underpeople" as servants of man—in one of the most imaginative science fiction stories I have ever read—to a couple of rapier-sharp satires on our own bureaucratic-technological society, as it might develop if left to the inexorable forward march of our advertising agencies and our monster industrial organizations.

Now twelve stories cannot, of course, hope to begin to ring all the changes on the myriad themes of science fiction. Those "changes" seem to me to be almost infinite, so varied does the output of writers in the field continue to be. On the other hand, I hope you will agree that the dozen selections have pretty well surveyed the high spots of the science fiction topography. And, as a matter of fact, some of the tales actually do touch on the fringes of the scientist-nonscientist controversy currently raging around C. P. Snow, et al. However, they do so in a fashion far removed from current realities. Even at their most bitterly satiric, they are true and fascinating extrapolations— science fiction at its best. But let it be added that whatever else they may be, in terms of satire, prophecy, or sheer storytelling, none of them truly is *scientific,* as we understand the term. All are *fictional.*

In any event, there is hardly a story in this collection of

vivid imaginings that will not make you think. If this is an unaccustomed exercise for you, well and good; now is the time to begin. But if you think you think already, fine!—here are several items which will give you some practice. As you read, you may have to engage in more than a bit of consideration of the state of our world as it is now and as it may become if we don't "do something about it." What that something should be, I have not the faintest idea. All I am interested in as I offer you these science fiction dreams is that you should (a) thoroughly enjoy reading them and (b) realize that science fiction is not just Adventure—that is, not just Space Opera, or Bug-Eyed Monsters and pretty girls, or Alien Invaders from Outer Space, or Weird Worlds or Tomorrows. In addition to all those things, which it can and does deal with, science fiction also is instinct with ideas, with imaginative questionings about the human condition as we find it in our own lives, the lives of those around us—and in the world at large.

So enjoy yourself—but keep your mind working while you do!

GROFF CONKLIN

Due Process

by Algis Budrys

FRANK HERTZOG of International Tours, Incorporated, scratched himself behind one disproportionately large ear and lifted one shaggy eyebrow. He sat turned sideways to his desk, with his feet up on an extended drawer. His visitor sat stiffly in a chair placed at the opposite corner of the desk, so that Hertzog's glance shot diagonally toward his visitor and, at his convenience, over the visitor's shoulder at the ocean horizon far away and far below.

Hertzog nibbled jerkily at his upper lip. "Now, let me just get this clear in my own mind," he said to the prim little man in the other chair. "You want cash in advance?"

"No later than July 14th midnight," the prim man affirmed. "It's very important that the money should have reached our office in Basle by that time." The little man sat with his thighs and knees pressed together, his back upright and his arms at his sides, with his hands clasped in his lap. He wore a black suit and a white shirt with a black string tie. He had a pale, boney face, and gray-black hair which had been clipped close at the sides and brushed flat on the top of his head with a white part straight down the middle. Motionless beads of perspiration covered his forehead.

"And as soon as the money is in your office, you'll have our order loaded on the first tube train out."

"That is correct," the prim little man said. He was a liquor salesman. "I must remind you that today is July 1st."

"Well, now," Frank Hertzog complained, "that seems like an awfully funny way to do business, all of a sudden. We've been good customers of yours for years. No ITI cruise ship serves anything but your brands."

"Naturally," the little salesman said. "Our brands are the best in the world."

9

"So's ITT's credit rating. I don't understand this, Mr. Keller, I really don't. The account's been settled every month. It almost sounds as if you don't want our business. There *are* other wholesalers in this world, you know."

Mr. Keller gestured nervously. "Please, Mr. Hertzog. None of our competitors are organized to give you service equal to ours."

"Up to now they haven't been, you mean. But you're forcing me to wonder whether a little less service and a great deal more courtesy wouldn't be worth it."

"Mr. Hertzog, I—" The little salesman suddenly leaned forward urgently. "It may cost me my job to speak frankly to you, Mr. Hertzog. You understand."

Hertzog leaned back and looked narrowly at Keller. "I'm not sure I do, Mr. Keller. You and my company have been dealing with each other for some time. In cases where a salesman has been handling the same account for years, it becomes a moot point whether he represents his employer or his account. A tacit arrangement of mutual advantage between salesman and account gradually evolves into being. This is a fact as old as salesmanship. I'm a little bit surprised at your reluctance to comply with business ethics, Mr. Keller. I really am. I wish you would say whatever is on your mind. I can't say I care for your implication that anything you tell me in confidence might pass beyond this room."

Keller's pale lips trembled at their corners. "Mr. Hertzog, you put me in a difficult position. You're clearly in the right, and yet—"

"If I'm in the right, Mr. Keller, then let's have it. What's going on?"

The little man sighed. "Very well, Mr. Hertzog." His voice fell, and he leaned forward to compensate for it, his eyes unconsciously darting about the room before he went on. "You know there's been a change in the top management of my company? What has occurred is that the new directors are much more favorably inclined toward Capetown than toward Atlantis."

"That's ridiculous!" Hertzog snapped. "Atlantis is the logical port facility for Europe. It's true that transshipping goods into the tube train terminal here and running them through the tunnel under the Bay of Biscay and the contaminated coastline does add an expense. But shipping overland across Africa from Capetown is even more costly."

Keller spread his hand placatingly. "Please, Mr. Hertzog. You know this, and I know this. In time, even my directors will know this. But at the moment they have been beguiled by this new notion of zeppelin freighters. They have been shown plans for lighter-than-air craft with cargo capacities comparable to those of a steamship, and they have attended test flight demonstrations. They are impressed by the majesty of these huge constructions—you understand, Mr. Hertzog, they are like children. They will grow up, but meanwhile—" Keller shook his head.

"Let them try zeppelin lighterage from Capetown to Europe across the African interior. One or two line squalls will grow 'em up fast. Insurance rates are a great urge toward maturity," Hertzog growled.

"Exactly. Exactly," Keller agreed. "But in the meantime they are convinced that Capetown will become the great cosmopolitan center of the Eastern Hemisphere, and that Atlantis will wither, out here on the ocean with nothing to sustain it. So they have instituted strict new policies. Please, Mr. Hertzog—one or two demonstrations of prompt, ready cash payment on your part, and they will think again. I realize it is an imposition on your self-esteem, but a truly great man can afford to be above such things." His voice became a conspiratorial whisper. "After all, Mr. Hertzog, once the Capetown bubble has burst, you'll be in a position to demand unheard-of discounts—"

"Yes," Hertzog said. "Yes, I see." He stood up and strolled aimlessly about the office, his hands clasped behind his back. He stared out through the window without focusing his eyes, and wrinkled his nose, eventually coming to a halt beside the settee where Keller had left his brief case. "All right, Mr. Keller, I'll have a bonded messenger at your Basle office by July 14th midnight," he said. He fumbled with the handle of Keller's brief case, swinging his hand absently backward and forward. Keller took it from him with a touch of asperity.

"Thank you very much, Mr. Hertzog. I was sure you would understand the situation."

"Yes," Hertzog said vaguely. "Yes," he repeated, watching the salesman leave.

Hertzog pressed Hoke Bannister's call stud on his desk, then walked back to the glass wall of his office and looked out. The stacked tiers of Atlantis rose up out of the ocean all

around him, the water swelling around the massive concrete
pilings on which they rested. It was a stormy day. The water
was green and white under a gray sky, and rain swept in an
exhilarating sheet across the invisible glass. Inside a two-
mile perimeter, the water was calm. At the perimeter, where
sonic turbulence broke up the wave action, leaping towers
of foam clashed together and surrounded Atlantis in a ram-
part of froth. Frank Hertzog was smiling fondly through the
glass when Hoke Bannister let himself in.

"Yeah?" he said, rummaging through the liquor cabinet.
He was an ugly, wide man who had recently acquired the
habit of five-dollar Havana cigars. His mouth was broad
enough so that he could keep one between his teeth at nearly
all times and still talk and drink.

"What would you do for thirty thousand dollars, Hoke?"
Hertzog asked him, returning to his desk.

"Thirty thousand dollars? You mean, what kind of rules
would I break? Few. Thirty thousand dollars keep a man
comfortable all his life, if he plays it careful, but no kicks,
you know? You don't take chances with that little bit of
capital."

"What would you do for the standard salesman's commission on a thirty-thousand-dollar order?"

"You mean Keller?" Bannister finished putting his drink
together and closed up the cabinet. "I was right, sending
him up here, yeah?"

"Yeah," Hertzog said, looking down at the buttons on his
desk. "Yeah."

Bannister took a gulp of his drink. He stared at it, snatched
open the liquor cabinet, and held up the crystal whisky de-
canter he'd used. "What in blazes have you fed me?" he
choked.

Hertzog looked up. "I wanted you to try some of that.
There's a local chemical outfit that's been trying to make
scotch out of plankton."

"Frank, don't turn Keller's outfit loose yet," Bannister
said.

"No," Hertzog said, "no, I'm not going to." He pushed a
button. "Paulette," he said. "Got that stuff for me?"

"Yes, Frank. Coming up." A slot clicked back on Hertzog's
desk, and a clipped sheaf of photostats slid up to fall flat on
the desk. "I've put what I think is the relevant copy on
top," Paulette's efficient voice said out of the air. Hertzog

frowned down at the photostats. "Yes. I see you have.
Thank you. And get hold of Thad Traven, will you, in the
City Council building? That's right—he's the clerk. Make me a
cocktail date for this afternoon. One of those plush and
ebony places in Pleasure House ought to be just right, I
think."

Thad Traven was thin and dark, with a mouth that over
the years had been compressed within its original dimensions, so that after his lips folded under out of sight there
was still a slit in his jaw for a half inch on either side.

"I can tell you're a steady man, Thad," Frank Hertzog said
to him. "A planner. A man who weighs all the possibilities
before he moves."

"No one's ever caught me looking foolish," Traven agreed.
He sipped his sherry Martini and let his glance run over the
faded tattoo of a mermaid on Hertzog's bare forearm.

"Yeah, well, I'm just a sort of Johnny-come-lately, you
might say," Hertzog said apologetically. "When you come
right down to it, all I am is a seaman roustabout whose father
happened to leave him a travel agency. Oh," he said, cutting
off any protest by Traven, "I've been lucky and managed to
build up the business, and all that. Got a few dollars in my
pocket. You know. But I'm really just a guy who hasn't got
the sense not to whack off on foolish chances. Every once in a
long while, a gamble like that will pay off for somebody.
I've been lucky, like I say. When I need to know something
—I mean, when it's something that takes a sophisticated man
with a trained mind, why, I've got to come to a man like
yourself for help."

Traven smiled. "You're more flattering than I perhaps deserve."

"No, no, I mean it, Thad. For instance, a man like me,
that runs a travel agency, is naturally interested in other
places in the world besides Atlantis. Sometimes it seems to
me that it wouldn't be a bad idea to develop some interests
in Europe or Africa—Sevastopol, say, or Capetown. I mean,
besides opening branch offices. Take a real hand in local business. But if I had just gone ahead and done that, I would have
found myself in real trouble with the civic government, here,
because I didn't understand it was better to keep our hands off
the Mainland. Whereas, if I'd come to you, I'm sure you would
have been glad to explain it to me."

"Of course, Frank. The prime tenet of the Conservative Party is that, here in our isolation from the Mainland, we are in an ideal position to avoid their difficulties. As long as our only real link to them is the freight tube, we stand in the position of acting as their clearing house. If we actively participate in their affairs, then we may well become embroiled in their attempts to deal with the results of the devastation. As long as we remain aloof, we are in the position of collecting our handling charges and letting it go at that. Involvement with the Mainland may easily entail added responsibilities for which we have no desire."

"Now," Hertzog explained eagerly, "I can see that, once it's been explained to me. Before, I thought that, inasmuch as we're descended from people who pushed the tube through from the Mainland and built this place, we were still somehow bound to those countries."

Traven smiled. "It's been a hundred years, Frank. None of the original sponsoring governments are still in existence. There is no legal basis for any such notion."

"No, I can see that, now, listening to you. But I needed to have it clarified."

Traven took a meditative sip of his drink. "Well, now," he said deprecatingly, "you didn't do so badly in that affair with William Waring. If he had been permitted to organize his investment syndicate, the weight of that much capitalization would have swung the civic elections to a slate of candidates pledged toward intervention in mainland affairs. You saved a great deal for many people in addition to yourself, there."

"Oh, well, he was all mixed up with a try at defrauding ITI of twenty thousand dollars. That's a lot of money. I was pretty surprised when I knocked him over and found out there was more to it than that. Just some more luck, Thad. But, you know, that was what got me thinking."

"Oh?"

"Yes, well I've been thinking that there Waring was setting up this business, which could have broken me, and I didn't have the faintest idea of it. If I'd had somebody who could tell me what was going on in civic politics, I wouldn't have been in the dark." He finished his drink and pointed to Traven's glass. "Have another?"

"Why, yes, thank you," Traven said carefully.

Hertzog signaled to the watchful waiter, and went on. "The elections run off next week, don't they?"

"As a matter of fact, they do—the first Tuesday after the Fourth of July. But they'll be pretty much a formality, this year. All the Mainland Interventionists withdrew after Waring was exposed. Not all of them were his candidates, of course, but even the legitimate ones were tarred with his brush."

"Uh-huh. Let's see, now . . . I'm not up to this stuff, like I said . . . you're on the Conservative ticket this year as usual, aren't you?"

Traven's lips closed entirely. "Yes, I am. I'll be the candidate for City Clerk, as usual."

"Excuse me, Thad, but that's not too far up the totem pole, is it?"

"No, it isn't," Traven said shortly.

"It seems a shame. I don't know Mayor Phillips to speak to, but it doesn't seem to me he's such an all-around hotshot."

"He is at party politicking," Traven said bitterly. "The rest of us have to settle for what's doled out to us."

"Hm-m-m. Seems like a funny way to run things. Doesn't seem fair to me."

"It isn't. But what can you expect? Atlantis is populated by people who don't have to work very hard for their money, or even think too deeply about anything. Hardly twenty per cent of them even bother to vote, and most of those are brought in by Phillips' organization. Of course, I can hardly complain about that. But, still—"

"Seems to me you *can* complain. If you don't go along with Phillips, you haven't got a chance—as long as the vote stays low."

"But who has the resources to set up a rival organization? It takes money—money for air time, money for advertising, for posters, for rallies. Who has that sort of money?"

"Well, now," Hertzog said, twisting his glass lazily in his fingers and looking at it thoughtfully.

"Good Heavens, Frank! You don't know what you're saying! And in any case, it's too late this year—"

"For a write-in candidate?"

"Write-in? No— But the campaigning, man! There's barely a week left!"

"Well, you know, Thad, ITI owns the water taxis, one of the helicopter services, and four of the hotels. We buy half the air time. We take a standard full page ad in all three newspapers every day. On TV, we've got the Sonny Weams show, 'Cactus and Hashknife Al,' 'Are You Smarter Than Your Wife?' and the Williamton Sandberg Mills news-in-depth program. How would it be if you campaigned for mayor on something like, say, the Progressive Reform ticket, with a big get-out-the-vote push and posters staring everybody in the face every time he got into a boat or hailed a 'copter? Think you could stir out, say, forty, forty-five per cent of the vote?"

Traven was pale. "Great Heavens, Frank, that's not legal! A corporation can't throw its treasury behind a candidate like that. And what would your Board of Directors say?"

"Comes to that, Thad, I'm the Board of Directors."

"But still you can't—"

"Not even if I run for dogcatcher in agate type at the bottom of each ad? I want to be dogcatcher, Thad. I have a burning passion to become dogcatcher. I'm going to campaign like crazy. But I need somebody to head the ticket. How's about it?"

"Frank, I . . . do you mean this?"

Hertzog dipped two fingers into the breast pocket of his sport shirt, took out two crumpled five-dollar bills and a slip of paper. He opened the paper and dropped it on the tablecloth in front of Traven. It was a certified ITI check for two hundred thousand dollars, made out to the Progressive Reform Party Campaign Fund.

"Of course," Hertzog said, "we're going to need a campaign issue. How about this? Phillips and the Conservative Party are alienating business interests on the Mainland which are getting annoyed at our aloofness—and our handling charges. We're losing business. Show 'em the figures—we're handling all the perishables, but the hard goods are being shipped by slow freight into Archangelsk and railroaded overland down to the Black Sea. And someday they'll put a north-south railroad across Africa. Yes, through the jungle, if we press 'em enough. Guarantee the populace a shorter work day and lower real estate taxes, if negotiations show we can increase our yearly gross by shading the handling charges a fraction."

Traven hesitated thoughtfully. "I'm not sure that jibes with my earlier public pronouncements."

"Yours? Mayor Phillips', you mean. You're coming out

in the open, now. Swinging with both fists. Blowing the lid
off. You're not one of Waring's gangsters—you're a respectable ex-Conservative who's had enough."

"Hm-m-m. Hm-m-m." Traven smiled broadly. "I believe I
can do it. Yes, it might be just the right kind of ammunition."

"Yes, it might. Well, Thad, you're the experienced man, so
I'll leave it to you to set up the campaign headquarters and
hire the public relations people. I'm sending a young fellow
from my office—Bannister's his name—to just lend a strong
back and maintain a liaison with the ITI treasury, in case you
run short—but I'll keep my fumble fingers out of this. Good
luck."

Traven picked up the check, studied it fascinatedly for a
moment, and put it in his billfold. "Er . . . thank you, Frank."

"Think nothing of it, Thad," Hertzog said, standing up.
He left the two five dollar bills on the table and motioned to
the waiter. "I'll see you at the polls," he said to Traven.

"Ah . . . Frank . . . suppose Phillips challenges me on my
assertions?"

"Well, if it worries you, they're perfectly safe. Matter of
public record. Study the Standard & Poore and the Dun &
Bradstreet reports for the last thirty years. It's all in there."
He waved a hand in farewell and left the cocktail lounge.

Frank Hertzog lived in a blister apartment, two rooms
anchored to the side of one of the ITI building's pylons,
four hundred feet below sea level. It was quiet down there,
and hard to get to. He stood in his kitchenette, carefully heating a pan of cocoa until it was just warmed. He poured
the cocoa into a stone mug with half an inch of scotch in
its bottom and went out into his living room, biting the
corner out of a bacon, lettuce, and tomato sandwich spread
with mustard. "How'd it go today?" he said to Hoke Bannister, who was standing in the middle of the rug and trying
his hand with the dart board.

"Well, ol' Thad Traven's got the Conservatives in a fit,
and the city in an uproar. Can't turn around without being
hit by a Traven ad. Sonny Weanis is telling jokes on Phillips,
'Are You Smarter Than Your Wife?' is full of questions
about freight tonnages, and Hashknife Al is racing Cactus in
the Dakota land rush."

"The Dakota land rush!" Hertzog shook his head. "Those
were the days, Hoke! When a man wanted to travel some-

where, he climbed on his trusty old paint and hunkered off into the sunset. That reminds me—sign this, will you?" He pulled a wrinkled sheaf of paper out of his hip pocket and handed it over.

"What is it?" Bannister asked.

"A messenger bond. An officer of the company has to sign it."

"Why can't you?"

"I'm the messenger. I'm leaving for Basle in twenty minutes with thirty thousand dollars. It's a little before Keller's deadline, but I imagine they won't mind getting it a few days ahead of time."

Bannister scrawled his name in the space indicated and put the bond away. "Got a plane waiting?"

"No. You don't get any sensation of travel, going that fast. I've got a few hours' time. I'm going to take the tube."

"Don't forget to come back before the polls close tomorrow. Every vote counts, you know."

"Yes. *What* am I running for?"

"District assemblyman. That's almost as good as dog-catcher."

"I was afraid of that." He picked up his overnight bag and pushed the buzzer for the pylon elevator, which hissed to a stop and appeared behind a sliding door in the living room wall. "Mind the store," he said.

"Woof," Bannister answered.

The tube terminal was a hundred yards square and a hundred feet high, with two circular doors, massive, twenty yards in diameter, dripping with condensation across their bolt-studded faces, side by side like a pair of shut eyes in the far wall. Two railed cradles rested on girdered feet, extending the tubes' profile into the vault, and threw their complex shadows upon the worn concrete flooring, where the maintenance crew swarmed. There was a passenger platform built out from the wall, its forward edge curved in and under to fit flush against the nearside cradle. Hertzog waited patiently, along with a small group of other people carrying suitcases.

In the cradle, the train was being made up. It consisted of three cars, two of them freight capsules and the third with a skimpy passenger compartment at one end, and at the moment all the freight holds were open, clamshell doors ajar like rudimentary wings held aloft down the train's length.

Loading cranes dropped down from the roof, lowering pre-packaged bundles of freight into calculated spaces in the holds, so that the interior of the train gradually built up into a solid mass much like one of those key-chain puzzles in which odd-shaped pieces of plastic interlock to form pistols, airplanes, and other charms. Shaped like a chrysalis jointed at two points, the train lay waiting to slide into the air lock, blind except for the three grimy portholes of the passenger compartment. The chamber echoed to every dropped tool and every scramble of a maintenance man's shoes up or down the cradle's latticework. The crane cables whined through their sheaves, and the stevedores bellowed at each other over the racket.

Each of the cranes seemed to bring down its last load at the same moment. A siren wound its way up to maximum audible pitch, and the clamshell doors first banged themselves shut and then pulled their retracting arms in after them. The passenger door spat open, and Hertzog boarded with his fellow passengers. As soon as the last of them was inside, the door thudded home. They found seats and the train started without preamble, inching laboriously through the raised air lock hatch.

The hatch closed behind them, and they waited in darkness. The pumps evacuated the lock, and then the tubeway door dilated, the sound of metal scraping over metal transmitted through the train with uncompromising clarity.

"A couple of bucks a week extra for oil wouldn't do the city any harm," Hertzog muttered to himself. The warning hooter made him drop his feet into the stirrups. The train slid forward, seemed to find its footing and shot ahead, motors singing, building up acceleration with considerable speed as it dropped down the initial incline, then, when it hit the long level stretch, settling down to a steady two hundred miles per hour, down the evacuated tube under the sea, toward the long, bleak, deadly coastal plain over which the tube ran within its massive concrete shield, toward the mountains which were the western frontier of life in Europe.

The line was single-tracked except where it paired at the terminals. And just before the tube broke the surface at the shore of France, there was a siding into which Hertzog's train was switched while an outbound train rumbled by. Hertzog peered curiously out through the portholes at the emergency platform along the siding. There were, supposedly, elaborate automatic provisions for shunting off trains with internal malfunctions and holding them here, just as there were safety blocks which kept two trains from meeting head-on in the tube proper. They seemed to work—either because everything was so efficiently designed or because there was a high *esprit de corps* among the air-suited trackwalkers who maintained the right of way.

Here on the shunt track, idling beside the wall of the main tube, the train was once more in an air lock, so that the passengers could, if need be, escape from a disaster to the dubious shelter of a substation which did not communicate with the surface. Hertzog got out of his chair and pulled the switch on the compartment door. It hissed back with an explosion of compressed air, opening on a bleak concrete platform with rust stains washed over its surface and grime everywhere.

"Please," a recorded voice said over the train's automatic public address system, "Do not exit except in genuine emergency. Please close the door."

Hertzog shrugged and reclosed the door. He went back to his seat. "Just wondered if it could be done," he said innocently to no one in particular.

Balse was disquieting for Frank Hertzog. For one thing, the buildings straggled every which way up hill and down dale. For another, everybody wore drab, soberly cut clothing. "Look like a bunch of bankers," Hertzog muttered to himself, getting on an elevator in the liquor distributor's office building.

"I beg your pardon, sir?" the elevator operator said unctuously, with a repressed sniff for Hertzog's clothing.

"Fourteen, Charlie," Hertzog said.

"Yes, sir."

"You in somebody's army, Charlie?"

"I beg your pardon?"

"You forgot to say 'Sir.' "

"Sorry, sir."

"Horsefeathers!"

"I beg—"

"Stop it, Charlie. I couldn't stand it. Why don't you come on out to Atlantis and get yourself a decent job?"

"Atlantis, sir?"

There was no mistaking the connotation in the operator's voice.

"Y'know, we only eat babies on ritual occasions, any more. Most of us have lost our taste for 'em entirely, and have to sort of force ourselves. Personally, for instance, I don't think they're any good at all, boiled, the way they serve 'em. Roast, now, that's a different story, but you hardly ever get 'em that way, any m—"

"Fourteen, sir," the opertor said stiffly.

"Thank you, Charlie," Hertzog said, and stepped out facing the hall door of the liquor house. "Don't take any wooden propaganda, now."

The president of the liquor wholesalers was a man named Mott, with a receding chin and prominent teeth. "Mr. Hertzog," he said, fluttering his hands, "I don't know what to say."

"Well, then, say it," Hertzog drawled, leaning back in his chair.

"Ah . . . it's not usual for the customer's Chairman of the Board to personally deliver so much cash."

"Ahead of time," Hertzog added.

"Ah . . . yes. Now, well, frankly, Mr. Hertzog, I don't know—"

"Weren't you expecting it?"

"Expecting it? Oh, yes, yes, we certainly were, but not until—"

"You can't ship until the 15th, even with the cash on hand today, is that it?"

"Well, yes," Mott said gratefully. "I'm gratified that you understand."

"Yes," Hertzog said. "So am I. We could have gone around in circles forever, couldn't we?" He stood up and shook Mott's hand. "Have to be pushing along now. Pleasure to've met you. Mott." He strolled out, caught a taxi to the tube terminal, and went home, whistling a song which began with: "If all little girls were like Mercedes Benzes—"

It was well over a week, now, since he had been elected assemblyman for his district, and Frank Hertzog had gotten accustomed to the idea. It was nine o'clock on the night of July 14th, and he was riding down the pylon elevator with Hoke Bannister.

"So it's pretty well settled down all around," he said. "With a new administration in Atlantis, the Mainland governments

are holding off on any ideas they might have had about em-
bargoing freight through the tube. There are three American
shippers who are going to route their hard goods through
here, and if that works out as well as it ought to, there'll be
more. The transatlantic airfreighters don't care one way or
the other, so long as we don't try to build a fleet of cargo
airplanes of our own, and why should we? Our forte's
quality not luxury."

"So Atlantis hasn't got a competitor left in the world, that
it can't stand off on a fair basis, right?" Bannister said.

"Well . . . yeah," Hertzog said.

"Here's your place."

"Let's keep going on down. I want to drop in on the terminal for a minute."

"Suit yourself."

"Uh-huh. Well, anyway, it looks like Atlantis isn't going
to go bust for some time. That's nice. I plan to stay in this
town. The Mainland's all right to visit, but I wouldn't want
to live there. They take money too seriously over there. You
wouldn't believe how greedy they can get, sometimes—they'd
rather risk losing out on something really good than let
thirty thousand bucks go by."

"Yeah?"

"Uh-huh." The elevator sighed open at the terminal level.
Hertzog strolled casually toward a train that was making
up. "But I don't want you thinking every Mainlander's a
penny-snatcher with no real drive. Take those boys with their
zeppelin line from Capetown. That took a little something to
dream up. Their rates could come to within shouting distance of the tube. And what if there wasn't any tube . . . ah,
there, Mr. Keller!" he sang out, slapping the liquor salesman
on the shoulder.

The prim little man threw a startled glance backward. "Mr.
Hertzog!" he gasped. "Are you taking this train?"

"Thinking of it."

"Oh."

"Nothing like a trip abroad to widen the range of a man's
interests, I always say," Hertzog murmured, ushering Keller
and Bannister aboard the train. He guided the little man to a
seat, pressed him gently down into it, and fastened his seat
belt for him, talking all the while. "Actually, I'm much more
impressed with tube travel than I am by aircraft. You can
pretty much see what's going on, from an airplane or, say, a

zeppelin, but a tube train's different. Here are all these myste-
rious rushing noises, and machinery and things, going on all
around you in the dark, and all you can do is sit there and
trust to it that everybody's done their job right and nothing's
going to go wrong. That's the kind of thing that really puts a
strain on your credentials as a Twenty-first Century man—
the implicit faith in mechanisms you yourself don't control.
Isn't that so, Mr. Keller? Sit down, Hoke, we're about to
start, I think."

The train hunched into the air lock, and then slid out. Bannister was grinning at Hertzog. Keller was pale and silent,
a satchel between his feet.

"But, you know, Mr. Keller, when you come right down to
it, it's the little things that really classify a culture's technology. We tend to be impressed by big, obvious mechanisms
that clank and groan and tell you they're working, but the
really efficient machine shouldn't intrude itself on civilized
activities like conversation or high-level business, and
shouldn't require elaborate installations that advertise its
presence. For example, Mr. Keller, we have photostat machines now that can progressively work their way through a
bundle of documents, or the contents of a brief case, and
photograph each side of each sheet of paper, in turn, without
anyone's knowing it. Right through the brief case, if need be.
You can build that kind of machine into a wall, or a picture on that wall, or into almost anything, with the photo-
graphic head built into the ring on a man's finger." He
reached into his breast pocket and took out the photostat
Paulette had put on top of the stack. "Yours, Mr. Keller?"

Keller took it in shaky fingers and looked at it. "This is
really too bad," he whispered. "Really too bad."

"Oh, I don't know," Hertzog said. He turned to Bannister.
"That's an escrow agreement between Mr. Keller as a private
party and the zeppelin freighting company. I wondered
whether he'd dare trust it to a safe deposit box, and it
turned out he didn't. It calls for a payment of one hundred
thousand dollars—and here I'm quoting exactly—'upon the
occasion of interruption in Atlantis-Mainland tube service
for a period beginning midnight, July 14th.' It's in the nature
of a bet. Mr. Keller has wagered that such an interruption
will occur, and the zeppelin company has wagered that it
won't."

Bannister said: "Oh?"

"Quite. Hoke, if you'll be good enough to peep into Mr. Keller's satchel, there, I'm confident you'll find what we might call an infernal machine."

"Sorry," Keller whispered, shrunken into his seat, his blue lips barely moving. "I'm sorry."

"Cheer up, Mr. Keller," Hertzog said. He stood up and unscrewed the bulb of the lamp over their three chairs, and replaced it with a socket adaptor. From another pocket, he took a personal intercom and plugged the antenna into the socket. He dialed a telephone number. "Mr. Traven please. Frank Hertzog calling. Wake him up." He waited, grinning at the other passengers in the compartment, while Bannister, with respectfully raised eyebrows, dismantled Mr. Keller's time bomb.

"Traven? I want the tubes shut down for repairs. That's right. Twenty-four hours from this midnight. Service and repair. Uh-huh. Vitally necessary. Results will be improved service. Yes, siree. And while you're ordering that service, have 'em put in a platform watchman at the siding station, and draft plans for doubletracking and elminating the siding as soon as they can. Yeah. We'll chip in, sure. Thank you. G'night, Traven."

He unplugged the intercom and replaced the bulb. Handing the intercom and adaptor to Keller, he said: "All ITI employes carry these. Here's yours. Good for anywhere in the world, out in the open, and any electrical connection to Atlantis underground or under water."

"You . . . you're not going to—"

"Take revenge? On you? You were only the zep company's tool. You can make the agreement stand up in court. Collect your hundred thousand from them. *They*'re the guys I want to jolt."

"Oh."

"Time bomb, all right," Bannister said. "Set to go off at midnight."

"Uh-huh. You know what this means, Hoke, with the tube shut down for the next day?"

"What?"

"It means we're going to have to fly back."

"Very simple business," Hertzog explained, his feet up on one end of his living room couch. "The zep boys had to use a man who knew the tube and habitually rode it. Keller filled their bill. But he was a company man, so he told his bosses. The bosses (A) didn't like Atlantis or Atlanteans any more than any other Mainland business did, before we changed city governments, and (B) were greedy to get me to pay for one more shipment, which they knew they couldn't deliver because the tube would be blown up. With the tube gone, Atlantis wouldn't have swung any weight with Mainland courts. I could have tried to sue for my money and never gotten within a mile of it.

"Now, Keller was figuring on the long view. He had his hundred thousand in escrow, which looked like a sure thing to his fussy mind, and he probably would have gotten a little more for delivering his company's business to the zeppelin line. Then there was his commission on the liquor sale, and his extra commission for making a sale on which there wouldn't have to be a delivery. A little bit from everybody, you might say.

"But—he came up here and told me that cock and bull story, and told me too much. He even told me when the bomb would go off—just safely after the last night train from Atlantis pulled into Basle. Well, that was a little too much. He tried to get too many things out of too many people, and he fell on his face. We were able to scrag him. Greed, Hoke, is not a useful emotion in a man who wants to make money."

"He made a hundred thousand."

"Hm-m-m . . . no, he didn't make it. That's going to be his trouble. He didn't earn it. He's the incompetent type that couldn't earn it in any way—not even a crooked way.

"And, of course, he and his money will be soon parted. Employers who pay large sums to have violent things done— say of the order of destroying a major transportation system —are of precisely the mental type to see that the incompetent employee does not enjoy his money. I'm afraid I don't have quite the right kind of psychology to give our little Mr. Keller what he did verily earn.

"Which reminds me . . . we're in the wholesale liquor business. When I found out Keller's bosses knew about his little extracurricular scheme, I got so mad I bought 'em out. A management like that ought to be shot—permitting a thirty-thousand gross profit to make 'em blow the gaff on millions more! People like that—" Hertzog shook his head. "No sense of responsibility."

"So that's how Keller's an ITI employee," Bannister said, opening a bottle. "Through the liquor house. I was wondering, when you gave him the intercom."

Hertzog smiled gently, ruminatively. "Technically, that's the answer. Privately . . . well, I expect to hear via that intercom, just precisely how Keller and his unearned increment are separated. I think he'll make a horrid noise about it."

Earthmen Bearing Gifts

by Fredric Brown

DHAR RY sat alone in his room, meditating. From outside the door he caught a thought wave equivalent to a knock, and, glancing at the door, he willed it to slide open.

It opened. "Enter, my friend," he said. He could have projected the idea telepathically; but with only two persons present, speech was more polite.

Ejon Khee entered. "You are up late tonight, my leader," he said.

"Yes, Khee. Within an hour the Earth rocket is due to land, and I wish to see it. Yes, I know, it will land a thousand miles away, if their calculations are correct. Beyond the horizon. But if it lands even twice that far the flash of the atomic explosion should be visible. And I have waited long for first contact. For even though no Earthman will be on that rocket, it will still be first contact—for them. Of course our telepath teams have been reading their thoughts for many centuries, but—this will be the first *physical* contact between Mars and Earth."

Khee made himself comfortable on one of the low chairs. "True," he said. "I have not followed recent reports too closely, though. Why are they using an atomic warhead? I know they suppose our planet is uninhabited, but still—"

"They will watch the flash through their lunar telescopes and get a—what do they call it?—a spectroscopic analysis. That will tell them more than they know now (or think they know; much of it is erroneous) about the atmosphere of our planet and the composition of its surface. It is—call it a sighting shot, Khee. They'll be here in person within a few oppositions. And then—"

27

Mars was holding out, waiting for Earth to come. What was left of Mars, that is; this one small city of about nine hundred beings. The civilization of Mars was older than that of Earth, but it was a dying one. This was what remained of it: one city, nine hundred people. They were waiting for Earth to make contact, for a selfish reason and for an unselfish one.

Martian civilization had developed in a quite different direction from that of Earth. It had developed no important knowledge of the physical sciences, no technology. But it had developed social sciences to the point where there had not been a single crime, let alone a war, on Mars for fifty thousand years. And it had developed fully the parapsychological sciences of the mind, which Earth was just beginning to discover.

Mars could teach Earth much. How to avoid crime and war to begin with. Beyond those simple things lay telepathy, telekinesis, empathy . . .

And Earth would, Mars hoped, teach them something even more valuable to Mars: how, by science and technology —which it was too late for Mars to develop now, even if they had the type of minds which would enable them to develop these things—to restore and rehabilitate a dying planet, so that an otherwise dying race might live and multiply again.

Each planet would gain greatly, and neither would lose.

And tonight was the night when Earth would make its first sighting shot. Its next shot, a rocket containing Earthmen, or at least an Earthman, would be at the next opposition, two Earth years, or roughly four Martian years, hence. The Martians knew this, because their teams of telepaths were able to catch at least some of the thoughts of Earthmen, enough to know their plans. Unfortunately, at that distance, the connection was one-way. Mars could not ask Earth to hurry its program. Or tell Earth scientists the facts about Mars' composition and atmosphere which would have made this preliminary shot unnecessary.

Tonight Ry, the leader (as nearly as the Martian word can be translated), and Khee, his administrative assistant and closest friend, sat and meditated together until the time was near. Then they drank a toast to the future—in a beverage based on menthol, which had the same effect on Martians as alcohol on Earthmen—and climbed to the roof of the building in which they had been sitting. They watched toward the north, where the rocket should land. The stars shone brilliantly and unwinkingly through the atmosphere.

In Observatory No. 1 on Earth's moon, Rog Everett, his eye at the eyepiece of the spotter scope, said triumphantly, "Thar she blew, Willie. And now, as soon as the films are developed, we'll know the score on that old planet Mars." He straightened up—there'd be no more to see now—and he and Willie Sanger shook hands solemnly. It was an historical occasion.

"Hope it didn't kill anybody. Any Martians, that is. Rog, did it hit dead center in Syrtis Major?"

"Near as matters. I'd say it was maybe a thousand miles off, to the south. And that's damn close on a fifty-million-mile shot. Willie, do you really think there are any Martians?"

Willie thought a second and then said, "No."

He was right.

Things

by Zenna Henderson

VIAT CAME BACK from the camp of the Strangers, his crest shorn, the devi ripped from his jacket, his mouth slack and drooling and his eyes empty. He sat for a day in the sun of the coveti center, not even noticing when the eager children gathered and asked questions in their piping little voices. When the evening shadow touched him, Viat staggered to his feet and took two steps and was dead.

The mother came then, since the body was from her and could never be alien, and since the emptiness that was not Viat had flown from his eyes. She signed him dead by pinning on his torn jacket the kiom—the kiom she had fashioned the day he was born, since to be born is to begin to die. He had not yet given his heart, so the kiom was still hers to bestow. She left the pelu softly alight in the middle of the kiom because Viat had died beloved. He who dies beloved walks straight and strong on the path to the Hidden Ones by the light of the pelu. Be the pelu removed, he must wander forever, groping in the darkness of the unlighted kiom.

So she pinned the kiom and wailed him dead.

There was a gathering together after Viat was given back to the earth. Backs were bent against the sun, and the coveti thought together for a morning. When the sun pointed itself into their eyes, they shaded them with their open palms and spoke together.

"The Strangers have wrought an evil thing with us." Dobi patted the dust before him. "Because of them, Viat is not. He came not back from the camp. Only his body came, breathing until it knew he would not return to it."

"And yet, it may be that the Strangers are not evil. They came to us in peace. Even, they brought their craft down on barrenness instead of scorching our fields." Deci's eyes

30

were eager on the sky. His blood was hot with the wonder of a craft dropping out of the clouds, bearing Strangers. "Perhaps there was no need for us to move the coveti."

"True, true," nodded Dobi. "They may not be of themselves evil, but it may be that the breath of them is death to us, or perhaps the falling of their shadows or the silent things that walk invisible from their friendly hands. It is best that we go not to the camp again. Neither should we permit them to find the coveti."

"Cry them not forbidden, yet!" cried Deci, his crest rippling, "we know them not. To taboo them now would not be fair. They may come bearing gifts—"

"For gifts given, something always is taken. We have no wish to exchange our young men for a look at the Strangers." Dobi furrowed the dust with his fingers and smoothed away the furrows as Viat had been smoothed away.

"And yet," Veti's soft voice came clearly as her blue crest caught the breeze, "it may be that they will have knowledge for us that we have not. Never have we taken craft into the clouds and back."

"Yes, yes!" Deci's eyes embraced Veti, who held his heart. "They must have much knowledge, many gifts for us."

"The gift of knowledge is welcome," said Tefu in his low rumble. "But gifts in the hands have fangs and bonds."

"The old words!" cried Deci. "The old ways do not hold when new ways arrive!"

"True," nodded Dobi. "If the new is truly a way and not a whirlwind or a trail that goes no place. But to judge without facts is to judge in error. I will go to the Strangers."

"And I." Tefu's voice stirred like soft thunder.

"And I? And I?" Deci's words tumbled on themselves and the dust stirred with his hurried rising.

"Young—" muttered Tefu.

"Young eyes to notice what old eyes might miss," said Dobi. "Our path is yours." His crest rippled as he nodded to Deci.

"Deci!" Veti's voice was shaken by the unknown. "Come not again as Viat came. The heart you bear with you is not your own."

"I will come again," cried Deci, "To fill your hands with wonders and delights." He gave each of her cupped palms a kiss to hold against his return.

Time is not hours and days, or the slanting and shortening of shadows. Time is a held breath and a listening ear.

Time incredible passed before the ripple through the grass, the rustle through reeds, the sudden sound of footsteps where it seemed no footsteps could be. The rocks seemed to part to let them through.

Dobi led, limping, slow of foot, flattened of crest, his eyes hidden in the shadow of his bent head. Then came Tefu, like one newly blind, groping, reaching, bumping, reeling until he huddled against the familiar rocks in the fading sunlight.

"Deci?" cried Veti, parting the crowd with her cry. "Deci?"

"He came not with us," said Dobi. "He watched us go."

"Willingly?" Veti's hands clenched over the memory of his mouth. "Willingly? Or was there force?"

"Willingly?" The eyes that Tefu turned to Veti saw her not. They looked within at hidden things. "Force? He stayed. There were no bonds about him." He touched a wondering finger to one eye and then the other. "Open," he rumbled. "Where is the light?"

"Tell me," cried Veti. "Oh, tell me!"

Dobi sat in the dust, his big hands marking it on either side of him.

"They truly have wonders. They would give us many strange things for our devi." His fingers tinkled the fringing of his jacket. "Fabrics beyond our dreams. Tools we could use. Weapons that could free the land of every flesh-hungry kutu."

"And Deci? And Deci?" Veti voiced her fear again.

"Deci saw all and desired all. His devi were ripped off before the sun slid an arm's reach. He was like a child in a meadow of flowers, clutching, grabbing, crumpling, and finding always the next flower fairer."

Wind came in the silence and poured itself around bare shoulders.

"Then he will return," said Veti, loosening her clenched hand. "When the wonder is gone."

"As Viat returned?" Tefu's voice rumbled. "As I have returned?" He held his hand before his eyes and dropped his fingers one by one. "How many fingers before you? Six? Four? Two?"

"You saw the Strangers, before we withdrew the coveti. You saw the strange garments they wore, the shining round-

ness, the heavy glitter and thickness. Our air is not air for
them. Without the garments, they would die."

"If they are so well wrapped against the world, how
could they hurt?" cried Veti. "They cannot hurt Deci. He
will return."

"I returned," murmured Tefu. "I did but walk among
them and the misting of their finished breath has done
this to me. Only time and the Hidden Ones know if sight
is through for me.

"One was concerned for me. One peered at me when
first my steps began to waver. He hurried me away from
the others and sat away from me and watched with me
as the lights went out. He was concerned for me—or was
studying me. But I am blind."

"And you?" asked Veti of Dobi. "It harmed you not?"

"I took care," said Dobi. "I came not close after the
first meeting. And yet—" he turned the length of his thigh.
From hip to knee the split flesh glinted like the raking of
a mighty claw. "I was among the trees when a kutu screamed
on the hill above me. Fire lashed out from the Strangers
and it screamed no more. Startled, I moved the branches
about me and—s-s-s-s-st!" His finger streaked beside his
thigh.

"But Deci—"

Dobi scattered his dust handprint with a swirl of his
fingers. "Deci is like a scavenging mayu. He follows, hand
out-stretched. 'Wait wait,' he cried when we turned to go.
'We can lead the world with these wonders.'

"Why should we lead the world? Now there is no first
and no last. Why should we reach beyond our brothers to
grasp things that dust will claim?"

"Wail him dead, Veti," rumbled Tefu. "Death a thousand
ways surrounds him now. And if his body comes again,
his heart is no longer with us. Wail him dead."

"Yes," nodded Dobi. "Wail him dead and give thanks
that our coveti is so securely hidden that the Strangers can
never come to sow among us the seeds of more Viats and
Tefus.

"The Strangers are taboo. The coveti path is closed."

So Veti wailed him dead, crouching in the dust of the
coveti path, clutching in her hands the kiom Deci had given
her with his heart.

Viat's mother sat with her an hour—until Veti broke
her wail and cried, "Your grief is not mine. You pinned

Viat's kiom. You folded his hands to rest. You gave him back to the earth. Wail not with me. I wail for an emptiness—for an un-knowledge. For a wondering and a fearing. You know Viat is on the trail to the Hidden Ones. But I know not of Deci. Is he alive? Is he dying in the wilderness with no pelu to light him into the darkness? Is he crawling now, blind and maimed up the coveti trail? I wail a death with no hope. A hopelessness with no death. I wail alone."

And so she wailed past the point of tears, into the aching dryness of grief. The coveti went about its doing, knowing she would live again when grief was spent.

Then came the day when all faces swung to the head of the coveti trail. All ears flared to the sound of Veti's scream and all eyes rounded to see Deci stagger into the coveti.

Veti flew to him, her arms out-stretched, her heart believing before her mind could confirm. But Deci winced away from her touch and his face half snarled as his hand, shorn of three fingers and barely beginning to regenerate, motioned her away.

"Deci!" cried Veti, "Deci?"

"Let—let—me breathe." Deci leaned against the rocks. Deci who could outrun a kutu, whose feet had lightness and swiftness beyond all others in the coveti. "The trail takes the breath."

"Deci!" Veti's hands still reached, one all unknowingly proffering the kiom. Seeing it, she laughed and cast it aside. The death mark with Deci alive before her? "Oh, Deci!" And then she fell silent as she saw his maimed hand, his ragged crest, his ravaged jacket, his seared legs—his eyes —His eyes! They were not the eyes of the Deci who had gone with eagerness to see the Strangers. He had brought the Strangers back in his eyes.

His breath at last came smoothly and he leaned to Veti, reaching as he did so, into the bundle by his side.

"I promised," he said, seeing Veti only. "I have come again to fill your hands with wonder and delight."

But Veti's hands were hidden behind her. Gifts from Strangers are suspect.

"Here," said Deci, laying an ugly angled thing down in the dust before Veti. "Here is death to all kutus, be they six-legged or two. Let the Durlo coveti say again the Klori stream is theirs for fishing," he muttered. "Nothing is theirs now save by our sufferance. I give you power, Veti."

Veti moved back a pace.

"And here," he laid a flask of glass beside the weapon. "This is for dreams and laughter. This is what Viat drank of—but too much. They call it water. It is a drink the Hidden Ones could envy. One mouthful and all memory of pain and grief, loss and unreachable dreams is gone.

"I give you forgetfulness, Veti."

Veti's head moved denyingly from side to side.

"And here." He pulled forth, carelessly, arms-lengths of shining fabric that rippled and clung and caught the sun. His eyes were almost Deci's eyes again.

Veti's heart was moved, woman-wise, to the fabric and her hands reached for it, since no woman can truly see a fabric unless her fingers taste its body, flow, and texture.

"For you, for beauty. And this, that you might behold yourself untwisted by moving waters." He laid beside the weapon and the water a square of reflecting brightness. "For you to see yourself as Lady over the world as I see myself Lord."

Veti's hands dropped again, the fabric almost untasted. Deci's eyes again were the eyes of a stranger.

"Deci, I waited not for *things*, these long days." Veti's hands cleansed themselves together from the cling of the fabric. Her eyes failed before Deci and sought the ground, jerking away from the strange things in the dust. "Come, let us attend to your hurts."

"But no! But see!" cried Deci. "With these strange things our coveti can rule all the valley and beyond and beyond!"

"Why?"

"Why?" echoed Deci. "To take all we want. To labor no more save to ask and receive. To have power—"

"Why?" Veti's eyes still questioned. "We have enough. We are not hungry. We are clothed against the changing seasons. We work when work is needed. We play when work is done. Why do we need more?"

"Deci finds quiet ways binding," said Dobi. "Rather would he have shouting and far, swift going. And sweat and effort and delicious fear pushing him into action. Soon come the kutu hunting days, Deci. Save your thirst for excitement until then."

"Sweat and effort and fear!" snarled Deci. "Why should I endure that when with this—" He snatched up the weapon and with one wave of his hand sheared off the top of Tefu's house. He spoke into the dying thunder of the discharge. "No kutu alive could unsheath its fangs after that, except as death draws back the sheath to mock its finished strength.

"And if so against a kutu," he muttered. "How much more so against the Durlo coveti?"

"Come, Deci," cried Veti. "Let us bind your wounds. As time will heal them, so time will heal your mind of these Strangers."

"I want no healing," shouted Deci, anger twisting his haggard face. "Nor will you after the Strangers have been here and proffered you their wonders in exchange for this foolish fringing devi." Contempt tossed his head. "For the devi in our coveti, we could buy their sky craft, I doubt not."

"They will not come," said Dobi. "The way is hidden. No Stranger can ever find our coveti. We have but to wait until—"

"Until tomorrow!" Deci's crest tossed rebelliously, his voice louder than need be. Or perhaps it seemed so from the echoes it raised in every heart. "I told—"

"You told?" Stupidly, the echo took words.

"*You told?*" Disbelief sharpened the cry.

"You told!" Anger spurted into the words.

"I told!" cried Deci. "How else reap the benefits that the Strangers—"

"Benefits!" spat Dobi. "Death!" His foot spurned the weapon in the dust. "Madness!" The flask gurgled as it moved. "Vanity!" Dust clouded across the mirror and streaked the shining fabric. "For such you have betrayed us to death."

"But no!" cried Deci. "*I* lived. Death does not always come with the Strangers." Sudden anger roughened his voice. "It's the old ways! You want no change! But all things change. It is the way of living things. Progress—"

"All change is not progress," rumbled Tefu, his hands hiding his blindness.

"Like it or not," shouted Deci. "Tomorrow the Strangers come! You have your choice, all of you!" His arm circled the crowd. "Keep to your homes like Pegu or come forward with your devi and find with me a power, a richness—"

"Or move the coveti again," said Dobi. "Away from betrayal and foolish greed. We have a third choice."

Deci caught his breath.

"Veti?" his whisper pled. "Veti? We do not need the rest

of the coveti. You and I together. We can wait for the strangers. Together we can have the world. With this weapon not one person in this coveti or any other can withstand us. We can be the new people. We can have our own coveti, and take what we want—anything, anywhere. Come to me, Veti."

Veti looked long into his eyes. "Why did you come back?" she whispered with tears in her voice. Then anger leaped into her eyes. *"Why did you come back!"* There was the force of a scream in her harsh words. She darted suddenly to the rocks. She snatched the kiom from the dust where it had fallen. Before Deci knew what was happening, she whirled on him and pinned death upon his ragged jacket. Then with a swift, decisive twist, she tore away the pelu and dropped it to the dust.

Deci's eyes widened in terror, his hand clutched at the kiom but dared not touch it.

"No!" he screamed, "No!"

Then Veti's eyes widened and her hands reached also for the kiom, but no power she possessed could undo what she had done and her scream rose with Deci's.

Then knowing himself surely dead and dead unbeloved, already entering the eternity of darkness of the unlighted kiom, Deci crumpled to the ground. Under his cheek was the hardness of the weapon, under his outflung hand, the beauty of the fabric, and the sunlight, bending through the water, giggled crazily on his chin.

One dead unbeloved is not as much as a crushed flower by the path. For the flower at least there is regret for its ended beauty.

So knowing Deci dead, the coveti turned from him. There was for memory of him only an uncertainty to Veti's feet and a wondering shock in Veti's eyes as she turned with the others to prepare to move the coveti.

The wind came and poured over the dust and the things and Deci.

And Deci lay waiting for his own breath to stop.

The Top

by George Sumner Albee

"9:07 A.M. TO Jonathan Gerber *from* L. Lester Leath," read the pale green memorandum slip on the desk. "Kindly save your day for me. Attached is an elevator pass for your permanent possession. Suggest you visit 13th Floor this morning, but no higher. LLL."

"So—after all these years," said Jonathan to himself as he drew the pass, the first he had ever actually touched, from its glassine envelope. It was, of course, a miniature pyramid. One metal surface bore the firm name, Allied, the other a photoengraving of his, Jonathan's, own head and shoulders. When or where he had been photographed he had no idea: recently, it must have been, for he was wearing a tie he had just bought; evidently the company police had caught him with a fast lens as he entered or left the building. "Miss Kindhands," he spoke to his secretary over the intercom, "cancel my appointments. Mr. Leath wants me to stand by."

The golden pyramid in his hand, he strode down the lustrous corridor to the elevator bank. "Thirteen," he said.

The elevator operator, though he had known his face and his fuzzy Harris tweed suit for years, faltered in alarm.

"It's all right," Jonathan assured him, and turned over his hand to show the pass.

"Yes, sir," said the man. He breathed the two words as a musician might breathe two soft, low notes on a flute. Then he came to attention, shut the bronze door and pushed his button.

"Fourteen years, or is it sixteen?" murmured Jonathan to himself, and descended, even as the elevator carried him upward in power and prestige, through the tiers of memory to his first days in the building.

He recalled, smiling, how he had had his doubts about

38

the elevators. As morning after morning they had lifted him to the advertising department on the eighth floor he had felt against all reason that there was trickery, that he was being carried not up but down, down, down into catacombs beneath Allied's gigantic stepped-back pyramid. The little electric bulbs in the car blinking 1 and 2 and 3 had not convinced him he was traveling upward; the motion was so smooth nothing could be felt; when the noiseless door opened nobody could have said where he was. Long empty corridors, narrow as the galleries of a mine, stretched away without end, their plastic panels gleaming under the light from squares of milk glass in the ceiling. There were no windows anywhere in the building, and the radiance entering through the glass brick might have come from deftly concealed electric lamps; there was nothing to prove it was daylight.

"Fantasy," Jonathan had rebuked himself. "I'm lucky; phenomenally lucky. Here I am, only twenty-seven, at Allied! Anybody else would give his eye teeth to be where I am." Nowadays he used colloquialisms to capture more readers for his ads, but in the past he had used them innocently for pleasure.

He had been a copywriter in a New York advertising agency when one afternoon the firm's senior partners had called him in and told him that the almost legendary firm in Minnesota wanted to hire him. If Jonathan refused the paltry gift of himself, it had been made clear, the agency might henceforth find it embarrassing to employ him. So might other agencies. So, feeling like an Aztec youth chosen for the stone altar, honored but doubtful, he had taken the train for Minnesota, finding chocolates and crimson roses in his stateroom. Oh, there had been qualms.

Nor had his first impression of L. Lester Leath been reassuring. Leath's soundproof office with its pale gray paint and pale gray furniture, its glass brick glowing with the dim light that might be sunshine and might not, had been rather like a bank of fog. And it had been difficult to tell where the fog left off and Leath himself began. His face was the color of mist, his hair might have been aluminum on which moisture had condensed, his white fingers had moved across his desk like small wraiths, while his voice had the soft, mournful boom of a deep-toned steamer whistle heard across miles of veiled sea.

It had taken Jonathan awhile to become accustomed to Leath's voice and its miracles of misty circumlocution.

"What will my job be?" he had asked, and Leath had replied that jobs were for the lowly and words were not to be used inaccurately. "I mean, what will my work be?" Jonathan had corrected himself. And Leath had answered: "Work! Ah, work! It was work which made the fathers of our nation giants on the land. It was work which made America what it is today, the light and beacon of a troubled world. People have grown soft, they ask for security. Ah, the best security, the only security is work." A third time, Jonathan had tried. And Leath had said: "What products will you advertise? My boy, Allied has no products. Let us say rather that Allied creates and develops semi-finished materials which enable small manufacturers, under the free enterprise system, to enrich or otherwise improve certain items for the ultimate benefit of the consumer, Mr. and Mrs. America. Your subject will be Allied itself. I have brought you to us because you have a nice flair for words. I was deeply stirred by your headline for the shotgun ad—*A Lad and His Dog*. And the little piece you wrote for the diaper people, what did you call it?—*Babies Are Fallen Stars*. Just give me words like that for Allied. Give me patriotism, friendship, nobility, love—"

Thus, fourteen years ago—could it be sixteen, could it be seventeen?—Jonathan had begun his task of writing, for millions of newspaper readers, little essays without subjects. When his first institutional copy appeared in print he had feared that people would laugh. But nobody had laughed. On the contrary, letters of praise had come in from every corner of the country. His ad which listed George Washington's virtues and named Allied as their modern inheritor had won the National Advertising Council's platinum-and-ruby medal. His ad stating that Allied conducted its business affairs according to precepts learned from a toilworn mother's lips by Honest Abe Lincoln had been singled out for a special scroll by the Junior Chamber of Commerce. Ever since, he had been writing such pieces with a growing appreciation of their worth, eloquence and dignity. And meanwhile L. Lester Leath had shown him only admiration and kindliness, and Allied had raised his salary from ten thousand dollars a year to seventeen-five and from seventeen-five to twenty-three-two. Each year he was awarded, in addition, a bonus of Class C preferred stock which he would forfeit only if he left the company before retirement age.

He was expected on the thirteenth floor. A burly young guard, in a gray uniform, no doubt a recruit from a college

football squad, saluted him. "Mr. Gerber? I'm to show you
anything you want to see," he said deferentially.

"I don't really know what I want to see, I'm afraid," said
Jonathan, smiling. "This is my first visit."

"Mr. Leath said you might like me to introduce you to the
divisional managers, sir."

"Then let's do that," replied Jonathan equably. "By all
means."

The guard marched ahead, opening bronze doors. In fifteen divisional office suites Jonathan shook hands with eight
bald thin men and seven bald fat men. These were not the
directors. These were merely the decision-and-risk-takers,
devoted family men who were paid a hundred thousand a
year and died early, of coronary attacks. Jonathan inspected
their graph room, their elaborate communications room,
their restaurant, their small three-bed hospital. "I see the
hospital has its own elevator," he observed to the guard. "If
a man dies at his desk you can get him out of the building
without anybody getting so much as a peek at him."

"The Planning Board doesn't slip up on many details, sir,"
replied the man.

Jonathan, in his fourth or fifth year with the company, had
had a personal encounter with Allied's precision technique
for just such fatalities. One day in the elevator an engineer
named Jacks had paled, gasped and fallen. While Jonathan
knelt over him the operator had stopped the car between
floors, telephoning calmly to the starter in the lobby for
instructions; then the cage had dropped fast and deep into
the cellars. Guards with a stretcher had met it.

"I'm afraid he's dead," Jonathan had said.

"Oh, no sir," the chief guard had replied. "He's fainted,
that's all, or else he's indisposed."

"You'll get him right to a doctor?"

"Just step back into the car, sir," the chief had said.

That had been all there was to it. Later Jonathan had been
unable to pry an unequivocal answer from the elevator operator, from the guards, from anybody. On the obituary
page of the newspaper, on the third day, there had been a
brief paragraph to the effect that one D. M. Jacks, engineer
"of this city," had passed away, but not so much as a word
had indicated that the man worked for Allied. Jacks had
simply disappeared. The company did not ignore death, it
by-passed it. When a man died his assistant took his place.
In a corporation with tens of thousands of employes some-

body was bound to die every day, and work could not be repeatedly interrupted.

Back once more on his own floors, Jonathan put his head into Leath's handsomely decorated anteroom. "If he wants me," he said, "I'm back."

"The doctor is with him now," said Miss Tablein, Leath's confidential secretary. "But stay near your phone, please."

At his desk, with nothing to do but wait and stare at the reader-acceptance graphs on the wall, Jonathan asked himself what could be in the wind. Leath was anything but impulsive; the permanent pass, the visit to Thirteen were in themselves a promotion. Nothing lay above Thirteen but Fourteen, since nobody at all was permitted to go up to Fifteen where the president's suite filled the pyramid's tip. Was he, Jonathan wondered, actually to join the Planning Board? He could rise no higher in the advertising department without taking Leath's own job.

He would have the answer soon enough, he told himself, whatever it might be. With a shrug he took the pass from his pocket, scrutinized his likeness on it, and laughed. Gone, gone were the waxen curls of youth! In reminiscent, sentimental mood he tried to recall how he had looked at twenty-seven. He could not manage it. "But I do remember," he said to himself with a smile, "that I was skeptical. Oh, was I skeptical!" He had, he remembered, in his suspicion of the elevators, actually paced off the corridors to make sure the lower floors of the pyramid were broader than the upper. He had done worse than that. He had played truant from his desk to explore the cellars—finding, of course, nothing evil, finding nothing at all.

Then—Jonathan recalled, smiling—having learned what he could about the building he had tried to discover what Allied's products were. Flair for words or not, it had seemed absurd to him at first to write ads without knowing what they were about. And he had been able to learn a little. He had found, for example, that the company's four thousand products bore alphabetic names ranging from *Aab*, an adulterant for milk-shakes, to *Zyz*, which were rotors for tractor magnetos. But his collection of *Aabs* and *Zyzes* had soon bored him.

The buzzer on his desk, tuned to G Sharp, sounded. With the dexterity of practice Jonathan lifted his telephone from its cradle and perched it like a parakeet on his shoulder.

"Gerber here," he said.

It was Leath's secretary. "The doctor is still with him," she said. "His ulcers must be unusually bad this morning, or maybe he's been hearing the ticking again. But I have some instructions for you. Kindly have your lunch, make a tour of Fourteen at one o'clock and report back here at two."

"What's cooking, Miss Tablein?" Jonathan asked her. The secretaries regarded slang as evidence of democracy and passed the word around that you were adorable, if you used it. A girl worked away her fingernails and her youth for a boss who was sufficiently adorable.

"I don't know," Miss Tablein answered. "It must be important, though. A Major Project."

"I eat my lunch at twelve with the Junior Executive Group, you know. The directors don't go out to lunch until a quarter past one. If I go up to Fourteen while they're out the place will be deserted. What does he want me to do up there, do you know?"

"Just look around, I guess," said Miss Tablein. "I wish I were going with you. Mr. Gerber, promise me one thing. Promise me, when you get back, you'll tell me if Mr. Waffen really has a gold-plated toilet seat."

"I will," promised Jonathan; but he knew he would not tell.

He ate lunch with two of his assistants, younger men still in their indoctrination period. The grapevine telegraph, he discovered to his amusement, had already tapped out the news of his golden pass. The boys showed him scrubbed, bright, eager faces; they writhed each time he opened his mouth, out of respect.

Shortly after one he rode up to Fourteen in the elevator. It was noticeably smaller than Thirteen; evidently the step-back was sharper than it appeared from the street. Another guard, saluting, informed him that there were eight directors' offices and a conference room, and that he was free to go anywhere he liked. "They're worth seeing, sir," he added. And they were. Several offices had barber chairs, gigantic television receivers and bars stocked with private blends. One had a cigar humidor the size of a bank vault, one a target range for air pistols, one a Finnish *sauna* bath. The most interesting was a room which duplicated the after-deck of a cabin cruiser, complete with angling chair and a rack for rods and reels. Not an assistant, not a secretary was to be seen. Not a memorandum desecrated the rich polished wood of the vast desks.

"Tell me," Jonathan said to the guard, "how often do these Planning Board men come in?"

"Well, they're here for the annual meeting, sir," replied the man. "Otherwise they come in only when Mr. Satherwaite sends for them, I guess." Hanscomb Ludlow Satherwaite II was Allied's president, who had his suite in the point of the pyramid and who was photographed, growing no older in the photographs from year to year, but never seen.

"Do any of them live in Minnesota? Forgive my curiosity. This is my first visit."

The guard chuckled. "Why, sir, you're forgetting they all have planes and pilots nowadays. Mr. Ippinger, now, he has four hundred thousand acres in Louisiana he keeps for the shrimping, so he lives there. Mr. Latchwell owns an island off the coast of Mexico; he has a castle and a little army; that's why he wears his red and blue uniforms and his leather boots with the stars on them."

"I've seen Mr. Latchwell in the elevators, of course."

Jonathan at one time or another had glimpsed most of the portly, imposing directors. There was one, undoubtedly the fisherman, who wore white canvas trousers and a white cap with a green celluloid bill. Another went bare-toed in rawhide sandals for his health. There was method behind their little eccentricities, of course; they put them on as a demonstration of equality, as wise old Leath had patiently explained to him more than once.

Thanking the guard, he went down again. "It's 1:55," he said, putting his bald head into Leath's anteroom.

"Come in and wait here," said Miss Tablein, peering over her glasses. "Tell me. Oh, you must tell me! Is it really—"

"Our directors work much too hard," said Jonathan, his tone disapproving, "for any such nonsense. But of course I understand you were just having a little fun."

"Oh, I did so want to know!"

Was Miss Tablein's loyalty questionable? She might just possibly, said Jonathan to himself, prove to be a dangerous fellow worker. He read *Dear Folks*, the Allied house organ, until the signal lamp flashed and Miss Tablein said he might go in. Good news or bad—and he scarcely saw how it could be bad—he would have it now.

"Good afternoon, my son," said L. Lester Leath.

His face was as white as a sheet of the *Gga* the company manufactured as an intermediate for the dentifrice industry, and smudged with shadow. One corner of his mouth sagged.

His left eye was an owl's, the pupil enormous and fierce.

"Lester!" cried Jonathan, shocked. "You're ill!"

"I'm not ill, I'm dying," replied the advertising manager without emotion. "I will die at my desk this afternoon, presumably within the next five or ten minutes."

"Let me drive you home!"

"No; I want it this way," said Leath in a voice that was a wisp of fog. "I want my death, as well as my life, to be a demonstration of service to Allied and all that it stands for. But time is short, my son. Tomorrow morning an Inter-Office Memo, Form 114B Blue, will announce that you are succeeding me as chief of the department. You'll start at fifty thousand. Your stock bonus will be comparable."

"Thank you, Lester."

"Your first act of office, I hope, will be to hire an assistant who blazes with our sacred fire. I suggest that you do what I did—comb the agencies for a young Jonathan Gerber and train him, as for twenty-one years I have trained you."

It was a gray afternoon. No sunlight at all was filtering through the glass brick. The room, it seemed to Jonathan, was crowded with bars of fog lying one on top of another like two-by-twelves stacked in a lumberyard. In dimness, in shimmer and shadow L. Lester Leath's face came and went, an image floating free in space, bobbling lazily like a barrel on a foggy sea.

"It's been such a joy to serve Allied that I haven't counted the years," said Jonathan. He had learned well. Such pronouncements were now effortless for him. But it was a bit of a blow nevertheless: "Has it really been so long?" he asked.

"It has, my son," said Leath, the sagging lip blurring his voice. "And I know I leave the department in good hands. Did you go up to Thirteen?"

"Yes; of course."

"Fourteen?"

"Of course. It was your order."

Leath swayed. With an effort he gathered together his failing energy. "Before you take over," he said, his voice fading, "there is one more thing, one final rite. You must meet our President. Go up to Fifteen." He sagged on his executive's posture chair.

"Lester!" Jonathan sprang forward.

Ever so slowly, Leath raised a white forefinger towards the ceiling. "Fifteen," he whispered, and died.

Tenderly Jonathan closed behind him the soundproof door that was now his own. "Miss Tablein," he said, "please call the janitor. Mr. Leath is no longer with Allied."

Down the corridor, at the elevator bank, a car appeared the instant he pressed the button, almost as if news of his eminence had somehow travelled down the dark shaft along the bell wire. "The top," he directed the operator brusquely, exhibiting his pass the merest flick.

The little lamps blinked; the door slid open.

"But I said I wanted the top," Jonathan protested indignantly. He was the advertising manager; he earned fifty thousand a year; his time was too valuable to Allied for him to permit a menial to waste it. "This is Fourteen, not Fifteen."

"Sorry, sir," said the operator. "This is as high as we go. Speak to the guard."

"I will indeed!" shouted Jonathan. The guard was already at his elbow; the chap who had conducted him through the director's suites. "What is this?" Jonathan demanded of him. "I want Fifteen, damn it!"

"Quite right, sir. Over here, sir," said the guard. He led the way to a plain bronze door with neither knob nor keyhole. "Just drop your pass into this slot. It operates an electrical circuit and opens the door. You do the same thing on the other side when you come down."

"Do you mean to say," asked Jonathan, incredulous, "Mr. Satherwaite walks this last flight each time he comes up here?"

"I've never seen him, sir, but he must."

From coast to coast hundreds of Allied plants were awhir, a hundred and ninety-three thousand Allied fellow workers were turning out four thousand products. Here at the center of the country sat this colossal pyramid which was the center of the whole thing; here on the topmost floor of the pyramid clicked the mind which in its genius comprehended and guided all. And here, here was he, Jonathan Gerber, about to shake the hand of supremacy! Eyes alight, shoulders squared, Jonathan dropped his pass into the thin slot, walked through the door and shut it after him.

Facing him was a simple staircase of painted steel with a hand-rail. Climbing it, past rough walls of orange hollow tile which had not been plastered, he marveled. How fitting that Mr. Satherwaite, with his immeasurable power, should despise its trappings! Many and many a time, in his writings,

Jonathan had said that Allied's president was a simple man, and as always the fiction had created the fact: he was. At the top of the staircase he stepped onto a bare concrete floor littered with scraps of building paper, pots of dried paint and dead flies. The air smelt like a Stilton cheese. Trying a door at his left, he peered into a black cavern in which greased steel elevator cables slipped over great spoked wheels. He tried a door at his right and gazed into another cavern exactly like it.

For five minutes, for ten, he stood in the musty heat turning slowly round and round, looking for he knew not what—a secret door, a cache, a blackboard on which his predecessors might have left, if nothing more, at least their signatures. But he saw only the paint pots, the flies and four small windows like round eyes, one in each inward-sloping wall. Cobwebs and grime covered the windows; but here and there on them, he saw, the scurf had been rubbed away, as by a sleeved elbow. Stepping to the nearest he broadened the clear spot on it and looked out.

He saw a segment of the town, which might have been a ramshackle clutter of blackened boards, and, beyond that, the endless plain of Minnesota. And he saw, something he had forgotten, that it was winter on the prairie. Dry snow, driven by the wind, smoked over farmhouses and fences. Where the land could be seen at all, it was blue with cold. And more snow was coming, and more cold. For it was true that summer was a vacation, an interlude; winter was the reality, the constant companion; winter lay ever a few miles to the north, waiting to reclaim its property. Blue lay the earth, veined with white like the deep sea, and the veins were ice.

"So cold, so cold—" murmured Jonathan, and shivered.

And, slapping the dust from his warm, fuzzy tweed suit, he summoned as raiment for his face awe and dedication in the proper proportions and tramped down the staircase, his heels ringing on the painted steel, bits of plaster gritty as sand beneath his sole. His hand, all the way, cherished the safety-rail.

"This would be no time to slip and fall," he warned himself cautiously. "No, no, I mustn't slip now."

My Object
All Sublime . . .

by Poul Anderson

WE MET in line of business. Michaels' firm wanted to start
a subdivision on the far side of Evanston and discovered that
I held title to some of the most promising acreage. They
made me a good offer, but I was stubborn; they raised it
and I stayed stubborn; finally the boss himself looked me
up. He wasn't entirely what I'd expected. Aggressive, of
course, but in so polite a way that it didn't offend, his man-
ners so urbane you rarely noticed his lack of formal education. Which lack he was remedying quite fast, anyhow,
via night classes and extension courses as well as omnivorous
reading.

We went out for a drink while we talked the matter over.
He led me to a bar that had little of Chicago about it:
quiet, shabby, no jukebox, no television, a bookshelf and
several chess sets, but none of the freaks and phonies who
usually infest such places. Besides ourselves, there were
only half a dozen customers—a professor-emeritus type
among the books, some people arguing politics with a degree of factual relevancy, a young man debating with the
bartender whether Bartok was more original than Schoen-
berg or vice versa. Michaels and I found a corner table
and some Danish beer.

I explained that I didn't care about money one way or
another, but objected to bulldozing some rather good-looking
countryside in order to erect still another chrome-plated
slum. Michaels stuffed his pipe before answering. He was a
lean, erect man, long-chinned and Roman-nosed, his hair
grizzled, his eyes dark and luminous. "Didn't my representa-
tive explain?" he said. "We aren't planning a row of identical

split-level sties. We have six basic designs in mind, with variations, to be located in a pattern . . . so."

He took out pencil and paper and began to sketch. As he talked, his accent thickened, but the fluency remained. And he made his own case better than anyone had done for him. Like it or not, he said, this was the middle twentieth century and mass production was here to stay. A community need not be less attractive for being ready-made, could in fact gain an artistic unity. He proceeded to show me how.

He didn't press me too hard, and conversation wandered. "Delightful spot, this," I remarked. "How'd you find it?"

He shrugged. "I often prowl about, especially at night. Exploring."

"Isn't that rather dangerous?"

"Not in comparison," he said with a touch of grimness.

"Uh . . . I gather you weren't born over here?"

"No. I didn't arrive in the United States until 1946. What they called a DP, a displaced person. I became Thad Michaels because I got tired of spelling out Tadeusz Michalowski. Nor did I want any part of old-country sentimentalism; I'm a zealous assimilationist."

Otherwise he seldom talked much about himself. Later I got some details of his early rise in business, from admiring and envious competitors. Some of them didn't yet believe it was possible to sell a house with radiant heating for less than twenty thousand dollars and show a profit. Michaels had found ways to make it possible. Not bad for a penniless immigrant.

I checked up and found he'd been admitted on a special visa, in consideration of services rendered the U. S. Army in the last stages of the European war. Those services had taken nerve as well as quick-wittedness.

Meanwhile our acquaintance developed. I sold him the land he wanted, but we continued to see each other, sometimes in the tavern, sometimes at my bachelor apartment, most often in his lakeshore penthouse. He had a stunning blonde wife and a couple of bright, well-mannered boys. Nonetheless he was a lonely man, and I fulfilled his need for friendship.

A year or so after we first met, he told me the story.

I'd been invited over for Thanksgiving dinner. Afterward we sat around and talked. And talked. And talked. When we

had ranged from the chances of an upset in the next city
election to the chances of other planets following the same
general course of history as our own, Amalie excused herself and went to bed. This was long past midnight. Michaels
and I kept on talking. I had not seen him so excited before. It
was as if that last subject, or some particular word, had
opened a door for him. Finally he got up, refilled our
whisky glasses with a motion not altogether steady, and
walked across the living room (noiseless on that deep green
carpet) to the picture window.

The night was clear and sharp. We overlooked the city,
streaks and webs and coils of glittering color, ruby, amethyst,
emerald, topaz, and the dark sheet of Lake Michigan; almost
it seemed we could glimpse endless white plains beyond.
But overhead arched the sky, crystal black, where the Great
Bear stood on his tail and Orion went striding along the
Milky Way. I had not often seen so big and frosty a view.

"After all," he said, "I know what I'm talking about."

I stirred, deep in my armchair. The fire on the hearth
spat tiny blue flames. Besides this, only one shaded lamp
lit the room, so that the star swarms had also been visible
to me when I passed by the window earlier. I gibed a little.
"Personally?"

He glanced back toward me. His face was stiff. "What
would you say if I answered yes?"

I sipped my drink. King's Ransom is a noble and comforting brew, most especially when the Earth itself seems
to tone with a deepening chill. "I'd suppose you had your
reasons and wait to see what they were."

He grinned one-sidedly. "Oh, well, I'm from this planet
too," he said. "And yet—yet the sky is so wide and strange,
don't you think the strangeness would affect men who went
there? Wouldn't it seep into them, so they carried it back in
their bones, and Earth was never quite the same afterward?"

"Go on. You know I like fantasies."

He stared outward, and then back again, and suddenly he
tossed off his drink. The violent gesture was unlike him.
But so had his hesitation been.

He said in a harsh tone, with all the former accent: "Okay,
then, I shall tell you a fantasy. It is a story for winter,
though, a cold story, that you are best advised not to take
so serious."

I drew on the excellent cigar he had given me and waited in the silence he needed.

He paced a few times back and forth before the window, eyes to the floor, until he filled his glass anew and sat down near me. He didn't look at me but at a picture on the wall, a somber, unintelligible thing which no one else liked. He seemed to get strength from it, for he began talking, fast and softly.

"Once upon a time, a very, very long time in the future, there was a civilization. I shall not describe it to you, for that would not be possible. Could you go back to the time of the Egyptian pyramid builders and tell them about this city below us? I don't mean they wouldn't believe you; of course they wouldn't, but that hardly matters. I mean they would not understand. Nothing you said could make sense to them. And the way people work and think and believe would be less comprehensible than those lights and towers and machines. Not so? If I spoke to you of people in the future living among great blinding energics, and of genetic changelings, and imaginary wars, and talking stones, and a certain blind hunter, you might feel anything at all, but you would not understand.

"So I ask you only to imagine how many thousands of times this planet has circled the sun, how deeply buried and forgotten we are; and then also to imagine that this other civilization thinks in patterns so foreign that it has ignored every limitation of logic and natural law, to discover means of traveling in time. So, while the ordinary dweller in that age (I can't exactly call him a citizen, or anything else for which we have a word, because it would be too misleading) —the average educated dweller knows in a vague, uninterested way that millennia ago some semi-savages were the first to split the atom—only one or two men have actually been here, walked among us, studied and mapped us and returned with a file of information for the central brain, if I may call it by such a name. No one else is concerned with us, any more than you are concerned with early Mesopotamian archeology. You see?"

He dropped his gaze to the tumbler in his hand and held it there, as if the whisky were an oracular pool. The silence grew. At last I said, "Very well. For the sake of the story, I'll accept the premise. I imagine time travelers would be unnoticeable. They'd have techniques of disguise and so on. Wouldn't want to change their own past."

"Oh, no danger of that," he said. "It's only that they couldn't learn much if they went around insisting they were from the future. Just imagine."

I chuckled.

Michaels gave me a shadowed look. "Apart from the scientific," he said, "can you guess what use there might be for time travel?"

"Well," I suggested, "trade in objects of art or natural resources. Go back to the dinosaur age and dig up iron before man appeared to strip the richest mines."

He shook his head. "Think again. They'd only want a limited number of Minoan statuettes, Ming vases, or Third World Hegemony dwarfs, chiefly for their museums. If 'museum' isn't too inaccurate a word. I tell you, they are *not* like us. As for natural resources, they're beyond the point of needing any; they make their own."

He paused, as if before a final plunge. Then: "What was this penal colony the French abandoned?"

"Devil's Island?"

"Yes, that was it. Can you imagine a better revenge on a condemned criminal than to maroon him in the past?"

"Why, I should think they'd be above any concept of revenge, or even of deterrence by horrible examples. Even in this century, we're aware that that doesn't work."

"Are you sure?" he asked quietly. "Side by side with the growth of today's enlightened penology, haven't we a corresponding growth of crime itself? You were wondering, some time ago, how I dared walk the night streets alone. Furthermore, punishment is a catharsis of society as a whole. Up in the future they'd tell you that public hangings did reduce the crime rate, which would otherwise have been still higher. Somewhat more important, these spectacles made possible the eighteenth century birth of real humanitarianism." He raised a sardonic brow. "Or so they claim in the future. It doesn't matter whether they are right, or merely rationalizing a degraded element in their own civilization. All you need assume is that they do send their very worst criminals back into the past."

"Rather rough on the past," I said.

"No, not really. For a number of reasons, including the fact that everything they cause to happen has already happened . . . Damn! English isn't built for talking about these paradoxes. Mainly, though, you must remember that they don't waste all this effort on ordinary miscreants. One has to be a very rare criminal to deserve exile in time. And the worst crime in the world depends on the particular year of the world's history. Murder, brigandage, treason, heresy, narcotics peddling, slaving, patriotism, the whole catalogue, all have rated capital punishment in some epochs, and been lightly regarded in others, and positively commended in still others. Think back and see if I'm not right."

I regarded him for a while, observing how deep the lines were in his face and recalling that at his age he shouldn't be so gray. "Very well," I said. "Agreed. But would not a man from the future, possessing all its knowledge—"

He set his glass down with audible force. "*What* knowledge?" he rapped. "Use your brains! Imagine yourself left naked and alone in Babylon. How much Babylonian language or history do you know? Who's the present king, how much longer will he reign, who'll succeed him? What are the laws and customs you must obey? You remember that eventually the Assyrians or the Persians or someone will conquer Babylon and there'll be hell to pay. But when? How? Is the current war a mere border skirmish or an all-out struggle? If the latter, is Babylon going to win? If not, what peace terms will be imposed? Why, there wouldn't be twenty men today who could answer those questions without looking up the answers in a book. And you're not one of them; nor have you been given a book."

"I think," I said slowly, "I'd head for the nearest temple, once I'd picked up enough of the language. I'd tell the priest I could make . . . oh . . . fireworks—"

He laughed, with small merriment. "How? You're in Babylon, remember. Where do you find sulfur and saltpeter? If you can get across to the priest what you want, and somehow persuade him to obtain the stuff for you, how do you compound a powder that'll actually go off instead of just fizzing? For your information, that's quite an art. Hell, you couldn't even get a berth as a deckhand. You'd be lucky if you ended up scrubbing floors. A slave in the fields is a likelier career. Isn't it?"

The fire sank low.

"All right," I conceded. "True."

"They pick the era with care, you know." He looked back

toward the window. Seen from our chairs, reflection on the glass blotted out the stars, so that we were only aware of the night itself.

"When a man is sentenced to banishment," he said, "all the experts confer, pointing out what the periods of their specialties would be like for this particular individual. You can see how a squeamish, intellectual type, dropped into Homeric Greece, would find it a living nightmare, whereas a rowdy type might get along fairly well—might even end up as a respected warrior. If the rowdy was not the blackest of criminals, they might actually leave him near the hall of Agamemnon, condemning him to no more than danger, discomfort, and homesickness.

"Oh, God," he whispered. "The homesickness!"

So much darkness rose in him as he spoke that I sought to steady him with a dry remark: "They must immunize the convict to every ancient disease. Otherwise this'd only be an elaborate death sentence."

His eyes focused on me again. "Yes," he said. "And of course the longevity serum is still active in his veins. That's all, however. He's dropped in an unfrequented spot after dark, the machine vanishes, he's cut off for the rest of his life. All he knows is that they've chosen an era for him with . . . such characteristics . . . that they expect the punishment will fit his crime."

Stillness fell once more upon us, until the clock on the mantel became the loudest thing in the world, as if all other sound had frozen to death outside. I glanced at its dial. The night was old; soon the east would be turning pale.

When I looked back, he was still watching me, disconcertingly intent. "What was your crime?" I asked.

He didn't seem taken aback, only said wearily, "What does it matter? I told you the crimes of one age are the heroisms of another. If my attempt had succeeded, the centuries to come would have adored my name. But I failed."

"A lot of people must have got hurt," I said. "A whole world must have hated you."

"Well, yes," he said. And after a minute: "This is a fantasy I'm telling you, of course. To pass the time."

"I'm playing along with you," I smiled.

His tension eased a trifle. He leaned back, his legs stretched across that glorious carpet. "So. Given as much of the fantasy as I've related, how did you deduce the extent of my alleged guilt?"

"Your past life. When and where were you left?"

He said, in as bleak a voice as I've ever heard, "Near Warsaw, in August, 1939."

"I don't imagine you care to talk about the war years."

"No, I don't."

However, he went on when enough defiance had accumulated: "My enemies blundered. The confusion following the German attack gave me a chance to escape from police custody before I could be stuck in a concentration camp. Gradually I learned what the situation was. Of course, I couldn't predict anything. I still can't; only specialists know, or care, what happened in the twentieth century. But by the time I'd become a Polish conscript in the German forces, I realized this was the losing side. So I slipped across to the Americans, told them what I'd observed, became a scout for them. Risky—but if I'd stopped a bullet, what the hell? I didn't; and I ended up with plenty of sponsors to get me over here; and the rest of the story is conventional."

My cigar had gone out. I relit it, for Michaels' cigars were not to be taken casually. He had them especially flown from Amsterdam.

"The alien corn," I said.

"What?"

"You know. Ruth in exile. She wasn't badly treated, but she stood weeping for her homeland."

"No, I don't know that story."

"It's in the Bible."

"Ah, yes. I really must read the Bible sometime." His mood was changing by the moment, toward the assurance I had first encountered. He swallowed his whisky with a gesture almost debonair. His expression was alert and confident.

"Yes," he said, "that aspect was pretty bad. Not so much the physical conditions of life. You've doubtless gone camping and noticed how soon you stop missing hot running water, electric lights, all the gadgets that their manufacturers assure us are absolute necessities. I'd be glad of a gravity reducer or a cell stimulater if I had one, but I get along fine without. The homesickness, though, that's what eats you. Little things you never noticed, some particular food, the way people walk, the games played, the small-talk top-

ics. Even the constellations. They're different in the future.
The sun has traveled that far in its galactic orbit.

"But, voluntary or forced, people have always been emi-
grating. We're all descended from those who could stand the
shock. I adapted."

A scowl crossed his brows. "I wouldn't go back now even
if I were given a free pardon," he said, "the way those trai-
tors are running things."

I finished my own drink, tasting it with my whole tongue
and palate, for it was a marvelous whisky, and listened to
him with only half an ear. "You like it here?"

"Yes," he said. "By now I do. I'm over the emotional
hump. Being so busy the first few years just staying alive,
and then so busy establishing myself after I came to this
country, that helped. I never had much time for self-pity.
Now my business interests me more and more, a fascinating
game, and pleasantly free of extreme penalties for wrong
moves. I've discovered qualities here that the future has lost
. . . I'll bet you have no idea how exotic this city is. Think.
At this moment, within five miles of us, there's a soldier on
guard at an atomic laboratory, a bum freezing in a doorway,
an orgy in a millionaire's apartment, a priest making ready
for sunrise rites, a merchant from Araby, a spy from Mus-
covy, a ship from the Indies . . ."

His excitement softened. He looked from the window
and the night, inward, toward the bedrooms. "And my wife
and kids," he finished, most gently. "No, I wouldn't go back,
no matter what happened."

I took a final breath of my cigar. "You *have* done rather
well."

Liberated from his gray mood, he grinned at me. "You
know, I think you believe that yarn."

"Oh, I do." I stubbed out the cigar, rose, and stretched.
"The hour is late. We'd better be going."

He didn't notice at once. When he did, he came out of
his chair like a big cat. *"We?"*

"Of course." I drew a nerve gun from my pocket. He
stopped in his tracks. "This sort of thing isn't left to chance.
We check up. Come along, now."

The blood drained from his face. "No," he mouthed, "no,
no, no, you can't, it isn't fair, not to Amalie, the children—"

"That," I told him, "is part of the punishment."

I left him in Damascus, the year before Tamerlane sacked it.

Human Man's Burden

by Robert Sheckley

EDWARD FLASWELL bought his planetoid, sight unseen, at the Interstellar Land Office on Earth. He selected it on the basis of a photograph, which showed little more than a range of picturesque mountains. But Flaswell loved mountains and as he remarked to the Claims Clerk, "Might be gold in them thar hills, mightn't thar, pardner?"

"Sure, pal, sure," the clerk responded, wondering what man in his right mind would put himself several light-years from the nearest woman of any description whatsoever. No man in his right mind would, the clerk decided, and gave Flaswell a searching look.

But Flaswell was perfectly sane. He just hadn't stopped to consider the problem.

Accordingly, Flaswell put down a small sum in credits and made a large promise to improve his land every year. As soon as the ink was dry upon his deed, he purchased passage aboard a second-class drone freighter, loaded it with an assortment of second-hand equipment and set out for his holdings.

Most novice pioneers find they have purchased a sizable chunk of naked rock. Flaswell was lucky. His planetoid, which he named Chance, had a minimal manufactured atmosphere that he could boost to breathable status. There was water, which his well-digging equipment tapped on the twenty-third attempt. He found no gold in them thar hills, but there was some exportable thorium. And best of all, much of the soil was suitable for the cultivation of dir, olge, smis and other luxury fruits.

As Flaswell kept telling his robot foreman, "This place is going to make me rich!"

"Sure, Boss, sure," the robot always responded.

The planetoid had undeniable promise. Its development was an enormous task for one man, but Flaswell was only twenty-seven years old, strongly built and of a determined frame of mind. Beneath his hand, the planetoid flourished. Months passed and Flaswell planted his fields, mined his picturesque mountains and shipped his goods out by the infrequent drone freighter that passed his way.

One day, his robot foreman said to him, "Boss Man, sir, you don't look too good, Mr. Flaswell, sir."

Flaswell frowned at this speech. The man he had bought his robots from had been a Human Supremicist of the most rabid sort, who had coded the robots' responses according to his own ideas of the respect due Human People. Flaswell found this annoying, but he couldn't afford new response tapes. And where else could he have picked up robots for so little money?

"Nothing wrong with me, Gunga-Sam," Flaswell replied.

"Ah! I beg pardon! But this is not so, Mr. Flaswell, Boss. You have been talking to yourself in the fields, you should excuse my saying it."

"Aw, it's nothing."

"And you have the beginning of a tic in your left eye, sahib. And your fingers are trembling. And you are drinking too much. And—"

"That's enough, Gunga-Sam. A robot should know his place," Flaswell said. He saw the hurt expression that the robot's metal face somehow managed to convey. He sighed and said, "You're right, of course. You're always right, old friend. What's the matter with me?"

"You are bearing too much of the Human Man's Burden."

"Don't I know it!" Flaswell ran a hand through his unruly black hair. "Sometimes I envy you robots. Always laughing, carefree, happy—"

"It is because we have no souls."

"Unfortunately I do. What do you suggest?"

"Take a vacation, Mr. Flaswell, Boss," Gunga-Sam suggested, and wisely withdrew to let his master think.

Flaswell appreciated his servitor's kindly suggestion, but a vacation was difficult. His planetoid, Chance, was in the Throcian System, which was about as isolated as one could get in this day and age. True, he was only a fifteen-day flight from the tawdry amusements of Cythera III and not much farther from Nagóndicon, where considerable fun could be obtained for the strong in stomach. But distance is money, and money was the very thing Flaswell was trying to make on Chance.

He planted more crops, dug more thorium and began to grow a beard. He continued to mumble to himself in the fields and to drink heavily in the evenings. Some of the simple farm robots grew alarmed when Flaswell lurched past and they began praying to the outlawed Combustion God. But loyal Gunga-Sam soon put a stop to this ominous turn of events.

"Ignorant mechanicals!" he told them. "The Boss Human, he all right. Him strong, him good! Believe me, brothers, it is even as I say!"

But the murmurings did not cease, for robots look to Humans to set an example. The situation might have gotten out of hand if Flaswell had not received, along with his next shipment of food, a shiny new Roebuck-Ward catalogue.

Lovingly he spread it open upon his crude plastic table and, by the glow of a simple cold-light bulb, began to pore over its contents. What wonders there were for the isolated pioneer! Home distilling plants, and moon makers, and portable solidovision, and—

Flaswell turned a page, read it, gulped and read it again. It said:

MAIL ORDER BRIDES!

Pioneers, why suffer the curse of loneliness alone? Why bear the Hu-Man's Burden singly? Roebuck-Ward is now offering, for the first time, a limited selection of *Brides for the Frontiersman*!

The Roebuck-Ward Frontier Model Bride is carefully selected for strength, adaptability, agility, perseverance, pioneer skills and, of course, a measure of comeliness. These girls are conditioned to any planet, since they possess a relatively low center of gravity, a skin properly pigmented for all climates, and short, strong toe and fingernails. Shapewise, they are well-proportioned and yet not distractingly contoured, a quality which the hard-working pioneer should appreciate.

The Roebuck-Ward Frontier Model comes in three general sizes (see specifications below) to suit any man's taste. Upon receipt of your request, Roebuck-Ward will quick-freeze one and ship her to you by third-class Drone Freight. In this way, your express charges are kept to an absolute minimum.

Why not order a Frontier Model Bride *TODAY*?

Flaswell called for Gunga-Sam and showed him the advertisement. Silently the mechanical read, then looked his master full in the face.

"This is surely it, effendi," the foreman said.

"You think so, huh?" Flaswell stood up and began to pace nervously around the room. "But I wasn't planning on getting married just yet. I mean what kind of a way is this to get married? How do I know I'll like her?"

"It is proper for Human Man to have Human Woman."

"Yeah, but—"

"Besides, do they quick-freeze a preacher and ship *him* out, too?"

A slow smile broke over Flaswell's face as he digested his servant's shrewd question. "Gunga-Sam," he said, "as usual, you have gone directly to the heart of the matter. I guess there's a sort of moratorium on the ceremony while a man makes up his mind. Too expensive to quick-freeze a preacher. And it *would* be nice to have a gal around who could work her share."

Gunga-Sam managed to convey an inscrutable smile.

Flaswell sat down and ordered a Frontier Model Bride, specifying the small size, which he felt was plenty big enough. He gave Gunga-Sam the order to radio.

The next few weeks were filled with excitement for Flaswell and he began to scan the skies anxiously. The robots picked up the mood of anticipation. In the evenings, their carefree songs and dances were interspersed with whispering and secret merriment. The mechanicals said to Gunga-Sam over and over again, "Hey, Foreman! The new Human Woman Boss, what will she be like?"

"It's none of your concern," Gunga-Sam told them. "That's Human Man business and you robots leave it alone."

But at the end, he was watching the skies as anxiously as anyone.

During those weeks, Flaswell meditated on the virtues of Frontier Woman. The more he thought about it, the more he liked the idea. No pretty, useless, helpless painted woman for him! How pleasant it would be to have a cheerful, common-sense, down-to-gravity gal who could cook, wash, pretty up the place, boss the house robots, make clothes, put up jellies. . . .

So he dreamed away the time and bit his nails to the quick.

At last the drone freighter flashed across the horizon, landed, jettisoned a large packing case, and fled in the direction of Amyra IV.

The robots brought the case to Flaswell.

"Your new bride, sir!" they shouted triumphantly, and flung their oilcans in the air.

Flaswell immediately proclaimed a half-day holiday and soon he was alone in his living room with the great frigid box marked *"Handle with Care. Woman Inside."*

He pressed the defrosting controls, waited the requisite hour, and opened the box. Within was another box, which required two hours to defrost. Impatiently he waited, pacing up and down the room and gnawing on the remnants of his fingernails.

And then the time was up, and with shaking hands, Flaswell opened the lid and saw—

"Hey, what is this?" he cried.

The girl within the box blinked, yawned like a kitten, opened her eyes, sat up. They stared at each other and Flaswell knew that something was terribly wrong.

She was clothed in a beautiful, impractical white dress and her name, *Sheila,* was worked upon it in gold thread. The next thing Flaswell noticed was her slenderness, which was scarcely suitable for hard work on outplanet conditions. Her skin was a creamy white, obviously the kind that would blister under his planetoid's fierce summer sun. Her hands were long-fingered, red-nailed, elegant—completely unlike anything the Roebuck-Ward Company had promised. As for her legs and other parts, Flaswell decided they would be very well on Earth, but not here, where a man must pay attention to his work.

She couldn't even be said to have a low center of gravity. Quite the contrary.

Flaswell felt, not unreasonably, that he had been swindled, duped, made a fool of.

Sheila stepped out of the crate, walked to a window and looked out over Flaswell's flowering green fields and his picturesque mountains beyond them.

"But where are the palm trees?" she asked.

"Palm trees?"

"Of course. They told me that Srinigar V had palm trees."

"This is not Srinigar V," Flaswell said.

"But aren't you the Pasha of Srae?" Sheila gasped.

"Certainly not. I am a Frontiersman. Aren't you a Frontier Model Bride?"

"Do I *look* like a Frontier Model Bride?" Sheila snapped, her eyes flashing. "I am the Ultra Deluxe Luxury Model Bride and I was supposed to go to the sub-tropical paradise planet of Srinigar V."

"We've both been cheated. The shipping department must have made an error," Flaswell said gloomily.

The girl looked around Flaswell's crude living room and a wince twinged her pretty features. "Oh, well. I suppose you can arrange transportation for me to Srinigar V."

"I can't even afford to go to Nagóndicon," Flaswell said. "I will inform Roebuck-Ward of their error. They will undoubtedly arrange transportation for you, when they send me my Frontier Model Bride."

Sheila shrugged her shoulders. "Travel broadens one," she said.

Flaswell nodded. He was thinking hard. This girl had, it was obvious, no pioneering qualities. But she was amazingly pretty. He saw no reason why her stay shouldn't be a pleasant one for both.

"Under the circumstances," Flaswell said, with an ingratiating smile, "we might as well be friends."

"Under what circumstances?"

"We are the only two Human People on the planet." Flaswell rested a hand lightly on her shoulder. "Let's have a drink. Tell me all about yourself. Do you—"

At that moment, he heard a loud sound behind. He turned and saw a small, squat robot climbing from a compartment in the packing case.

"What do *you* want?" Flaswell demanded.

"I," said the robot, "am a Marrying Robot, empowered by the government to provide legal marriages in space. I am further directed by the Roebuck-Ward Company to act as guardian, duenna and protector for the young lady in my charge, until such time as my primary function, to perform a ceremony of marriage, has been accomplished."

"Uppity damned robot," Flaswell grumbled.

"What did you expect?" Sheila asked. "A quick-frozen Human preacher?"

"Of course not. But a robot duenna—"

"The very best kind," she assured him. "You'd be surprised at how some men act when they get a few light-years from Earth."

"I would?" Flaswell said disconsolately.

"So I'm told," Sheila replied, demurely looking away from him. "And after all, the promised bride of the Pasha of Srae should have a guardian of some sort."

"Dearly beloved," the robot intoned, "we are here gathered to join—"

"Not now," Sheila said loftily. "Not this one."

"I'll have the robots fix a room for you," Flaswell growled, and walked away, mumbling to himself about Human Man's Burden.

He radioed Roebuck-Ward and was told that the proper model Bride would be sent at once and the interloper shipped elsewhere. Then he returned to his farming and mining, determined to ignore the presence of Sheila and her duenna.

Work continued on Chance. There was thorium to be mined out of the soil and new wells to dig. Harvest time was soon at hand, and the robots toiled for long hours in the green-blossomed fields, and lubricating oil glistened on their honest metal faces, and the air was fragrant with the perfume of the dir flowers.

Sheila made her presence felt with subtle yet surprising force. Soon there were plastic lampshades over the naked cold-light bulbs and drapes over the stark windows and scatter rugs on the floors. And there were many other changes around the house that Flaswell felt rather than saw.

His diet underwent a change, too. The robot chef's memory tape had worn thin in many spots, so all the poor mechanical could remember how to make was beef Stroganoff, cucumber salad, rice pudding and cocoa. Flaswell had, with considerable stoicism, been eating these dishes ever since he came to Chance, varying them occasionally with shipwreck rations.

Then Sheila took the robot chef in hand. Patiently she impressed upon his memory tape the recipes for beef stew, pot roast, tossed green salad, apple pie, and many others. The eating situation upon Chance began to improve markedly.

But when Sheila put up smis jelly in vacuum jars, Flaswell began to have doubts.

Here, after all, was a remarkably practical young lady, in spite of her expensive appearance. She could do all the things a Frontier Wife could do. And she had other attributes. What did he need a regular Roebuck-Ward Frontier Model for?

After mulling this for a while, Flaswell said to his foreman, "Gunga-Sam, I am confused."

"Ah?" said the foreman, his metal face impassive.

"I guess I need a little of that robot intuition. She's doing very well, isn't she, Gunga-Sam?"

"The Human Woman is taking her proper share of Human Person's Burden."

"She sure is. But can it last? She's doing as much as any Frontier Model Wife could do, isn't she? Cooking, canning—"

"The workers love her," Gunga-Sam said with simple dignity. "You did not know, sir, but when that rust epidemic broke out last week, she toiled night and day, bringing relief and comforting the frightened younger robots."

"She did all that?" Flaswell gasped, shaken. "But a girl of her background, a luxury model—"

"It does not matter. She is a Human Person and she has the strength and nobility to take on Human Person's Burden."

"Do you know," Flaswell said slowly, "this has convinced me. I really believe she is fit to stay here. It's not her fault she isn't a Frontier Model. That's a matter of screening and conditioning, and you can't change that. I'm going to tell her she can stay. And then I'll cancel the other Roebuck order."

A strange expression glowed in the foreman's eyes, an expression almost of amusement. He bowed low and said, "It shall be as the master wishes."

Flaswell hurried out to find Sheila.

She was in the sick bay, which had been constructed out of an old toolshed. With the aid of a robot mechanic, she was caring for the dents and dislocations that are the peculiar lot of metal-skinned beings.

"Sheila," Flaswell said, "I want to speak to you."

"Sure," she answered absently, "as soon as I tighten this bolt."

She locked the bolt cleverly into place, and tapped the robot with her wrench.

"There, Pedro," she said, "try that leg now."

The robot stood up gingerly, put weight on the leg, found that it held. He capered comically around the Human Woman, saying, "You sure fixed it, Boss Lady. Gracias, ma'am."

And he danced out into the sunshine.

Flaswell and Sheila watched him go, smiling at his antics. "They're just like children," Flaswell said.

"One can't help but love them," Sheila responded. "They're so happy, so carefree—"

"But they haven't got souls," Flaswell reminded her.

"No," she agreed somberly. "They haven't. What did you wish to see me about?"

"I wanted to tell you—" Flaswell looked around. The sick bay was an antiseptic place, filled with wrenches, screwdrivers, hacksaws, ballpeen hammers and other medical equipment. It was hardly the atmosphere for the sort of announcement he was about to make.

"Come with me," he said.

They walked out of the hospital and through the blossoming green fields, to the foot of Flaswell's spectacular mountains. There, shadowed by craggy cliffs, was a still, dark pool of water overhung with giant trees, which Flaswell had force-grown. Here they paused.

"I wanted to say this," Flaswell said. "You have surprised me completely, Sheila. I expected you would be a parasite, a purposeless person. Your background, your breeding, your appearance all pointed in this direction. But I was wrong. You have risen to the challenge of a Frontier environment, have conquered it triumphantly, and have won the hearts of everybody."

"Everybody?" Sheila asked very softly.

"I believe I can speak for every robot on the planetoid.

They idolize you. I think you belong here, Sheila."

The girl was silent for a long while, and the wind murmured through the boughs of the giant force-grown trees, and ruffled the black surface of the lake.

Finally she said, "Do *you* think I belong here?"

Flaswell felt engulfed by her exquisite perfection, lost in the topaz depths of her eyes. His breath came fast, he touched her hand, her fingers clung.

"Sheila. . . ."

"Yes, Edward. . . ."

"Dearly beloved," a strident metallic voice barked, "we are here gathered—"

"Not now, you fool!" Sheila cried.

The Marrying Robot came forward and said sulkily, "Much as I hate to interfere in the affairs of Human People, my taped coefficients are such that I must. To my way of thinking, physical contact is meaningless. I have, by way of experiment, clashed limbs with a seamstress robot. All I got for my troubles was a dent. Once I thought I experienced something, an electric something that shot through me giddily and made me think of slowly shifting geometric forms. But upon examination, I discovered the insulation had parted from a conductor center. Therefore, the emotion was invalid."

"Uppity damned robot," Flaswell growled.

"Excuse my presumption. I was merely trying to explain that I personally find my instructions unintelligible—that is, to prevent any and all physical contact until a ceremony of marriage has been performed. But there it is; those are my orders. Can't I get it over with now?"

"No!" said Sheila.

The robot shrugged his shoulders fatalistically and slid into the underbrush.

"Can't stand a robot who doesn't know his place," said Flaswell. "But it's all right."

"What?"

"Yes," Flaswell said, with an air of conviction. "You are as good as any Frontier Model Wife and far prettier. Sheila, will you marry me?"

The robot, who had been thrashing around in the underbrush, now slid eagerly toward them.

"No," said Sheila.

"No?" Flaswell repeated uncomprehendingly.

"You heard me. No! Absolutely no!"

"But why? You fit so well here, Sheila. The robots adore you. I've never seen them work so well—"

"I'm not interested in your robots," she said, standing very straight, her hair disheveled, her eyes blazing. "And I am not interested in your planetoid. And I am most emphatically not interested in you. I am going to Srinigar V, where I will be the pampered bride of the Pasha of Srae!"

They stared at each other, Sheila white-faced with anger, Flaswell red with confusion.

The Marrying Robot said, "Now should I start the ceremony? Dearly beloved. . . ."

Sheila whirled and ran toward the house.

"I don't understand," the Marrying Robot said plaintively. "It's all very bewildering. When does the ceremony take place?"

"It doesn't," Flaswell said, and stalked toward the house, his brows beetling with rage.

The robot hesitated, sighed metallically and hurried after the Ultra Deluxe Luxury Model Bride.

All that night, Flaswell sat in his room, drank deeply and mumbled to himself. Shortly after dawn, the loyal Gunga-Sam knocked and slipped into the room.

"Women!" Flaswell snarled to his servitor.

"Ah?" said Gunga-Sam.

"I'll never understand them," Flaswell said. "She led me on. I thought she wanted to stay here. I thought. . . ."

"The mind of Human Man is murky and dark," said Gunga-Sam, "but it is as crystal compared to the mind of Human Woman."

"Where did you get that?" Flaswell asked.

"It is an ancient robot proverb."

"You robots. Sometimes I wonder if you *don't* have souls."

"Oh, no, Mr. Flaswell, Boss. It is expressly written in our Construction Specifications that robots are to be built with no souls, to spare them anguish."

"A very wise provision," Flaswell said, "and something they might consider with Human People, too. Well, to hell with her. What do you want?"

"I came to tell you, sir, that the drone freighter is landing."

Flaswell turned pale. "So soon? Then it's bringing my new bride!"

"Undoubtedly."

"And it will take Sheila away to Srinigar V."

"Assuredly, sir."

Flaswell groaned and clutched his head. Then he straightened and said, "All right, all right. I'll see if she's ready."

He found Sheila in the living room, watching the drone freighter spiral in. She said, "The very best of luck, Edward. I hope your new bride fulfills all your expectations."

The drone freighter landed and the robots began removing a large packing case.

"I had better go," Sheila said. "They won't wait long." She held out her hand.

Flaswell took it.

He held her hand for a moment, then found he was holding her arm. She did not resist, nor did the Marrying Robot break into the room. Flaswell suddenly found that Sheila was in his arms. He kissed her and felt exactly like a small sun going nova.

Finally she said, "Wow," huskily, in a not quite believing voice.

Flaswell cleared his throat twice. "Sheila, I love you. I can't offer you much luxury here, but if you'd stay—"

"It's about time you found out you love me, you dope!" she said. "Of course I'm staying!"

The next few minutes were ecstatic and decidedly vertiginous. They were interrupted at last by the sound of loud robot voices outside. The door burst open and the Marrying Robot stamped in, followed by Gunga-Sam and two farm mechanicals.

"Really!" the Marrying Robot said. "It is unbelievable! To think I'd see the day when robot pitted himself against robot!"

"What happened?" Flaswell asked.

"This foreman of yours *sat* on me," the Marrying Robot said indignantly, "while his cronies held my limbs. I was merely trying to enter this room and perform my duty as set forth by the government and the Roebuck-Ward Company."

"Why, Gunga-Sam!" Flaswell said, grinning.

The Marrying Robot hurried up to Sheila. "Are you damaged? Any dents? Any short-circuits?"

"I don't think so," said Sheila breathlessly.

Gunga-Sam said to Flaswell, "The fault is all mine, Boss,

sir. But everyone knows that Human Man and Human Woman need solitude during the courtship period. I merely performed what I considered my duty to the Human Race in this respect, Mr. Flaswell, Boss, sahib."

"You did well, Gunga-Sam," Flaswell said. "I'm deeply grateful and—oh, Lord!"

"What is it?" Sheila asked apprehensively.

Flaswell was staring out the window. The farm robots were carrying the large packing case toward the house.

"The Frontier Model Bride!" said Flaswell. "What'll we do, darling? I canceled you and legally contracted for the other one. Do you think we can break the contract?"

Sheila laughed. "Don't worry. There's no Frontier Model Bride in that box. Your order was canceled as soon as it was received."

"It was?"

"Certainly." She looked down, ashamed. "You'll hate me for this—"

"I won't," he promised. "What is it?"

"Well, Frontiersmen's pictures are on file at the Company, you know, so Brides can see what they're getting. There *is* a choice—for the girls, I mean—and I'd been hanging around the place so long, unable to get unclassified as an Ultra Deluxe, that I—I made friends with the head of the order department. And," she said all in a rush, "I got myself sent here."

"But the Pasha of Srae—"

"I made him up."

"But why?" Flaswell asked puzzledly. "You're so pretty—"

"That everybody expects me to be a toy for some spoiled, pudgy idiot," she finished with a good deal of heat. "I don't want to be! I want to be a wife! And I'm just as good as any chunky, homely female!"

"Better," he said.

"I can cook and doctor robots and be practical, can't I? Haven't I proved it?"

"Of course, dear."

She began to cry. "But nobody would believe it, so I had to trick you into letting me stay long enough to—to fall in love with me."

"Which I did," he said, drying her eyes for her. "It's all worked out fine. The whole thing was a lucky accident."

What looked like a blush appeared on Gunga-Sam's metallic face.

"You mean it wasn't an accident?" Flaswell exclaimed.

"Well, sir, Mr. Flaswell, effendi, it is well-known that Human Man needs *attractive* Human Woman. The Frontier Model sounded a little severe and Memsahib Sheila is a daughter of a friend of my former master. So I took the libery of sending the order directly to her. She got her friend in the order department to show her your picture and ship her here. I hope you are not displeased with your humble servant for disobeying."

"Well, I'll be damned," Flaswell finally got out. "It's like I always said—you robots understand Human People better than anyone." He turned to Sheila. "But what *is* in that packing case?"

"My dresses and my jewelry, my shoes, my cosmetics, my hair styler, my—"

"But—"

"You want me to look nice when we go visiting, dear," Sheila said. "After all, Cythera III is only fifteen days away. I looked it up before I came."

Flaswell nodded resignedly. You had to expect something like this from an Ultra Deluxe Luxury Model Bride.

"Now!" Sheila said, turning to the Marrying Robot.

The robot didn't answer.

"Now!" Flaswell shouted.

"You're quite sure?" the robot queried sulkily.

"Yes! Get started!"

"I just don't understand," the Marrying Robot said. "Why now? Why not last week? Am I the only sane one here? Oh, well. Dearly beloved. . . ."

And the ceremony was held at last. Flaswell proclaimed a three-day holiday and the robots sang and danced and celebrated in their carefree robot fashion.

Thereafter, life was never the same on Chance. The Flaswells began to have a modest social life, to visit and be visited by couples fifteen and twenty days out, on Cythera III, Tham and Randico I. But the rest of the time, Sheila was an irreproachable Frontier Wife, loved by the robots and idolized by her husband. The Marrying Robot, following his instruction manual, retrained himself as an accountant and bookkeeper, skills for which his mentality was peculiarly well-suited. He often said the whole place would go to pieces if it weren't for him.

And the robots continued to dig thorium from the soil,

and the dir, olge and smis blossomed, and Flaswell and Sheila shared together the responsibility of Human People's Burden.

Flaswell was always quite vocal on the advantages of shopping at Roebuck-Ward. But Sheila knew that the real advantage was in having a foreman like the loyal, soulless Gunga-Sam.

On the Fourth Planet

by J. F. Bone

THE UL KWORN paused in his search for food, extended his eye and considered the thing that blocked his path.

He hadn't noticed the obstacle until he had almost touched it. His attention had been focused upon gleaning every feeder large enough to be edible from the lichens that covered his feeding strip. But the unexpected warmth radiating from the object had startled him. Sundown was at hand. There should be nothing living or non-living that radiated a fraction of the heat that was coming from the gleaming metal wall which lay before him. He expanded his mantle to trap the warmth as he pushed his eye upward to look over the top. It wasn't high, just high enough to be a nuisance. It curved away from him toward the boundaries of his strip, extending completely across the width of his land.

A dim racial memory told him that this was an artifact, a product of the days when the Folk had leisure to dream and time to build. It had probably been built by his remote ancestors millennia ago and had just recently been uncovered from its hiding place beneath the sand. These metal objects kept appearing and disappearing as the sands shifted to the force of the wind. He had seen them before, but never a piece so large or so well-preserved. It shone as though it had been made yesterday, gleaming with a soft silvery luster against the blue-black darkness of the sky.

As his eye cleared the top of the wall, he quivered with shock and astonishment. For it was not a wall as he had thought. Instead, it was the edge of a huge metal disc

72

fifty raads in diameter. And that wasn't all of it. Three thick columns of metal extended upward from the disc, leaning inward as they rose into the sky. High overhead, almost beyond the range of accurate vision, they converged to support an immense cylinder set vertically to the ground. The cylinder was almost as great in diameter as the disc upon which his eye first rested. It loomed overhead, and he had a queasy feeling that it was about to fall and crush him. Strange jointed excrescences studded its surface, and in its side, some two-thirds of the way up, two smaller cylinders projected from the bigger one. They were set a little distance apart, divided by a vertical row of four black designs, and pointed straight down his feeding strip.

The Ul Kworn eyed the giant structure with disgust and puzzlement. The storm that had uncovered it must have been a great one to have blown so much sand away. It was just his fortune to have the thing squatting in his path! His mantle darkened with anger. Why was it that everything happened to him? Why couldn't it have lain in someone else's way, upon the land of one of his neighbors? It blocked him from nearly three thousand square raads of life-sustaining soil. To cross it would require energy he could not spare. Why couldn't it have been on the Ul Caada's or the Ul Varsi's strip—or any other of the numberless Folk? Why did he have to be faced with this roadblock?

He couldn't go around it since it extended beyond his territory and, therefore, he'd have to waste precious energy propelling his mass up the wall and across the smooth shining surface of the disc—all of which would have to be done without food, since his eye could see no lichen growing upon the shiny metal surface.

The chill of evening had settled on the land. Most of the Folk were already wrapped in their mantles, conserving their energy until the dawn would warm them into life. But Kworn felt no need to estivate. It was warm enough beside the wall.

The air shimmered as it cooled. Microcrystals of ice formed upon the legs of the structure, outlining them in shimmering contrast to the drab shadowy landscape, with its gray-green cover of lichens stippled with the purple balls of the lichen feeders that clung to them. Beyond Kworn and his neighbors, spaced twenty raads apart, the mantled bodies of the Folk stretched in a long single line across the rolling landscape, vanishing into the darkness. Behind this line, a day's travel to the rear, another line of the Folk was following. Behind them was yet another. There were none ahead, for the Ul Kworn and the other Ul were the elders of the Folk and moved along in the first rank where their maturity and ability to reproduce had placed them according to the Law.

Caada and Varsi stirred restlessly, stimulated to movement by the heat radiating from the obstacle, but compelled by the Law to hold their place in the ranks until the sun's return would stimulate the others. Their dark crimson mantles rippled over the soil as they sent restless pseudopods to the boundaries of their strips.

They were anxious in their attempt to communicate with the Ul Kworn.

But Kworn wasn't ready to communicate. He held aloof as he sent a thin pseudopod out toward the gleaming wall in front of him. He was squandering energy; but he reasoned that he had better learn all he could about this thing before he attempted to cross it tomorrow, regardless of what it cost.

It was obvious that he would have to cross it, for the Law was specific about encroachment upon a neighbor's territory. *No member of the Folk shall trespass the feeding land of another during the Time of Travel except with published permission. Trespass shall be punished by the ejection of the offender from his place in rank.*

And that was equivalent to a death sentence.

He could ask Caada or Varsi for permission, but he was virtually certain that he wouldn't get it. He wasn't on particularly good terms with his neighbors. Caada was querulous, old and selfish. He had not reproduced this season and his vitality was low. He was forever hungry and not averse to slipping a sly pseudopod across the boundaries of his land to poach upon that of his neighbor. Kworn had warned him some time ago that he would not tolerate encroachment and would call for a group judgment if there was any poaching. And since the Folk were physically incapable of lying to one another, Caada would be banished. After that Caada kept his peace, but his dislike for Kworn was always evident.

But Varsi who held the land on Kworn's right was worse.

He had advanced to Ul status only a year ago. At that time there had been rumors among the Folk about illicit feeding and stealing of germ plasm from the smaller and weaker members of the race. But that could not be proved, and many young Folk died in the grim process of growing to maturity. Kworn shrugged. If Varsi was an example of the younger generation, society was heading hell-bent toward Emptiness. He had no love for the pushing, aggressive youngster who crowded out to the very borders of his domain, pressing against his neighbors, alert and aggressive toward the slightest accidental spillover into his territory. What was worse, Varsi had reproduced successfully this year and thus had rejuvenated. Kworn's own attempt had been only partially successful. His energy reserves hadn't been great enough to produce a viable offspring, and the rejuvenation process in his body had only gone to partial completion. It would be enough to get him to the winter feeding grounds. But as insurance he had taken a place beside Caada, who was certain to go into Emptiness if the feeding en route was bad.

Still, he hadn't figured that he would have Varsi beside him.

He consoled himself with the thought that others might have as bad neighbors as he. But he would never make the ultimate mistake of exchanging germ plasm with either of his neighbors, not even if his fertility and his position depended upon it. Cells like theirs would do nothing to improve the sense of discipline and order he had so carefully developed in his own. His offspring were courteous and honorable, a credit to the Folk and to the name of Kworn. A father should be proud of his offspring, so that when they developed to the point where they could have descendants, he would not be ashamed of what they would produce. An Ul, Kworn thought grimly, should have some sense of responsibility toward the all-important future of the race.

His anger died as he exerted synergic control. Anger was a waster of energy, a luxury he couldn't afford. He had little enough as it was. It had been a bad year. Spring was late, and winter had come early. The summer had been dry and the lichens in the feeding grounds had grown poorly. The tiny, bulbous lichen feeders, the main source of food for the Folk, had failed to ripen to their usual succulent fullness. They had been poor, shrunken things, hardly worth ingesting. And those along the route to the winter feeding grounds were no better.

Glumly he touched the wall before him with a tactile filament. It was uncomfortably warm, smooth and slippery to the touch. He felt it delicately, noting the almost microscopic horizontal ridges on the wall's surface. He palpated with relief. The thing was climbable. But even as he relaxed, he recoiled, the filament writhing in agony! The wall had burned his flesh! Faint threads of vapor rose from where he had touched the metal, freezing instantly in the chill air. He pinched off the filament in an automatic protective constriction of his cells. The pain ceased instantly, but the burning memory was so poignant that his mantle twitched and shuddered convulsively for some time before the reflexes died.

Thoughtfully he ingested his severed member. With a sense of numbing shock he realized that he would be unable to pass across the disc. The implications chilled him. If he could not pass, his land beyond the roadblock would be vacant and open to preemption by his neighbors. Nor could he wait until they had passed and rejoin them later. The Law was specific on that point. *If one of the Folk lags behind in his rank, his land becomes vacant and open to his neighbors. Nor can one who has lagged behind reclaim his land by moving forward. He who abandons his position, abandons it permanently.*

Wryly, he reflected that it was this very Law that had impelled him to take a position beside the Ul Caada. And, of course, his neighbors knew the Law as well as he. It was a part of them, a part of their cells even before they split off from their parent. It would be the acme of folly to expect that neighbors like Varsi or Caada would allow him to pass over their land and hold his place in rank.

Bitterness flooded him with a stimulation so piercing that Caada extended a communication filament to project a question. "What is this thing which lies upon your land and mine?" Caada asked. His projection was weak and feeble. It was obvious that he would not last for many more days unless feeding improved.

"I do not know. It is something of metal, and it bars my land. I cannot cross it. It burns me when I touch it."

A quick twinge of excitement rushed along Caada's filament. The old Ul broke the connection instantly, but not

before Kworn read the flash of hope that Kworn had kindled.
There was no help in this quarter, and the wild greed of Varsi
was so well-known that there was no sense even trying that
side.

A surge of hopelessness swept through him. Unless he
could find some way to pass this barrier he was doomed.

He didn't want to pass into Emptiness. He had seen too
many others go that way to want to follow them. For a
moment he thought desperately of begging Caada and Varsi
for permission to cross into their land for the short time that
would be necessary to pass the barrier, but reason asserted
itself. Such an act was certain to draw a flat refusal and,
after all, he was the Ul Kworn and he had his pride. He
would not beg when begging was useless.

And there was a bare possibility that he might survive if
he closed his mantle tightly about him and waited until all
the ranks had passed. He could then bring up the rear
. . . and, possibly, just possibly, there would be sufficient
food left to enable him to reach the winter feeding grounds.

And it might still be possible to cross the disc. There was
enough warmth in it to keep him active. By working all
night he might be able to build a path of sand across its
surface and thus keep his tissues from being seared by the
metal. He would be technically violating the law by moving
ahead of the others, but if he did not feed ahead, no harm
would be done.

He moved closer to the barrier and began to pile sand against
its base, sloping it to make a broad ramp to the top of the
disc. The work was slow and the sand was slippery. The
polished grains slipped away and the ramp crumbled time
after time. But he worked on, piling up sand until it reached
the top of the disc. He looked across the flat surface that
stretched before him.

Fifty raads!

It might as well be fifty zets. He couldn't do it. Already his
energy level was so low that he could hardly move, and to
build a raad-wide path across this expanse of metal was a
task beyond his strength. He drooped across the ramp, utterly exhausted. It was no use. What he ought to do was
open his mantle to Emptiness.

He hadn't felt the communication filaments of Caada and
Varsi touch him. He had been too busy, but now with Caada's
burst of glee, and Varsi's cynical, "A noble decision, Ul

Kworn. You should be commended," he realized that they knew everything.

His body rippled hopelessly. He was tired, too tired for anger. His energy was low. He contemplated Emptiness impassively. Sooner or later it came to all Folk. He had lived longer than most, and perhaps it was his time to go. He was finished. He accepted the fact with a cold fatalism that he never dreamed he possessed. Lying there on the sand, his mantle spread wide, he waited for the end to come.

It wouldn't come quickly, he thought. He was still far from the cellular disorganization that preceeded extinction. He was merely exhausted, and in need of food to restore his energy.

With food he might still have an outside chance of building the path in time. But there was no food. He had gleaned his area completely before he had ever reached the roadblock.

Lying limp and relaxed on the ramp beside the barrier, he slowly became conscious that the metal wasn't dead. It was alive! Rhythmic vibrations passed through it and were transmitted to his body by the sand.

A wild hope stirred within him. If the metal were alive it might hear him if he tried to communicate. He concentrated his remaining reserves of energy, steeled himself against the pain and pressed a communication filament against the metal.

"Help me!" he projected desperately. "You're blocking my strip! I can't pass!"

Off to one side he sensed Varsi's laughter and on the other felt Caada's gloating greed.

"I cannot wake this metal," he thought hopelessly as he tried again, harder than before, ignoring the pain of his burning flesh.

Something clicked sharply within the metal, and the tempo of the sounds changed.

"It's waking!" Kworn thought wildly.

There was a creaking noise from above. A rod moved out from the cylinder and twisted into the ground in Varsi's territory, to the accompaniment of clicking, grinding noises. A square grid lifted from the top of the cylinder and began rotating. And Kworn shivered and jerked to the tremendous power of the words that flowed through him. They were words, but they had no meaning, waves of sound that hammered at his receptors in an unknown tongue he could not understand. The language of the Folk had changed since the days of the ancients, he thought despairingly.

And then, with a mantle-shattering roar, the cylinders jutting overhead spouted flame and smoke. Two silvery balls trailing thin, dark filaments shot out of the great cylinder and buried themselves in the sand behind him. The filaments lay motionless in the sand as Kworn, wrapped defensively in his mantle, rolled off the ramp to the ground below.

The silence that followed was so deep that it seemed like Emptiness had taken the entire land.

Slowly Kworn loosened his mantle. "In the name of my first ancestor," he murmured shakily, "what was that?" His senses were shocked and disorganized by the violence of the sound. It was worse even than the roar and scream of the samshin that occasionally blew from the south, carrying dust, lichens, feeders, and even Folk who had been too slow or too foolish to hide from the fury of the wind.

Gingerly, Kworn inspected the damage to his mantle. It was minor. A tiny rip that could easily be repaired, a few grains of sand that could be extruded. He drew himself together to perform the repairs with the least possible loss of energy, and as he did, he was conscious of an emanation coming from the filaments that had been hurled from the cylinder.

Food!

And such food!

It was the distilled quintessence of a thousand purple feeders! It came to his senses in a shimmering wave of ecstasy so great that his mantle glowed a bright crimson. He stretched a pseudopod toward its source, and as he touched the filament his whole body quivered with anticipation. The barrier was blotted from his thoughts by an orgy of shuddering delight almost too great for flesh to endure. Waves of pleasure ran through his body as he swiftly extended to cover the filament. It could be a trap, he thought, but it made no difference. The demands of his depleted body and the sheer vacuole-constricting delight of this incredible foodstuff made a combination too potent for his will to resist, even if it had desired to do so. Waves of pleasure rippled through him as more of his absorptive surface contacted the filament. He snuggled against it, enfolding it completely, letting the peristaltic rushes sweep through him. He had never fed like this as long as he could recall. His energy levels swelled and pulsed as he sucked the last delight from the cord, and contemplated the further pleasure waiting for him in that other one lying scarcely twenty raads away.

Sensuously, he extended a pseudopod from his upper surface and probed for the other filament. He was filled to the top of his primary vacuole but the desire for more was stronger than ever—despite the fact that he knew the food in the other filament would bring him to critical level, would force him to reproduce. The thought amused him. As far back as he could remember, no member of the Folk had ever budded an offspring during the Time of Travel. It would be unheard of, something that would go down through the years in the annals of the Folk, and perhaps even cause a change in the Law.

The pseudopod probed, reached and stopped short of its goal. There was nothing around it but empty air.

Fear drove the slow orgasmic thoughts from his mind. Absorbed in gluttony, he hadn't noticed that the filament had tightened and was slowly drawing back into the cylinder from whence it came. And now it was too late! He was already over the rim of the metal disc.

Feverishly, he tried to disengage his absorptive surfaces from the filament and crawl down its length to safety, but he couldn't move. He was stuck to the dark cord by some strange adhesive that cemented his cells firmly to the cord. He could not break free.

The line moved steadily upward, dragging him inexorably toward a dark opening in the cylinder overhead. Panic filled him! Desperately he tried to loosen his trapped surfaces. His pseudopod lashed futilely in the air, searching with panic for something to grip, something to clutch that would stop this slow movement to the hell of pain that waited for him in the metal high overhead.

His searching flesh struck another's, and into his mind flooded the Ul Caada's terrified thought. The old one had reacted quicker than he, perhaps because he was poaching, but like himself he was attached and could not break free.

"Serves you right," Kworn projected grimly. "The thing was on my land. You had no right to feed upon it."

"Get me loose!" Caada screamed. His body flopped at the end of a thick mass of digestive tissue, dangling from the line, writhing and struggling in mindless terror. It was strange, Kworn thought, that fear should be so much stronger in the old than in the young.

"Cut loose, you fool," Kworn projected. "There isn't enough of you adhered to hurt if it were lost. A little body substance isn't worth your life. Hurry! You'll be too late if you don't. That metal is poisonous to our flesh."

"But it will be pain to cut my absorbing surface," Caada protested.

"It will be death if you don't."

"Then why don't you?"

"I can't," Kworn said hopelessly. "All my surface is stuck to the filament. I can't cut free." He was calm now, resigned to the inevitable. His greed had brought him to this. Perhaps it was a fitting punishment. But Caada need not die if he would show courage.

He rotated his eye to watch his struggling neighbor. Apparently Caada was going to take his advice. The tissue below the part of him stuck to the filament began to thin. His pseudopod broke contact. But his movements were slow and hesitant. Already his body mass was rising above the edge of the disc.

"Quick, you fool!" Kworn projected. "Another moment and you're dead!"

But Caada couldn't hear. Slowly his tissues separated as he reluctantly abandoned his absorptive surface. But he was already over the disc. The last cells pinched off and he fell, mantle flapping, full on the surface of the disc. For a moment he lay there quivering, and then his body was blotted from sight by a cloud of frozen steam, and his essence vanished screaming into Emptiness.

Kworn shuddered. It was a terrible way to die. But his own fate would be no better. He wrapped his mantle tightly around him as his leading parts vanished into the dark hole in the cylinder. In a moment he would be following Caada on the journey from which no member of the Folk had ever returned. His body disappeared into the hole.

—and was plunged into paradise!

His foreparts slipped into a warm, thick liquid that loosened the adhesive that bound him to the cord. As he slipped free, he slowly realized that he was not to die. He was bathed in liquid food! He was swimming in it! He was surrounded on all sides by incredible flavors so strange and delicious that his mind could not classify them! The filament had been good, but this—this was indescribable! He relaxed, his mantle spreading through the food, savoring, absorbing, digesting, metabolizing, excreting. His energy levels peaked. The nuclei of his germ plasm swelled, their chromosomes split, and a great bud formed and separated from his body. He had reproduced!

Through a deadening fog of somatic sensation, he realized dully that this was wrong, that the time wasn't right, that the space was limited, and that the natural reaction to abundant food supply was wrong. But for the moment he didn't care.

For thousands of seasons he had traveled the paths between equator and pole in a ceaseless hunt for food, growing and rejuvenating in good seasons, shrinking and aging in bad. He had been bound to the soil, a slave to the harsh demands of life and Nature. And now the routine was broken.

He luxuriated in his freedom. It must have been like this in the old days, when the waters were plentiful and things grew in them that could be eaten, and the Folk had time to dream young dreams and think young thoughts, and build their thoughts and dreams into the gleaming realities of cities and machines. Those were the days when the mind went above the soil into the air and beyond it to the moons, the sun and the evening stars.

But that was long ago.

He lay quietly, conscious of the change within him as his cells multiplied to replace those he had lost, and his body grew in weight and size. He was rejuvenated. The cells of his growing body, stimulated by the abundance of food, released memories he had forgotten he had ever possessed. His past ran in direct cellular continuity to the dawn of his race, and in him was every memory he had experienced since the beginning. Some were weak, others were stronger, but all were there awaiting an effort of recall. All that was required was enough stimulation to bring them out of hiding.

And for the first time in millennia the stimulus was available. The stimulus was growth, the rapid growth that only an abundant food supply could give, the sort of growth that the shrunken environment outside could not supply. With sudden clarity he saw how the Folk had shrunk in mind and body as they slowly adapted to the ever-increasing rigor of life. The rushing torrent of memory and sensation that swept through him gave him a new awareness of what he had been once and what he had become. His eye was lifted from the dirt and lichens.

What he saw filled him with pity and contempt. Pity for what the Folk had become; contempt for their failure to recognize it. Yet he had been no better than the others. It was only through the accident of this artifact that he had learned. The Folk *couldn't* know what the slow dwindling of their food supply had done to them. Over the millennia they had adapted, changing to fit the changing conditions, surviving only because they were more intelligent and more tenacious than the other forms of life that had become extinct. A thousand thousand seasons had passed since the great war that had devastated the world. A million years of slow adaptation to the barren waste that had been formed when the ultimate products of Folk technology were loosed on their creators, had created a race tied to a subsistence level of existence, incapable of thinking beyond the basic necessities of life.

The Ul Kworn sighed. It would be better if he would not remember so much. But he could suppress neither the knowledge nor the memories. They crowded in upon him, stimulated by the food in which he floated.

Beside him, his offspring was growing. A bud always grew rapidly in a favorable environment, and this one was ideal. Soon it would be as large as himself. Yet it would never develop beyond an infant. It could not mature without a transfer of germ plasm from other infants of the Folk. And there were no infants.

It would grow and keep on growing because there would be no check of maturity upon its cells. It would remain a partly sentient lump of flesh that would never be complete. And in time it would be dangerous. When it had depleted the food supply it would turn on him in mindless hunger. It wouldn't realize that the Ul Kworn was its father, or if it did, it wouldn't care. An infant is ultimately selfish, and its desires are the most important thing in its restricted universe.

Kworn considered his situation dispassionately.

It was obvious that he must escape from this trap before his offspring destroyed him. Yet he could think of no way to avoid the poison metal. He recognized it now, the element with the twelve protons in its nucleus, a light metal seldom used by the Folk even in the days of their greatness because of its ability to rapidly oxidize and its propensity to burst into brillant flame when heated. With sudden shock he realized that the artefact was nothing less than a gigantic torch!

Why had it been built like this? What was its function? Where had it come from? Why hadn't it spoken since it had released that flood of unintelligible gibberish before it had drawn him inside? Ever since he had entered this food tank it had been quiet except for a clicking, chattering whir that came from somewhere above him. He had the odd impression that it was storing information about him and the way he reacted in the tank.

And then, abruptly, it broke into voice. Cryptic words poured from it, piercing him with tiny knives of sound. The intensity and rapidity of the projections shocked him, left him quivering and shaking when they stopped as abruptly as they had begun.

In the quiet that followed, Kworn tried to recall the sequence of the noise. The words were like nothing he had ever heard. They were not the language of the Folk either past or present. And they had a flow and sequence that was not organic. They were mechanical, the product of a metal intelligence that recorded and spoke but did not think. The Folk had machines like that once.

How had it begun? There had been a faint preliminary, an almost soundless voice speaking a single word. Perhaps if he projected it, it would trigger a response. Pitching his voice in the same key and intensity he projected the word as best he could remember it.

And the voice began again.

Kworn quivered with excitement. Something outside the artefact was forcing it to speak. He was certain of it. As certain as he was that the artefact was recording himself and his offspring. But who—or what—was receiving the record? And why?

This could be a fascinating speculation, Kworn thought. But there would be time enough for that later. His immediate need was to get out. Already the food supply was running low, and his offspring was becoming enormous. He'd have to leave soon if he was ever going to. And he'd have to do something about his own growth. Already it was reaching dangerous levels. He was on the ragged edge of an another reproduction, and he couldn't afford it.

Regretfully, he began moving the cornified cells of his mantle and his underlayer toward his inner surfaces, arranging them in a protective layer around his germ plasm and absorptive cells. There would be enough surface absorption to take care of his maintenance needs, and his body could retain its peak of cellular energy. Yet the desire to feed and bud was almost overpowering. His body screamed at him for denying it the right that food would give it, but Kworn resisted the demands of his flesh until the frantic cellular urges passed.

Beside him his offspring pulsed with physical sensation. Kworn envied it even as he pitied it. The poor mindless thing could be used as a means to the end of his escape, but it was useless for anything else. It was far too large, and far too stupid, to survive in the outside world. Kworn extruded a net of hairlike pseudopods and swept the tank in which they lay. It was featureless, save for a hole where the filament had not completely withdrawn when it had pulled him into this place. A few places in the wall had a different texture than the others, probably the sense organs of the recorder. He rippled with satisfaction. There was a grille of poison metal in the top of the tank through which flowed a steady current of warm air. It would be pleasant to investigate this further, Kworn thought, but there was no time. His offspring had seen to that.

He placed his eye on a thin pseudopod and thrust it through the hole in the wall of the tank. It was still night outside, but a faint line of brightness along the horizon indicated the coming of dawn. The artifact glittered icily beneath him, and he had a feeling of giddiness as he looked down the vertiginous drop to the disc below. The dark blotch of Caada's burned body was almost invisible against the faintly gleaming loom of the still-warm disc. Kworn shuddered. Caada hadn't deserved a death like that. Kworn looked down, estimating the chances with his new intelligence, and then slapped a thick communication fibril against his offspring's quivering flesh and hurled a projection at its recoiling mass.

Considering the fact that its cells were direct derivations of his own, Kworn thought grimly, it was surprising how hard it was to establish control. The youngster had developed a surprising amount of individuality in its few xals of free existence. He felt a surge of thankfulness to the old Ul Kworn as the youngster yielded to his firm projection. His precursor had always sought compliant germ plasm to produce what he had called "discipline and order." It was, in fact, weakness. It was detrimental to survival. But right now that weakness was essential.

Under the probing lash of his projection the infant extruded a thick mass of tissue that met and interlocked with a similar mass of his own. As soon as the contact firmed, Kworn began flowing toward his eye, which was still in the half-open hole in the side of the tank.

The outside cold struck his sense centers with spicules of ice as he flowed to the outside, clinging to his offspring's gradually extending pseudopod. Slowly he dropped below the cylinder. The infant was frantic. It disliked the cold and struggled to break free, but Kworn clung limpetlike to his offspring's flesh as it twisted and writhed in an effort to return to the warmth and comfort into which it was born.

"Let go!" his offspring screamed. "I don't like this place."

"In a moment," Kworn said as he turned the vague writhings into a swinging pendulum motion. "Help me move back and forth."

"I can't. I'm cold. I hurt. Let me go!"

"Help me," Kworn ordered grimly, "or hang out here and freeze."

His offspring shuddered and twitched. The momentum of the swing increased. Kworn tightened his grip.

"You promised to let go!" his offspring wailed. "You prom—"

The infant's projection was cut off as Kworn loosed himself at the upward arc of the swing, spread his mantle and plummeted toward the ground. Fear swept through him as his body curved through the thin air, missing the edge of the disc and landing on the ground with a sense-jarring thud. Behind and above him up against the cylinder, the thick tendril of his offspring's flesh withdrew quickly from sight. For a moment the Ul Kworn's gaze remained riveted on the row of odd markings on the metal surface, and then he turned his attention to life.

There was no reason to waste the pain of regret upon that half sentient mass of tissue that was his offspring. The stupid flesh of his flesh would remain happy in the darkness with the dwindling food until its flesh grew great enough to touch the poison metal in the ceiling of the tank.

And then—

With a harsh projection of horror, the Ul Kworn moved, circling the artefact on Caada's vacated strip. And as he moved he concentrated energy into his high-level communication organs, and projected a warning of danger.

"Move!" he screamed. "Move forward for your lives!"

The line rippled. Reddish mantles unfolded as the Folk reacted. The nearest, shocked from estivation, were in motion even before they came to full awareness. Alarms like this weren't given without reason.

Varsi's reaction, Kworn noted, was faster than any of his fellows. The young Ul had some favorable self-preservation characteristics. He'd have to consider sharing some germ plasm with him at the next reproduction season, after all.

In a giant arc, the Folk pressed forward under the white glow of emerging dawn. Behind them the artifact began to project again in its strange tongue. But in mid-cry it stopped abruptly. And from it came a wail of mindless agony that tore at Kworn's mind with regret more bitter because nothing could be done about it.

His offspring had touched the poison metal.

Kworn turned his eye backwards. The artefact was shaking on its broad base from the violence of his offspring's tortured writhings. As he watched a brilliant burst of light flared from its top. Heat swept across the land, searing the lichens and a scattered few of the Folk too slow to escape. The giant structure burned with a light more brilliant than the sun and left behind a great cloud of white vapor that hung on the air like the menacing cloud of a samshin. Beneath the cloud the land was bare save for a few twisted pieces of smoking metal.

The roadblock was gone.

Kworn moved slowly forward, gleaning Caada's strip and half of his own which he shared with Varsi.

He would need that young Ul in the future. It was well to place him under an obligation. The new thoughts and old memories weren't dying. They remained, and were focused upon the idea of living better than at this subsistence level. It should be possible to grow lichens, and breed a more prolific type of lichen feeder. Water channeled from the canals would stimulate lichen growth a thousand-fold. And with a more abundant food supply, perhaps some of the Folk could be stimulated to think and apply ancient buried skills to circumvent Nature.

It was theoretically possible. The new breed would have to be like Varsi, tough, driving and selfishly independent. In time they might inherit the world. Civilization could arise again. It was not impossible.

His thoughts turned briefly back to the artefact. It still

bothered him. He still knew far too little about it. It was a fascinating speculation to dream of what it might have been. At any rate, one thing was sure. It was not a structure of his race. If nothing else, those cabalistic markings on the side of the cylinder were utterly alien.

Thoughtfully he traced them in the sand. What did they mean?

The Ballad of Lost C'mell

by Cordwainer Smith

SHE WAS A girly girl and they were true men, the lords of creation, but she pitted her wits against them and she won. It had never happened before, and it is sure never to happen again, but she did win. She was not even of human extraction. She was cat-derived, though human in outward shape, which explains the C in front of her name. Her father's name was C'mackintosh and her name was C'mell. She won her trick against the lawful and assembled Lords of the Instrumentality.

It all happened at Earthport, greatest of buildings, smallest of cities, standing twenty-five kilometers high at the Western edge of the Smaller Sea of Earth.

Jestocost had an office outside the fourth valve.

Jestocost liked the morning sunshine, while most of the other Lords of the Instrumentality did not, so that he had no trouble in keeping the office and the apartments which he had selected. His main office was ninety meters deep, twenty meters high, twenty meters broad. Behind it was the "fourth valve," almost a thousand hectares in extent. It was shaped helically, like an enormous snail. Jestocost's apartment, big as it was, was merely one of the pigeonholes in the muffler on the rim of Earthport. Earthport stood like an enormous wineglass, reaching from the magma to the high atmosphere.

Earthport had been built during mankind's biggest mechanical splurge. Though men had had nuclear rockets since the beginning of consecutive history, they had used chemical rockets to load the interplanetary ion-drive and nuclear-drive vehicles or to assemble the photonic sail-ships for interstellar cruises. Impatient with the troubles of taking things bit by bit into the sky, they had worked out a billion-ton rocket, only to find that it ruined whatever countryside it touched in landing. The Daimoni—people of Earth extraction, who came back from somewhere beyond the stars—had helped men build it of weatherproof, rustproof, timeproof, stressproof material. Then they had gone away and had never come back.

Jestocost often looked around his apartment and wondered what it might have been like when white-hot gas, muted to a whisper, surged out of the valve into his own chamber and the sixty-four other chambers like it. Now he had a back wall of heavy timber, and the valve itself was a great hollow cave where a few wild things lived. Nobody needed that much space any more. The chambers were useful, but the valve did nothing. Planoforming ships whispered in from the stars; they landed at Earthport as a matter of legal convenience, but they made no noise and they certainly had no hot gases.

Jestocost looked at the high clouds far below him and talked to himself.

"Nice day. Good air. No trouble. Better eat."

Jestocost often talked like that to himself. He was an individual, almost an eccentric. One of the top council of mankind, he had problems, but they were not personal problems. He had a Rembrandt hanging above his bed—the only Rembrandt known in the world, just as he was possibly the only person who could appreciate a Rembrandt. He had the tapestries of a forgotten empire hanging from his back wall. Every morning the sun played a grand opera for him, muting and lighting and shifting the colors so that he could almost imagine that the old days of quarrel, murder and high drama had come back to Earth again. He had a copy of Shakespeare, a copy of Colegrove and two pages of the Book of Eccelesiastes in a locked box beside his bed. Only forty-two people in the universe could read Ancient English, and he was one of them. He drank wine, which he had made by his own robots in his own vineyards on the Sunset coast. He was a man, in short, who had arranged his own life to live comfortably, selfishly and well on the personal side, so that he could give generously and impartially of his talents on the official side.

When he awoke on this particular morning, he had no

idea that a beautiful girl was about to fall hopelessly in love
with him—that he would find, after a hundred years and
more of experience in government, another government on
earth just as strong and almost as ancient as his own—that
he would willingly fling himself into conspiracy and danger
for a cause which he only half understood. All these things
were mercifully hidden from him by time, so that his only
question on arising was, should he or should he not have a
small cup of white wine with his breakfast. On the 173rd
day of each year, he always made a point of eating eggs.
They were a rare treat, and he did not want to spoil himself
by having too many, nor to deprive himself and forget a
treat by having none at all. He puttered around the room,
muttering, "White wine? White wine?"

C'mell was coming into his life, but he did not know it. She
was fated to win; that part, she herself did not know.

Ever since mankind had gone through the Rediscovery of
Man, bringing back governments, money, newspapers, national languages, sickness and occasional death, there had
been the problem of the underpeople—people who were not
human, but merely humanly shaped from the stock of Earth
animals. They could speak, sing, read, write, work, love and
die; but they were not covered by human law, which simply
defined them as "homunculi" and gave them a legal status
close to animals or robots. Real people from off-world were
always called "hominids."

Most of the underpeople did their jobs and accepted their
half-slave status without question. Some became famous—
C'mackintosh had been the first earth-being to manage a
thousand-meter broad-jump under normal gravity. His picture was seen in a thousand worlds. His daughter, C'mell,
was a girly girl, earning her living by welcoming human beings and hominids from the outworlds and making them
feel at home when they reached Earth. She had the privilege
of working at Earthport, but she had the duty of working
very hard for a living which did not pay well. Human beings and hominids had lived so long in an affluent society
that they did not know what it meant to be poor. But the
Lords of the Instrumentality had decreed that underpeople
—derived from animal stock—should live under the eco-
nomics of the Ancient World; they had to have their own
kind of money to pay for their rooms, their food, their pos-
sessions and the education of their children. If they became

bankrupt, they went to the Poorhouse, where they were killed painlessly by means of gas.

It was evident that humanity, having settled all of its own basic problems, was not quite ready to let Earth animals, no matter how much they might be changed, assume a full equality with man.

The Lord Jestocost, seventh of that name, opposed the policy. He was a man who had little love, no fear, freedom from ambition and a dedication to his job: but there are passions of government as deep and challenging as the emotions of love. Two hundred years of thinking himself right and of being outvoted had instilled in Jestocost a furious desire to get things done his own way.

Jestocost was one of the few true men who believed in the rights of the underpeople. He did not think that mankind would ever get around to correcting ancient wrongs unless the underpeople themselves had some of the tools of power —weapons, conspiracy, wealth and (above all) organization with which to challenge man. He was not afraid of revolt, but he thirsted for justice with an obsessive yearning which overrode all other considerations.

When the Lords of the Instrumentality heard that there was the rumor of a conspiracy among the underpeople, they left it to the robot police to ferret out.

Jestocost did not.

He set up his own police, using underpeople themselves for the purpose, hoping to recruit enemies who would realize that he was a friendly enemy and who would in course of time bring him into touch with the leaders of the underpeople.

If those leaders existed, they were clever. What sign did a girly girl like C'mell ever give that she was the spearhead of a criss-cross of agents who had penetrated Earthport itself? They must, if they existed, be very, very careful. The telepathic monitors, both robotic and human, kept every thought-band under surveillance by random sampling. Even the computers showed nothing more significant than improbable amounts of happiness in minds which had no objective reason for being happy.

The death of her father, the most famous cat-athlete which the underpeople had ever produced, gave Jestocost his first definite clue.

He went to the funeral himself, where the body was packed in an ice-rocket to be shot into space. The mourners were thoroughly mixed with the curiosity-seekers. Sport is international, inter-race, inter-world, inter-species. Hominids were there: true men, 100% human, they looked weird and horrible because they or their ancestors had undergone bodily modifications to meet the life conditions of a thousand worlds.

Underpeople, the animal-derived "homunculi," were there, most of them in their work clothes, and they looked more human than did the human beings from the outer worlds. None were allowed to grow up if they were less than half the size of man, or more than six times the size of man. They all had to have human features and acceptable human voices. The punishment for failure in their elementary schools was death. Jestocost looked over the crowd and wondered to himself, "We have set up the standards of the toughest kind of survival for these people and we give them the most terrible incentive, life itself, as the condition of absolute progress. What fools we are to think that they will not overtake us!" The true people in the group did not seem to think as he did. They tapped the underpeople peremptorily with their canes, even though this was an underperson's funeral, and the bear-men, bull-men, cat-men and others yielded immediately and with a babble of apology.

C'mell was close to her father's icy coffin.

Jestocost not only watched her; she was pretty to watch. He committed an act which was an indecency in an ordinary citizen but lawful for a Lord of the Instrumentality: he peeped her mind.

And then he found something which he did not expect.

As the coffin left, she cried, "Ee-telly-kelly, help me! help me!"

She had thought phonetically, not in script, and he had only the raw sound on which to base a search.

Jestocost had not become a Lord of the Instrumentality without applying daring. His mind was quick, too quick to be deeply intelligent. He thought by gestalt, not by logic. He determined to force his friendship on the girl.

He decided to await a propitious occasion, and then changed his mind about the time.

As she went home from the funeral, he intruded upon the circle of her grimfaced friends, underpeople who were trying to shield her from the condolences of ill-mannered but well-meaning sports enthusiasts.

She recognized him, and showed him the proper respect. "My Lord, I did not expect you here. You knew my father?"

He nodded gravely and addressed sonorous words of consolation and sorrow, words which brought a murmur of approval from humans and underpeople alike.

But with his left hand hanging slack at his side, he made the perpetual signal of *alarm! alarm!* used within the Earthport staff—a repeated tapping of the thumb against the third finger—when they had to set one another on guard without alerting the off-world transients.

She was so upset that she almost spoiled it all. While he was still doing his pious doubletalk, she cried in a loud clear voice:

"You mean *me?*"

And he went on with his condolences: ". . . and I do mean *you,* C'mell, to be the worthiest carrier of your father's name. *You* are the one to whom we turn in this time of common sorrow. *Who could I mean but you* if I say that C'mackintosh never did things by halves, and died young as a result of his own zealous conscience? Good-by, C'mell, I go back to my office."

She arrived forty minutes after he did.

He faced her straight away, studying her face.

"This is an important day in your life."

"Yes, my Lord, a sad one."

"I do not," he said, "mean your father's death and burial. I speak of the future to which we all must turn. Right now, it's you and me."

Her eyes widened. She had not thought that he was that kind of man at all. He was an official who moved freely around Earthport, often greeting important offworld visitors and keeping an eye on the bureau of ceremonies. She was a part of the reception team, when a girly girl was needed to calm down a frustrated arrival or to postpone a quarrel. Like the geisha of ancient Japan, she had an honorable profession; she was not a bad girl but a professionally flirtatious hostess. She stared at the Lord Jestocost. He did not *look* as though he meant anything improperly personal. But, thought she, you can never tell about men.

"You know men," he said, passing the initiative to her.

"I guess so," she said. Her face looked odd. She started to give him smile #3 (extremely adhesive) which she had learned in the girly-girl school. Realizing it was wrong, she tried to give him an ordinary smile. She felt she had made a face at him.

"Look at me," he said, "and see if you can trust me. I am going to take both our lives in my hands."

She looked at him. What imaginable subject could involve him, a Lord of the Instrumentality, with herself, an under-girl? They never had anything in common. They never would.

But she stared at him.

"I want to help the underpeople."

He made her blink. That was a crude approach, usually followed by a very raw kind of pass indeed. But his face was illuminated by seriousness. She waited.

"Your people do not have enough political power even to talk to us. I will not commit treason to the true-human race, but I am willing to give your side an advantage. If you bargain better with us, it will make all forms of life safer in the long run."

C'mell stared at the floor, her red hair soft as the fur of a Persian cat. It made her head seem bathed in flames. Her eyes looked human, except that they had the capacity of reflecting when light struck them; the irises were the rich green of the ancient cat. When she looked right at him, looking up from the floor, her glance had the impact of a blow. "What do you want from me?"

He stared right back. "Watch me. Look at my face. Are you sure, *sure* that I want nothing from you personally?"

She looked bewildered. "What else is there to want from me except personal things? I am a girly girl. I'm not a person of any importance at all, and I do not have much of an education. You know more, sir, than I will ever know."

"Possibly," he said, watching her.

She stopped feeling like a girly girl and felt like a citizen. It made her uncomfortable.

"Who," he said, in a voice of great solemnity, "is your own leader?"

"Commissioner Teadrinker, sir. He's in charge of all out-world visitors." She watched Jestocost carefully; he still did not look as if he were playing tricks.

He looked a little cross. "I don't mean him. He's part of my own staff. Who's your leader among the underpeople?"

"My father was, but he died."

Jestocost said. "Forgive me. Please have a seat. But I don't mean that."

She was so tired that she sat down into the chair with an innocent voluptuousness which would have disorganized any ordinary man's day. She wore girly girl clothes, which were close enough to the everyday fashion to seem agreeably modish when she stood up. In line with her profession, her clothes were designed to be unexpectedly and provocatively revealing when she sat down—not revealing enough to shock the man with their brazenness, but so slit, tripped and cut that he got far more visual stimulation than he expected.

"I must ask you to pull your clothing together a little," said Jestocost in a clinical turn of voice. "I am a man, even if I am an official, and this interview is more important to you and to me than any distraction would be."

She was a little frightened by his tone. She had meant no challenge. With the funeral that day, she meant nothing at all; these clothes were the only kind she had.

He read all this in her face.

Relentlessly, he pursued the subject.

"Young lady, I asked about your leader. You name your boss and you name your father. I want your leader."

"I don't understand," she said, on the edge of a sob, "I don't understand."

Then, he thought to himself, I've got to take a gamble. He thrust the mental dagger home, almost drove his words like steel straight into her face. "Who . . ." he said, slowly and icily, "is . . . Ee . . . telly . . . kelly?"

The girl's face had been cream-colored, pale with sorrow. Now she went white. She twisted away from him. Her eyes glowed like twin fires.

Her eyes . . . like twin fires.

(No undergirl, thought Jestocost as he reeled, could hypnotize me.)

Her eyes . . . were like cold fires.

The room faded around him. The girl disappeared. Her eyes became a single white, cold fire.

Within this fire stood the figure of a man. His arms were wings, but he had human hands growing at the elbows of his wings. His face was clear, white, cold as the marble of an ancient statue; his eyes were opaque white. "I am the E-telekeli. You will believe in me. You may speak to my daughter C'mell."

The image faded.

Jestocost saw the girl staring as she sat awkwardly on the chair, looking blindly through him. He was on the edge of making a joke about her hypnotic capacity when he saw that she was still deeply hypnotized, even after he had been released. She had stiffened and again her clothing had fallen into its planned disarray. The effect was not stimulating; it was pathetic beyond words, as though an accident had happened to a pretty child. He spoke to her.

He spoke to her, not really expecting an answer.

"Who are you?" he said to her, testing her hypnosis.

"I am he whose name is never said aloud," said the girl in a sharp whisper, "I am he whose secret you have penetrated. I have printed my image and my name in your mind."

Jestocost did not quarrel with ghosts like this. He snapped out a decision. "If I open my mind, will you search it while I watch you? Are you good enough to do that?"

"I am very good," hissed the voice in the girl's mouth.

C'mell arose and put her two hands on his shoulders. She looked into his eyes. He looked back. A strong telepath himself, Jestocost was not prepared for the enormous thought-voltage which poured out of her.

Look in my mind, he commanded, for the subject of *underpeople* only.

I see it, thought the mind behind C'mell.

Do you see what I mean to do for the underpeople?

Jestocost heard the girl breathing hard as her mind served as a relay to his. He tried to remain calm so that he could see which part of his mind was being searched. Very good so far, he thought to himself. An intelligence like that on Earth itself, he thought—and we of the Lords not knowing it!

The girl hacked out a dry little laugh.

Jestocost thought at the mind, Sorry. Go ahead.

This plan of yours—thought the strange mind—may I see more of it?

That's all there is.

Oh, said the strange mind, you want me to think for you.

Can you give me the keys in the Bank and Bell which pertain to destroying underpeople?

You can have the information keys if I can ever get them, thought Jestocost, but not the control keys and not the master switch of the Bell.

Fair enough, thought the other mind, and what do I pay for them?

You support me in my policies before the instrumentality. You keep the underpeople reasonable, if you can, when the time comes to negotiate. You maintain honor and good faith in all subsequent agreements. But how can I get the keys? It would take me a year to figure them out myself.

Let the girl look once, thought the strange mind, and I will be behind her. Fair?

Fair, thought Jestocost.

Break? thought the mind.

How do we re-connect? thought Jestocost back.

As before. Through the girl. Never say my name. Don't think it if you can help it. Break?

Break! thought Jestocost.

The girl, who had been holding his shoulders, drew his face down and kissed him firmly and warmly. He had never touched an underperson before, and it never had occurred to him that he might kiss one. It was pleasant, but he took her arms away from his neck, half-turned her around, and let her lean against him.

"Daddy!" she sighed happily.

Suddenly she stiffened, looked at his face, and sprang for the door. "Jestocost!" she cried. "Lord Jestocost! What am I doing here?"

"Your duty is done, my girl. You may go."

She staggered back into the room. "I am going to be sick," she said. She vomited on his floor.

He pushed a button for a cleaning robot and slapped his desk-top for coffee.

She relaxed and talked about his hopes for the underpeople. She stayed an hour. By the time she left they had a plan. Neither of them had mentioned E-telekeli, neither had put purposes in the open. If the monitors had been listening, they would have found no single sentence or paragraph which was suspicious.

When she had gone, Jestocost looked out of his window. He saw the clouds far below and he knew the world below him was in twilight. He had planned to help the underpeople, and he had met powers of which organized mankind had no conception or perception. He was righter than he had thought. He had to go on through.

But as partner—C'mell herself!

Was there ever an odder diplomat in the history of worlds?

In less than a week they had decided what to do. It was the Council of the Lords of the Instrumentality at which they would work—the brain center itself. The risk was high, but the entire job could be done in a few minutes if it were done at the Bell itself.

This is the sort of thing which interested Jestocost.

He did not know that C'mell watched him with two different facets of her mind. One side of her was alertly and wholeheartedly his fellow-conspirator, utterly in sympathy with the revolutionary aims to which they were both committed. The other side of her—was feminine.

She had a womanliness which was truer than that of any hominid woman. She knew the value of her trained smile, her splendidly kept red hair with its unimaginably soft texture, her lithe young figure with firm breasts and persuasive hips. She knew down to the last millimeter the effect which her legs had on hominid men. True humans kept few secrets from her. The men betrayed themselves by their unfulfillable desires, the women by their irrepressible jealousies. But she knew people best of all by not being one herself. She had to learn by imitation, and imitation is conscious. A thousand little things which ordinary women took for granted, or thought about just once in a whole lifetime, were subjects of acute and intelligent study to her. She was a girl by profession; she was a human by assimilation; she was an inquisitive cat in her genetic nature. Now she was falling in love with Jestocost, and she knew it.

Even she did not realize that the romance would sometime leak out into rumor, be magnified into legend, distilled into romance. She had no idea of the ballad about herself that would open with the lines which became famous much later:

> She got the which of the what-she-did,
> Hid the bell with a blot, she did,
> But she fell in love with a hominid.
> Where is the which of the what-she-did?

All this lay in the future, and she did not know it.

She knew her own past.

She remembered the off-Earth prince who had rested his head in her lap and had said, sipping his glass of motl by way of farewell:

"Funny, C'mell, you're not even a person and you're the most intelligent human being I've met in this place. Do you know it made my planet poor to send me here? And what did I get out of them? Nothing, nothing, and a thousand times nothing. But you, now. If you'd been running the government of Earth, I'd have gotten what my people need, and this world would be richer too. Manhome, they call it. Manhome, my eye! The only smart person on it is a female cat."

He ran his fingers around her ankle. She did not stir. That was part of hospitality, and she had her own ways of making sure that hospitality did not go too far. Earth police were watching her; to them, she was a convenience maintained for outworld people, something like a soft chair in the Earthport lobbies or a drinking fountain with acid-tasting water for strangers who could not tolerate the insipid water of Earth. She was not expected to have feelings or to get involved. If she had ever caused an incident, they would have punished her fiercely, as they often punished animals or underpeople, or else (after a short formal hearing with no appeal) they would have destroyed her, as the law allowed and custom encouraged.

She had kissed a thousand men, maybe fifteen hundred. She had made them feel welcome and she had gotten their complaints or their secrets out of them as they left. It was a living, emotionally tiring but intellectually very stimulating. Sometimes it made her laugh to look at human women with their pointed-up noses and their proud airs, and to realize that she knew more about the men who belonged to the human women than the human women themselves ever did.

Once a policewoman had had to read over the record of two pioneers from New Mars. C'mell had been given the job of keeping in very close touch with them. When the policewoman got through reading the report she looked at C'mell and her face was distorted with jealousy and prudish rage.

"Cat, you call yourself. Cat! You're a pig, you're a dog, you're an animal. You may be working for Earth but don't ever get the idea that you're as good as a person. I think it's a crime that the Instrumentality lets monsters like you greet real human beings from outside! I can't stop it. But may the Bell help you, girl, if you ever touch a real Earth man! If you ever get near one! If you ever try tricks here! Do you understand me?"

"Yes, ma'am," C'mell had said. To herself she thought, "That poor thing doesn't know how to select her own clothes or how to do her own hair. No wonder she resents somebody who manages to be pretty."

Perhaps the policewoman thought that raw hatred would be shocking to C'mell. It wasn't. Underpeople were used to hatred, and it was not any worse raw than it was when cooked with politeness and served like poison. They had to live with it.

But now, it was all changed.

She had fallen in love with Jestocost.

Did he love her?

Impossible. No, not impossible. Unlawful, unlikely, indecent—yes, all these, but not impossible. Surely he felt something of her love.

If he did, he gave no sign of it.

People and underpeople had fallen in love many times before. The underpeople were always destroyed and the real people brainwashed. There were laws against that kind of thing. The scientists among people had created the underpeople, had given them capacities which real people did not have (the thousand-yard jump, the telepath two miles underground, the turtle-man waiting a thousand years next to an emergency door, the cow-man guarding a gate without reward), and the scientists had also given many of the underpeople the human shape. It was handier that way. The human eye, the five-fingered hand, the human size—these were convenient for engineering reasons. By making underpeople the same size and shape as people, more or less, the scientists eliminated the need for two or three or a dozen different sets of furniture. The human form was good enough for all of them.

But they had forgotten the human heart.

And now she, C'mell, had fallen in love with a man, a true man old enough to have been her own father's grandfather.

But she didn't feel daughterly about him at all. She re-

membered that with her own father there was an easy com-
radeship, an innocent and forthcoming affection, which
masked the fact that he was considerably more cat-like than
she was. Between them there was an aching void of for-
ever-unspoken words—things that couldn't quite be said by
either of them, perhaps things that couldn't be said at all.
They were so close to each other that they could get no
closer. This created enormous distance, which was heart-
breaking but unutterable. Her father had died, and now
this true man was here, with all the kindness—

"That's it," she whispered to herself, "with all the kindness that none of these passing men have ever really shown.
With all the depth which my poor underpeople can never
get. Not that it's not in them. But they're born like dirt,
treated like dirt, put away like dirt when we die. How can
any of my own men develop real kindness? There's a special sort of majesty to kindness. It's the best part there is
to being people. And he has whole oceans of it in him.
And it's strange, strange, strange that he's never given his
real love to any human woman."

She stopped, cold.

Then she consoled herself and whispered on, "Or if he
did, it's so long ago that it doesn't matter now. He's got
me. Does he know it?"

The Lord Jestocost did know, and yet he didn't. He was
used to getting loyalty from people, because he offered
loyalty and honor in his daily work. He was even familiar
with loyalty becoming obsessive and seeking physical form,
particularly from women, children and underpeople. He had
always coped with it before. He was gambling on the fact
that C'mell was a wonderfully intelligent person, and that
as a girly girl, working on the hospitality staff of the Earthport police, she must have learned to control her personal
feelings.

"We're born in the wrong age," he thought, "when I
meet the most intelligent and beautiful female I've ever met,
and then have to put business first. But this stuff about
people and underpeople is sticky. Sticky. We've got to keep
personalities out of it."

So he thought. Perhaps he was right.

If the nameless one, whom he did not dare to remember,
commanded an attack on the Bell itself, that was worth
their lives. Their emotions could not come into it. The

Bell mattered: justice mattered: the perpetual return of mankind to progress mattered. He did not matter, because he had already done most of his work. C'mell did not matter, because their failure would leave her with mere underpeople forever. The Bell did count.

The price of what he proposed to do was high, but the entire job could be done in a few minutes if it were done at the Bell itself.

The Bell, of course, was not a Bell. It was a three-dimensional situation table, three times the height of a man. It was set one story below the meeting room, and shaped roughly like an ancient bell. The meeting table of the Lords of the Instrumentality had a circle cut out of it, so that the Lords could look down into the Bell at whatever situation one of them called up either manually or telepathically. The Bank below it, hidden by the floor, was the key memory-bank of the entire system. Duplicates existed at thirty-odd other places on Earth. Two duplicates lay hidden in interstellar space, one of them beside the ninety-million-mile gold-colored ship left over from the War against Raumsog and the other masked as an asteroid.

Most of the Lords were off-world on the business of the Instrumentality.

Only three beside Jestocost were present—the Lady Johanna Gnade, the Lord Issan Olascoaga and the Lord William Not-from-here. (The Not-from-heres were a great Norstrilian family which had migrated back to Earth many generations before.)

The E-telekeli told Jestocost the rudiments of a plan.

He was to bring C'mell into the chambers on a summons.

The summons was to be serious.

They should avoid her summary death by automatic justice, if the relays began to trip.

C'mell would go into partial trance in the chamber.

He was then to call the items in the Bell which E-telekeli wanted traced. A single call would be enough. E-telekeli would take the responsibility for tracing them. The other Lords would be distracted by him, E-telekeli.

It was simple in appearance.

The complication came in action.

The plan seemed flimsy, but there was nothing which Jestocost could do at this time. He began to curse himself for letting his passion for policy involve him in the intrigue.

It was too late to back out with honor; besides, he had given his word; besides, he liked C'mell—as a being, not as a girly girl—and he would hate to see her marked with disappointment for life. He knew how the underpeople cherished their identities and their status.

With heavy heart but quick mind he went to the council chamber. A dog-girl, one of the routine messengers whom he had seen many months outside the door, gave him the minutes.

He wondered how C'mell or E-telekeli would reach him, once he was inside the chamber with its tight net of telepathic intercepts.

He sat wearily at the table—

And almost jumped out of his chair.

The conspirators had forged the minutes themselves, and the top item was: "C'mell daughter to C'mackintosh, cat-stock (pure) lot 1138, confession of. Subject: conspiracy to export homuncular material. Reference: planet De Prinsensmacht."

The Lady Johanna Gnade had already pushed the buttons for the planet concerned. The people there, Earth by origin, were enormously strong but they had gone to great pains to maintain the original Earth appearance. One of their first-men was at the moment on Earth. He bore the title of the Twilight Prince (Prins van de Schemering) and he was on a mixed diplomatic and trading mission.

Since Jestocost was a little late, C'mell was being brought into the room as he glanced over the minutes.

The Lord Not-from-here asked Jestocost if he would preside.

"I beg you, sir and scholar," he said, "to join me in asking the Lord Issan to preside this time."

The presidency was a formality. Jestocost could watch the Bell and Bank better if he did not have to chair the meeting too.

C'mell wore the clothing of a prisoner. On her it looked good. He had never seen her wearing anything but girly-girl clothes before. The pale-blue prison tunic made her look very young, very human, very tender and very frightened. The cat family showed only in the fiery cascade of her hair and the lithe power of her body as she sat, demure and erect.

Lord Issan asked her: "You have confessed. Confess again."

"This man," and she pointed at a picture of the Twilight Prince, "wanted to go to the place where they torment human children for a show."

"What!" cried three of the Lords together.

"What place?" said the Lady Johanna, who was bitterly in favor of kindness.

"It's run by a man who looks like this gentleman here," said C'mell, pointing at Jestocost. Quickly, so that nobody could stop her, but modestly, so that none of them thought to doubt her, she circled the room and touched Jestocost's shoulder. He felt a thrill of contact-telepathy and heard bird-cackle in her brain. Then he knew that the E-telekeli was in touch with her.

"The man who has the place," said C'mell, "is five pounds lighter than this gentleman, two inches shorter, and he has red hair. His place is at the Cold Sunset corner of Earthport, down the boulevard and under the boulevard. Underpeople, some of them with bad reputations, live in that neighborhood."

The Bell went milky, flashing through hundreds of combinations of bad underpeople in that part of the city. Jestocost felt himself staring at the casual milkiness with unwanted concentration.

The Bell cleared.

It showed the vague image of a room in which children were playing Hallowe'en tricks.

The Lady Johanna laughed, "Those aren't people. They're robots. It's just a dull old play."

"Then," added C'mell, "he wanted a dollar and a shilling to take home. Real ones. There was a robot who had found some."

"What are those?" said Lord Issan.

"Ancient money—the real money of old America and old Australia," cried Lord William. "I have copies, but there are no originals outside the state museum." He was an ardent, passionate collector of coins.

"The robot found them in an old hiding place right under Earthport."

Lord William almost shouted at the Bell. "Run through every hiding place and get me that money."

The Bell clouded. In finding the bad neighborhoods it

had flashed every police point in the Northwest sector of the tower. Now it scanned all the police points under the tower, and ran dizzily through thousands of combinations before it settled on an old toolroom. A robot was polishing circular pieces of metal.

When Lord William saw the polishing, he was furious. "Get that here," he shouted. "I want to buy those myself!"

"All right," said Lord Issan. "It's a little irregular, but all right."

The machine showed the key search devices and brought the robot to the escalator.

The Lord Issan said, "This isn't much of a case."

C'mell sniveled. She was a good actress. "Then he wanted me to get a homunculus egg. One of the E-type, derived from birds, for him to take home."

Issan put on the search device.

"Maybe," said C'mell, "somebody has already put it in the disposal series."

The Bell and the Bank ran through all the disposal devices at high speed. Jestocost felt his nerves go on edge. No human being could have memorized these thousands of patterns as they flashed across the Bell too fast for human eyes, but the brain reading the Bell through his eyes was not human. It might even be locked into a computer of its own. It was, thought Jestocost, an indignity for a Lord of the Instrumentality to be used as a human spy-glass.

The machine blotted up.

"You're a fraud," cried the Lord Issan. "There's no evidence."

"Maybe the offworlder tried," said the Lady Johanna.

"Shadow him," said Lord William. "If he would steal ancient coins he would steal anything."

The Lady Johanna turned to C'mell. "You're a silly thing. You have wasted our time and you have kept us from serious inter-world business."

"It *is* inter-world business," wept C'mell. She let her hand slip from Jestocost's shoulder, where it had rested all the time. The body-to-body relay broke and the telepathic link broke with it.

"We should judge that," said Lord Issan.

"You might have been punished," said Lady Johanna.

The Lord Jestocost had said nothing, but there was a glow of happiness in him. If the E-telekeli was half as good as he seemed, the underpeople had a list of checkpoints and escape routes which would make it easier to hide from the capricious sentence of painless death which human authorities meted out.

There was singing in the corridors that night.

Underpeople burst into happiness for no visible reason.

C'mell danced a wild cat dance for the next customer who came in from the outworld stations, that very evening. When she got home to bed, she knelt before the picture of her father C'mackintosh and thanked the E-telekeli for what Jestocost had done.

But the story became known a few generations later, when the Lord Jestocost had won acclaim for being the champion of the underpeople and when the authorities, still unaware of E-telekeli, accepted the elected representatives of the underpeople as negotiators for better terms of life; and C'mell had died long since.

She had first had a long, good life.

She became a female chef when she was too old to be a girly girl. Her food was famous. Jestocost once visited her. At the end of the meal he had asked, "There's a silly rhyme among the underpeople. No human beings know it except me."

"I don't care about rhymes," she said.

"This is called 'The what-she-did.' "

C'mell blushed all the way down to the neckline of her capacious blouse. She had filled out a lot in middle age. Running the restaurant had helped.

"Oh, that rhyme!" she said. "It's silly."

"It says you were in love with a hominid."

"No," she said. "I wasn't." Her green eyes, as beautiful as ever, stared deeply into his. Jestocost felt uncomfortable. This was getting personal. He liked political relationships; personal things made him uncomfortable.

The light in the room shifted and her cat eyes blazed at him, she looked like the magical fire-haired girl he had known.

"I wasn't in love. You couldn't call it that . . ."

Her heart cried out, *It was you, it was you, it was you.*

"But the rhyme," insisted Jestocost, "says it was a hominid. It wasn't that Prins van de Schemering?"

"Who was he?" C'mell asked the question quietly, but her emotions cried out, *Darling, will you never, never know?*

"The strong man."

"Oh, him. I've forgotten him."

Jestocost rose from the table. "You've had a good life, C'mell. You've been a citizen, a committeewoman, a leader. And do you even known how many children you have had?"

"Seventy-three," she snapped at him. "Just because they're multiple doesn't mean we don't know them."

His playfulness left him. His face was grave, his voice kindly. "I meant no harm, C'mell."

He never knew that when he left she went back to the kitchen and cried for a while. It was Jestocost whom she had vainly loved ever since they had been comrades, many long years ago.

Even after she died, at the full age of five-score and three, he kept seeing her about the corridors and shafts of Earthport. Many of her great-granddaughters looked just like her and several of them practised the girly girl business with huge success.

They were not half-slaves. They were citizens (reserved grade) and they had photopasses which protected their property, their identity and their rights. Jestocost was the godfather to them all; he was often embarrassed when the most voluptuous creatures in the universe threw playful kisses at him. All he asked was fulfillment of his political passions, not his personal ones. He had always been in love, madly in love—

With justice itself.

At last, his own time came, and he knew that he was dying, and he was not sorry. He had had a wife, hundreds of years ago, and had loved her well; their children had passed into the generations of man.

In the ending, he wanted to know something, and he called to a nameless one (or to his successor) far beneath the ground. He called with his mind till it was a scream.

I have helped your people.

"Yes," came back the faintest of faraway whispers, inside his head.

I am dying. I must know. Did she love me?

"She went on without you, so much did she love you. She let you go, for your sake, not for hers. She really loved you. More than death. More than life. More than time. You will never be apart."

Never apart?

"Not, not in the memory of man," said the voice, and was then still.

Jestocost lay back on his pillow and waited for the day to end.

Thirty Days Had September

by Robert F. Young

THE SIGN IN the window said: SCHOOLTEACHER FOR SALE, DIRT CHEAP; and, in smaller letters: CAN COOK, SEW, AND IS HANDY AROUND THE HOUSE.

She made Danby think of desks and erasers and autumn leaves; of books and dreams and laughter. The proprietor of the little second-hand store had adorned her with a gay-colored dress and had slipped little red sandals on her feet, and she stood in her upright case in the window like a life-size doll waiting for someone to bring her to life.

Danby tried to move on down the spring street to the parking lot where he kept his Baby Buick. Laura probably had his supper all dialed and waiting on the table for him and she would be furious if he was late. But he went right on standing where he was, tall and thin, his youth not quite behind him, still lingering in his brown, wistful eyes, showing faintly in the softness of his cheeks.

His inertia annoyed him. He'd passed the store a thousand times on his way from the parking lot to his office and on his way from his office to the parking lot, but this was the first time he'd ever stopped and looked in the window.

But wasn't this the first time the window had ever contained something that he wanted?

Danby tried to face the question. Did he *want* a schoolteacher? Well hardly. But Laura certainly needed someone to help her with the housework and they couldn't afford an automatic maid, and Billy certainly could stand some extra-TV tutoring, with the boxtop tests coming up, and—

And— And her hair made him think of September sunlight, her face, of a September day. A September mist set-

110

tled around him and all of a sudden his inertia left him and he began to walk—but not in the direction he had intended to go. . . .

"How much is the schoolteacher in the window?" he asked.

Antiques of every description were scattered about the interior of the store. The proprietor was a little old man with bushy white hair and gingerbread eyes. He looked like an antique himself.

He beamed at Danby's question. "You like her, sir? She's very lovely."

Danby's face felt warm. "How much?" he repeated.

"Forty-nine ninety-five, plus five dollars for the case."

Danby could hardly believe it. With schoolteachers so rare, you'd think the price would go up, not down. And yet, less than a year ago, when he'd been thinking of buying a rebuilt third grade teacher to help Billy with his TV-schoolwork, the lowest-priced one he could find had run well over a hundred dollars. He would have bought her even at that, though, if Laura hadn't talked him out of it. Laura had never gone to real-school and didn't understand.

But forty-nine ninety-five! And she could cook and sew too! Surely Laura wouldn't try to talk him out of buying this one—

She definitely wouldn't if he didn't give her the chance. "Is— Is she in good condition?"

The proprietor's face grew pained. "She's been completely overhauled, sir. Brand new batteries, brand new motors. Her tapes are good for another ten years yet, and her memory banks will probably last forever. Here, I'll bring her in and show you."

The case was mounted on castors, but it was awkward to handle. Danby helped the old man push it out of the window and into the store. They stood it by the door where the light was brightest.

The old man stepped back admiringly. "Maybe I'm old-fashioned," he said, "but I still say that teleteachers will never compare to the real thing. You went to real-school, didn't you, sir?"

Danby nodded.

"I thought so. Funny the way you can always tell."

"Turn her on, please," Danby said.

The activator was a tiny button, hidden behind the left ear lobe. The proprietor fumbled for a moment before he found it; then there was a little *click!*, followed by a soft, almost inaudible, purring sound. Presently, color crept into the cheeks, the breast began to rise and fall; blue eyes opened—

Danby's fingernails were digging into the palms of his hands. "Make her say something."

"She responds to almost everything, sir," the old man said. "Words, scenes, situations . . . If you decide to take her and aren't satisfied, bring her back and I'll be glad to refund your money." He faced the case. "What is your name?" he asked.

"Miss Jones." Her voice was a September wind.

"Your occupation?"

"Specifically, I'm a fourth grade teacher, sir, but I can substitute for first, second, third, fifth, sixth, seventh, and eighth grades, and I'm well-grounded in the humanities. Also, I'm proficient in household chores, am a qualified cook, and can perform simple tasks, such as sewing on buttons, darning socks, and repairing rips and tears in clothing."

"They put a lot of extras in the later models," the old man said in an aside to Danby. "When they finally realized that teleducation was here to stay, they started doing everything they could to beat the cereal companies. But it didn't do any good." Then: "Step outside your case, Miss Jones. Show us how nice you walk."

She walked once around the drab room, her little red sandals twinkling over the dusty floor, her dress a gay little rainfall of color. Then she returned and stood waiting by the door.

Danby found it difficult to talk. "All right," he said finally. "Put her back in her case. I'll take her."

"Something for me, Dad?" Billy shouted. "Something for me?"

"Sure thing," Danby said, trundling the case up the walk and lifting it onto the diminutive front porch. "For your mother, too."

"Whatever it is, it better be good," Laura said, arms folded in the doorway. "Supper's stone cold."

"You can warm it up," Danby said. "Watch out, Billy!"

He lifted the case over the threshold, breathing a little hard, and shoved it down the short hall and into the living room. The living room was preempted by a pink-coated pitchman who had invited himself in via the 120″ screen and who was loudly proclaiming the superiority of the new 2061 Lincolnette convertible.

"Be careful of the rug!" Laura said.

"Don't get excited, I'm not going to hurt your rug," Danby said. "And will somebody please turn off TV so we can hear ourselves think!"

"I'll turn it off, Dad." Billy made nine-year-old strides across the room and killed the pitchman, pink coat and all.

Danby fumbled with the cover of the case, aware of Laura's breath on the back of his neck. "A schoolteacher!" she gasped, when it finally came open. "Of all the things for a grown man to bring home to his wife! A schoolteacher."

"She's not an ordinary schoolteacher," Danby said. "She can cook, she can sew, she— She can do just about anything. You're always saying you need a maid. Well now you've got one. And Billy's got someone to help him with his TV-lessons."

"How much?" For the first time Danby realized what a narrow face his wife had.

"Forty-nine ninety-five."

"Forty-nine ninety-five! George, are you crazy? Here I've been saving our money so we could turn in our Baby B. for a new Cadillette, and you go throwing it away on an old broken-down schoolteacher. What does *she* know about tel-education? Why, she's fifty years behind the times!"

"She's not going to help *me* with *my* TV-lessons!" Billy said, glowering at the case. "My TV-teacher said those old android teachers weren't good for anything. They— They used to *hit* kids!"

"They did not!" Danby said. "And I should know because I went to real-school all the way to eighth grade." He turned to Laura. "And she's not broken down either, and she's not fifty years behind the times, and she knows more about *real* education than your teleteachers ever will! And like I said, she can sew, she can cook—"

"Well, tell her to warm up our supper then!"

"I will!"

He reached into the case, depressed the little activator button, and, when the blue eyes opened, said: "Come with me, Miss Jones," and led her into the kitchen.

He was delighted at the way she responded to his instructions as to which buttons to push, which levers to raise and lower, which indicators to point at which numerals— Supper was off the table in a jiffy and back on again in the wink of an eye, all warm and steaming and delectable.

Even Laura was mollified. "Well . . ." she said.

"Well I guess!" Danby said. "I said she could cook, didn't I? Now you won't have to complain any more about jammed buttons and broken fingernails and—"

"All right, George. Don't rub it in."

Her face was back to normal again, still a little on the thin side of course, but that was part of its attractiveness under ordinary circumstances; that, and her dark, kindling eyes and exquisitely made-up mouth. She'd just had her breasts built up again and she really looked terrific in her new gold and scarlet loungerie. Danby decided he could have done far worse. He put his finger under her chin and kissed her. "Come on, let's eat," he said.

For some reason he'd forgotten about Billy. Glancing up from the table, he saw his son standing in the doorway, staring balefully at Miss Jones who was busy with the coffee.

"She's not going to hit me!" Billy said, answering Danby's glance.

Danby laughed. He felt better, now that half the battle was won. The other half could be taken care of later. "Of course she's not going to hit you," he said. "Now come over and eat your supper like a good boy."

"Yes," Laura said, "and hurry up. *Romeo and Juliet* is on the Western Hour and I don't want to miss a minute of it."

Billy relented. "Oh, all right!" he said. But he gave Miss Jones a wide berth as he walked into the kitchen and took his place at the table.

Romeo Montague twisted a cigarette with deft fingers, put it between sombrero-shadowed lips and lit it with a kitchen match. Then he guided his sleek palomino down the moonlit hillside to the Capulet ranch house.

"Guess I better be a mite keerful," he soliloquized. "These hyar Capulets, being sheepherders an' hereditary enemies o' my fambly, who are noble cattlemen, would gun me down afore I knowed what happened if'n they got the chance. But this gal I met at the wrassle tonight is worth a mite o' danger."

Danby frowned. He had nothing against rewriting the classics but it seemed to him that the rewrite men were overdoing the cattlemen-sheepmen deal. Laura and Billy didn't seem to mind, however. They were hunched forward in their viewchairs, gazing raptly at the 120″ screen. So maybe the rewrite men knew what they were doing at that.

Even Miss Jones seemed interested . . . but that was impossible, Danby quickly reminded himself. She *couldn't* be interested. No matter how intelligently her blue eyes might be focused on the screen, all she was doing, really, was sitting there wasting her batteries. He should have taken Laura's advice and turned her off—

But somehow he just hadn't had the heart. There was an element of cruelty in depriving her of life, even temporarily.

Now *there* was a ridiculous notion, if ever a man had one. Danby shifted irritably in his viewchair and his irritation intensified when he realized that he'd lost the thread of the play. By the time he regained it, Romeo had scaled the wall of the Capulet rancho, had crept through the orchard, and was standing in a gaudy garden beneath a low balcony.

Juliet Capulet stepped onto the balcony via a pair of anachronistic french doors. She was wearing a white cowgirl—or sheepgirl—suit with a thigh-length skirt, and a wide-brimmed sombrero crowned her bleached blond tresses. She leaned over the balcony railing, peered down into the garden. "Where ya'll at, Rome?" she drawled.

"Why this is ridiculous!" Miss Jones said abruptly. "The words, the costumes, the action, the place— Everything's wrong!"

Danby stared at her. He remembered suddenly what the proprietor of the secondhand store had said about her responding to scenes and situations as well as words. He'd assumed, of course, that the old man had meant scenes and situations directly connected with her duties as a teacher, not *all* scenes and situations.

An annoying little premonition skipped through Danby's mind. Both Laura and Billy, he noticed, had turned from their visual repast and were regarding Miss Jones with disbelieving eyes. The moment was a critical one.

He cleared his throat. "The play isn't really 'wrong,' Miss Jones," he said. "It's just been rewritten. You see, nobody would watch it in the original, and if no one watched it, what would be the sense of anyone sponsoring it?"

"But did they have to make it a *Western?*"

Danby glanced apprehensively at his wife. The disbelief in her eyes had been replaced by furious resentment. Hastily he returned his attention to Miss Jones.

"Westerns are the rage now, Miss Jones," he explained.

"It's sort of a revival of the early TV period. People like them, so naturally sponsors sponsor them and writers go way out of their way to find new material for them."

"But Juliet in a cowgirl suit! It's beneath the standards of even the lowest medium of entertainment."

"All right, George, that's enough." Laura's voice was cold. "I told you she was fifty years behind the times. Either turn her off or I'm going to bed!"

Danby sighed, stood up. He felt ashamed somehow as he walked over to where Miss Jones was sitting and felt for the little button behind her left ear. She regarded him calmly, her hands resting motionless on her lap, her breath coming and going rhythmically through her synthetic nostrils.

It was like committing murder. Danby shuddered as he returned to his viewchair. "You and your schoolteachers!" Laura said.

"Shut up!" Danby said.

He looked at the screen, tried to become interested in the play. It left him cold. The next program featured another play —a whodunit entitled *Macbeth*. That one left him cold, too. He kept glancing surreptitiously at Miss Jones. Her breast was still now, her eyes closed. The room seemed horribly empty.

Finally he couldn't stand it any longer. He stood up. "I'm going for a little ride," he told Laura, and walked out.

He backed the Baby B. out of the drivette and drove down the suburban street to the boulevard, asking himself over and over why an antique schoolteacher should affect him so. He knew it wasn't merely nostalgia, though nostalgia was part of it—nostalgia for September and real-school and walking into the classroom September mornings and seeing the teacher step out of her little closet by the blackboard the minute the bell rang and hearing her say, "Good morning, class. Isn't it a beautiful day for studying our lessons?"

But he'd never liked school any more than the other kids had, and he knew that September stood for something else besides books and autumn dreams. It stood for something he had lost somewhere along the line, something indefinable, something intangible; something he desperately needed now—

Danby wheeled the Baby B. down the boulevard, twisting in and around the scurrying automobilettes. When he turned down the side street that led to Friendly Fred's, he saw that there was a new stand going up on the corner. A big sign said: KING-SIZE CHARCOAL HOTS—HAVE A REAL HOT DOG GRILLED OVER A REAL FIRE! OPEN SOON!

He drove past, pulled into the parking lot beside Friendly Fred's, stepped out into the spring-starred night and let himself in by the side door. The place was crowded but he managed to find an empty stall. Inside, he slipped a quarter into the dispenser and dialed a beer.

He sipped it moodily when it emerged in its sweated paper cup. The stall was stuffy and smelt of its last occupant—a wino, Danby decided. He wondered briefly how it must have been in the old days when barroom privacy was unheard of and you had to stand elbow to elbow with the other patrons and everybody knew how much everybody else drank and how drunk everybody else got. Then his mind reverted to Miss Jones.

There was a small telescreen above the drink-dispenser, and beneath it were the words: GOT TROUBLES? TUNE IN FRIENDLY FRED, THE BARTENDER—HE'LL LISTEN TO YOUR WOES (*only 25¢ for 3 minutes*). Danby slipped a quarter in the coin slot. There was a little click and the quarter rattled in the coin return cup and Friendly Fred's recorded voice said, "Busy right now, pal. Be with you in a minute."

After a minute and another beer, Danby tried again. This time the two-way screen lit up and Friendly Fred's pink-jowled, cheerful face shimmered into focus. "Hi, George. How's it goin'?"

"Not too bad, Fred. Not *too* bad."

"But it could be better, eh?"

Danby nodded. "You guessed it, Fred. You guessed it." He looked down at the little bar where his beer sat all alone. "I . . . I bought a schoolteacher, Fred," he said.

"A *schoolteacher!*"

"Well I admit it's a kind of odd thing to buy, but I thought maybe the kid might need a little help with his TV-lessons—boxtop tests are coming up pretty soon and you know how kids feel when they don't send in the right answers and can't win a prize. And then I thought she—this is a special schoolteacher, you understand, Fred—I thought she could help Laura around the house. Things like that . . ."

His voice trailed away as he raised his eyes to the screen. Friendly Fred was shaking his friendly face solemnly. His pink jowls waggled. Presently: "George, you listen to me. You get rid of that teacher. Y'hear me, George? Get rid of her. Those android teachers are just as bad as the real old-fashioned kind—the kind that really breathed, I mean. You know what, George? You won't believe this, but I know. They usta hit kids. That's right. Hit them—" There was a buzzing noise and the screen started to flicker. "Time's up, George. Want another quarter's worth?"

"No thanks," Danby said. He finished his beer and left.

Did *everybody* hate schoolteachers? And, if so, why didn't everybody hate teleteachers too?

Danby pondered the paradox all next day at work. Fifty years ago it had looked as though android teachers were going to solve the educational problem as effectively as reducing the size and price of the prestige-cars at the turn of the century had solved the economic problem. But while android teachers had certainly obviated the teacher shortage, they'd only pointed up the other aspect of the problems—the school shortage. What good did it do to have enough teachers when there weren't enough classrooms for them to teach in? And how could you appropriate enough money to build new schools when the country was in constant need of newer and better super-highways?

It was silly to say that the building of public schools should have priority over the building of public roads, because if you neglected the country's highways you automatically weakened the average citizen's penchant to buy new cars, thereby weakening the economy, precipitating a depression, and making the building of new schools more impracticable than it had been in the first place.

When you came right down to it, you had to take your hat off to the cereal companies. In introducing teleteachers and teleducation, they had saved the day. One teacher standing in one room, with a blackboard on one side of her and a movie-screen on the other, could hold classes for fifty million pupils, and if any of those pupils didn't like the way she taught all he had to do was switch channels to one of the other teleducational programs sponsored by one of the other cereal companies. (It was up to each pupil's parents, of course, to see that he didn't skip classes, or tune in on the next grade before he passed the previous grade's boxtop tests.)

But the best part of the whole ingenious system was the happy fact that the cereal companies paid for everything, thereby absolving the taxpayer of one of his most onerous obligations and leaving his pocketbook more amenable to salestax, gas tax, tolls, and car-payments. And all the cereal companies asked in return for their fine public service was that the pupils—and preferably the parents, too—eat their cereal.

So the paradox wasn't a paradox after all. A schoolteacher was an anathema because she symbolized expense; a tele-teacher was a respected public servant because she symbolized the large economy-size package. But the difference, Danby knew, went much deeper.

While schoolteacher-hatred was partly atavistic, it was largely the result of the propaganda campaign the cereal companies had launched when first putting their idea into action. They were responsible for the widespread myth that android schoolteachers hit their pupils and they still revived that myth occasionally just in case there was anybody left who still doubted it.

The trouble was, most people were teleducated and there-fore didn't know the truth. Danby was an exception. He'd been born in a small town, the mountainous location of which had made TV reception impossible, and before his family migrated to the city he'd attended real-school. So he *knew* that schoolteachers didn't hit their pupils.

Unless Androids, Inc. had distributed one or two deficient models by mistake. And that wasn't likely. Androids, Inc. was a pretty efficient corporation. Look at what excellent service station attendants they made. Look at what fine stenographers, waitresses, and maids they put on the market.

Of course neither the average man starting out in business nor the average householder could afford them. But—Danby's thoughts did an intricate hop, skip, and a jump—wasn't that all the more reason why Laura should be satisfied with a makeshift maid?

But she wasn't satisfied. All he had to do was take one look at her face when he came home that night and he knew beyond the shadow of a doubt that she wasn't satisfied.

He had never seen her cheeks so pinched, her lips so thin. "Where's Miss Jones?" he asked.

"She's in her case," Laura said. "And tomorrow morning you're going to take her back to whoever you bought her from and get our forty-nine ninety-five refunded!"

"She's not going to hit *me* again!" Billy said from his In-dian squat in front of the TV screen.

Danby whitened. *"Did* she hit him?"

"Well, not exactly," Laura said.

"Either she did or she didn't," Danby said.

"Tell him what she said about my TV-teacher!" Billy shouted.

"She said Billy's teacher wasn't qualified to teach horses."

"And tell him what she said about Hector and Achilles!"

Laura sniffed. "She said it was a shame to make a cowboy-and-Indian melodrama out of a classic like the *Iliad* and call it education."

The story came out gradually. Miss Jones apparently had gone on an intellectual rampage from the moment Laura had turned her on in the morning to the moment Laura had turned her off. According to Miss Jones, everything in the Danby household was wrong, from the teleducation programs Billy watched on the little red TV set in his room and the Morning and Afternoon programs Laura watched on the big TV set in the living room, to the pattern of the wallpaper in the hallway (little red Cadillettes rollicking along interlaced ribbons of highways), the windshield picture window in the kitchen, and the dearth of books.

"Can you imagine?" Laura said. "She actually thinks books are still being published!"

"All I want to know," Danby said, "is did she hit him?"

"I'm coming to that—"

About three o'clock, Miss Jones had been dusting in Billy's room. Billy was watching his lessons dutifully, sitting at his little desk as nice and quiet as you please, absorbed in the efforts of the cowboys to take the Indian village of Troy, when all of a sudden Miss Jones swept across the room like a mad woman, uttered her sacrilegious remark about the alteration of the *Iliad*, and turned off the set right in the middle of the lesson. That was when Billy had begun to scream and when Laura had burst into the room and found Miss Jones gripping his arm with one hand and raising her other hand to deliver the blow.

"I got there in the nick of time," Laura said. "There's no telling what she might have done. Why, she might have killed him!"

"I doubt it," Danby said. "What happened after that?"

"I grabbed Billy away from her and told her to go back to her case. Then I shut her off and closed the cover. And believe me, George Danby, it's going to stay closed! And like I said, tomorrow morning you're going to take her back— if you want Billy and me to go on living in this house!"

Danby felt sick all evening. He picked at his supper,

languished through part of the Western Hour, glancing every now and then, when he was sure Laura wasn't looking, at the case standing mutely by the door. The heroine of the Western Hour was a dance hall girl—a 39-24-38 blonde named Antigone. Seemed that her two brothers had killed each other in a gun fight and the local sheriff—a character named Creon—had permitted only one of them a decent burial on Boot Hill, illogically insisting that the other be left out on the desert for the buzzards to pick at. Antigone couldn't see it that way at all, and she told her sister Ismene that if one brother rated a respectable grave, so did the other, and that she, Antigone, was going to see that he got one, and would Ismene please lend her a hand? But Ismene was chicken, so Antigone said All right, she'd take care of the matter herself; then an old prospector named Teiresias rode into town and—

Danby got up quietly, slipped into the kitchen, and let himself out the back door. He got behind the wheel and drove down to the boulevard, then up the boulevard, with all the windows open and the warm wind washing around him.

The hot dog stand on the corner was nearing completion. He glanced at it idly as he turned into the side street. There were a number of empty stalls at Friendly Fred's and he chose one at random. He had quite a few beers, standing there at the lonely little bar, and he did a lot of thinking. When he was sure his wife and son were in bed, he drove home, opened Miss Jones' case, and turned her on.

"Were you going to hit Billy this afternoon?" he asked.

The blue eyes regarded him unwaveringly, the lashes fluttering at rhythmic intervals, the pupils gradually adjusting themselves to the living room lamp Laura had left burning. Presently: "I'm incapable of striking a human, sir. I believe the clause is in my guarantee."

"I'm afraid your guarantee ran out some time ago, Miss Jones," Danby said. His voice felt thick and his words kept running together. "Not that it matters. You did grab his arm though, didn't you?"

"I had to, sir."

Danby frowned. He swayed a little, weaved back into the living room on rubbery legs. "Come over and sit down and tell me about it, Mish—Miss Jones," he said.

He watched her step out of her case and walk across the room. There was something odd about the way she walked. Her step was no longer light, but heavy; her body no longer delicately balanced, but awry. With a start, he realized that she was limping.

She sat down on the couch and he sat down beside her. "He kicked you, didn't he?" he said.

"Yes, sir. I had to hold him back or he'd have kicked me again."

There was a dull redness filling the room, coalescing before his eyes. Then, subtly, the redness dissipated before the dawning realization that here in his hand lay the very weapon he had needed: the psychological bludgeon with which he could quell all further objection to Miss Jones.

But a little of the redness still remained and it was permeated with regret. "I'm terribly sorry, Miss Jones. Billy's too aggressive, I'm afraid."

"He could hardly help being so, sir. I was quite astonished today when I learned that those horrid programs that he watches constitute his entire educational fare. His teleteacher is little more than a semi-civilized M.C. whose primary concern is selling his company's particular brand of corn flakes. I can understand now why your writers have to revert to the classics for ideas. Their creativity is snuffed out by clichés while still in its embryo-stage."

Danby was enchanted. He had never heard anyone talk that way before. It wasn't her words so much. It was the way she said them, the conviction that her voice carried despite the fact that her "voice" was no more than a deftly built speaker geared to tapes that were in turn geared to unimaginably intricate memory banks.

But sitting there beside her, watching her lips move, seeing her lashes descend ever so often over her blue blue eyes, it was as though September had come and sat in the room. Suddenly a feeling of utter peace engulfed him. The rich, mellow days of September filed one by one past his eyes and he saw why they were different from other days. They were different because they had depth and beauty and quietness; because their blue skies held promises of richer, mellower days to come—

They were different because they had *meaning*. . . .

The moment was so poignantly sweet that Danby never wanted it to end. The very thought of its passing racked him with unbearable agony and instinctively he did the only physical thing he could do to sustain it.

He put his arm around Miss Jones' shoulder.

She did not move. She sat there quietly, her breast rising

and falling at even intervals, her long lashes drifting down now and again like dark, gentle birds winging over blue limpid waters—

"The play we watched last night," Danby said. *"Romeo and Juliet*—Why didn't you like it?"

"It was rather horrible, sir. It was a burlesque, really—tawdry, cheap, the beauty of the lines corrupted and obscured."

"Do you know the lines?"

"Some of them."

"Say them. Please."

"Yes, sir. At the close of the balcony scene, when the two lovers are parting, Juliet says, *'Good night, good night! Parting is such sweet sorrow, That I shall say good night till it be morrow.'* And Romeo answers: *'Sleep dwell upon thine eyes, peace in thy breast! Would I were sleep and peace, so sweet to rest!'* Why did they leave that out, sir? Why?"

"Because we're living in a cheap world," Danby said, surprised at his sudden insight, "and in a cheap world, precious things are worthless. Shay—say the lines again please, Miss Jones."

"Good night, good night! Parting is such sweet sorrow, that I shall say good night till it be morrow—"

"Let me finish." Danby concentrated. *"Sleep dwell upon thine eyes, peace—"*

"—in thy breast—"

"Would I were sleep and peace, so—"

"—sweet—"

"—so sweet to rest!"

Abruptly Miss Jones stood up. "Good evening, madam," she said.

Danby didn't bother to get up. It wouldn't have done any good. He could see Laura well enough, anyway, from where he was sitting. Laura standing in the living room doorway in her new Cadillette pajamas and her bare feet that had made no sound in their surreptitious descent of the stairs. The two-dimensional cars that comprised the pajama pattern stood out in vermilion vividness and it was as though she was lying down and letting them run rampant over her body, letting them defile her breasts and her belly and her legs . . .

He saw her narrow face and her cold pitiless eyes and he knew it would be useless to try to explain, that she wouldn't—couldn't—understand. And he realized with sudden shocking clarity that in the world in which he lived September had been dead for decades, and he saw himself in the morning, loading the case into the Baby B. and driving down the glittering city streets to the little secondhand store and asking the proprietor for his money back and he saw himself afterwards, but he had to look away, and when he looked away he saw Miss Jones standing incongruously in the gaudy living room and heard her saying, over and over like a broken bewildered record, "Is something wrong, madam? Is something wrong?"

It was several weeks before Danby felt whole enough to go down to Friendly Fred's for a beer. Laura had begun speaking to him by then, and the world, while not quite the same as it had once been, had at least taken on some of the aspects of its former self. He backed the Baby B. out of the drivette and drove down the street and into the multicolored boulevard traffic. It was a clear June night and the stars were crystal pinpoints high above the fluorescent fire of the city. The hot dog stand on the corner was finished now, and open for business. Several customers were standing at the gleaming chrome counter and a waitress was turning sizzling wieners over a chrome charcoal brazier. There was something familiar about her gay rainfall of a dress, about the way she moved; about the way the gentle sunrise of her hair framed her gentle face— Her new owner was leaning on the counter some distance away, chatting with a customer.

There was a tightness in Danby's chest as he parked the Baby B. and got out and walked across the concrete apron to the counter—a tightness in his chest and a steady throbbing in his temples. There were some things you couldn't permit to happen without at least trying to stop them, no matter what the price for trying to stop them involved.

He had reached the section of the counter where the owner was standing and he was about to lean across the polished chrome and slap the smug fat face, when he saw the little cardboard sign propped against the chrome mustard jar, the sign that said, MAN WANTED. . . .

A hot dog stand was a long way from being a September classroom, and a schoolteacher dispensing hot dogs could never quite compare to a schoolteacher dispensing dreams; but if you wanted something badly enough, you took whatever you could get of it, and were thankful for even that. . . .

"I could only work nights," Danby said to the owner. "Say from six to twelve—"

"Why, that would be fine," the owner said. "I'm afraid I won't be able to pay you much at first, though. You see, I'm just starting out and—"

"Never mind that," Danby said. "When do I start?"

"Why, the sooner the better."

Danby walked around to where a section of the counter raised up on hidden hinges and he stepped into the stand proper and took off his coat. If Laura didn't like the idea, she could go to hell, but he knew it would be all right because the additional money he'd be making would make *her* dream—the Cadillette one—come true.

He donned the apron the owner handed him and joined Miss Jones in front of the charcoal brazier. "Good evening, Miss Jones," he said. She turned her head and the blue eyes seemed to light up and her hair was like the sun coming up on a hazy September morning. "Good evening, sir," she said, and a September wind sprang up in the June night and blew through the stand and it was like going back to school again after an endless empty summer.

The Cage

by Bertram Chandler

IMPRISONMENT IS ALWAYS a humiliating experience, no matter how philosophical the prisoner. Imprisonment by one's own kind is bad enough—but one can, at least, talk to one's captors, one can make one's wants understood; one can, on occasion, appeal to them man to man.

Imprisonment is doubly humiliating when one's captors, in all honesty, treat one as a lower animal.

The party from the survey ship could, perhaps, be excused for failing to recognize the survivors from the interstellar liner *Lode Star* as rational beings. At least two hundred days had passed since their landing on the planet without a name—an unintentional landing made when *Lode Star*'s Erenhaft generators, driven far in excess of their normal capacity by a breakdown of the electronic regulator, had flung her far from the regular shipping lanes to an unexplored region of Space. *Lode Star* had landed safely enough; but shortly thereafter (troubles never come singly) her Pile had got out of control and her Captain had ordered his First Mate to evacuate the passengers and such crew members not needed to cope with the emergency, and to get them as far from the ship as possible.

Hawkins and his charges were well clear when there was a flare of released energy, a not very violent explosion. The survivors wanted to turn to watch, but Hawkins drove them on with curses and, at times, blows. Luckily they were up wind from the ship and so escaped the fall-out.

When the fireworks seemed to be over Hawkins, accompanied by Dr. Boyle, the ship's surgeon, returned to the scene of the disaster. The two men, wary of radioactivity, were cautious and stayed a safe distance from the shallow, still smoking crater that marked where the ship had been. It was all too obvious to them that the Captain, his officers

126

and technicians, were now no more than an infinitesimal part of the incandescent cloud that had mushroomed up into the low overcast.

Thereafter the fifty-odd men and women, the survivors of *Lode Star*, had degenerated. It hadn't been a fast process—Hawkins and Boyle, aided by a committee of the more responsible passengers, had fought a stout rearguard action. But it had been a hopeless sort of fight. The climate was against them, for a start. Hot it was, always in the neighborhood of 85° Fahrenheit. And it was wet—a thin, warm drizzle falling all the time. The air seemed to abound with the spores of fungi—luckily these did not attack living skin but throve on dead organic matter, on clothing. They throve to an only slightly lesser degree on metals and on the synthetic fabrics that many of the castaways wore.

Danger, outside danger, would have helped to maintain morale. But there were no dangerous animals. There were only little smooth-skinned things, not unlike frogs, that hopped through the sodden undergrowth, and, in the numerous rivers, fishlike creatures ranging in size from the shark to the tadpole, and all of them possessing the bellicosity of the latter.

Food had been no problem after the first few hungry hours. Volunteers had tried a large, succulent fungus growing on the boles of the huge fern-like trees. They had pronounced it good. After a lapse of five hours they had neither died nor even complained of abdominal pains. That fungus was to become the staple diet of the castaways. In the weeks that followed other fungi had been found, and berries, and roots—all of them edible. They provided a welcome variety.

Fire—in spite of the all-pervading heat—was the blessing most missed by the castaways. With it they could have supplemented their diet by catching and cooking the little frog-things of the rain forest, the fishes of the streams. Some of the hardier spirits did eat these animals raw, but they were frowned upon by most of the other members of the community. Too, fire would have helped to drive back the darkness of the long nights, would, by its real warmth and light, have dispelled the illusion of cold produced by the ceaseless dripping of water from every leaf and frond.

When they fled from the ship most of the survivors had possessed pocket lighters—but the lighters had been lost when the pockets, together with the clothing surrounding them, had disintegrated. In any case, all attempts to start a fire in the days when there were still pocket lighters had failed—there was not, Hawkins swore, a single dry spot on the whole accursed planet. Now the making of fire was quite impossible: even if there had been present an expert on the rubbing together of two dry sticks he could have found no material with which to work.

They made their permanent settlement on the crest of a low hill. (There were, so far as they could discover, no mountains.) It was less thickly wooded there than the surrounding plains, and the ground was less marshy underfoot. They succeeded in wrenching fronds from the fern-like trees and built for themselves crude shelters—more for the sake of privacy than for any comfort that they afforded. They clung, with a certain desperation, to the governmental forms of the worlds that they had left, and elected themselves a council. Boyle, the ship's surgeon, was their chief. Hawkins, rather to his surprise, was returned as a council member by a majority of only two votes—on thinking it over he realized that many of the passengers must still bear a grudge against the ship's executive staff for their present predicament.

The first council meeting was held in a hut—if so it could be called—especially constructed for the purpose. The council members squatted in a rough circle. Boyle, the president, got slowly to his feet. Hawkins grinned wryly as he compared the surgeon's nudity with the pomposity that he seemed to have assumed with his elected rank, as he compared the man's dignity with the unkempt appearance presented by his uncut, uncombed gray hair, his uncombed and straggling gray beard.

"Ladies and gentlemen," began Boyle.

Hawkins looked around him at the naked, pallid bodies, at the stringy, lusterless hair, the long, dirty fingernails of the men and the unpainted lips of the women. He thought, I don't suppose I look much like an officer and a gentleman myself.

"Ladies and gentlemen," said Boyle. "We have been, as you know, elected to represent the human community upon this planet. I suggest that at this, our first meeting, we discuss our chances of survival—not as individuals, but as a race—"

"I'd like to ask Mr. Hawkins what our chances are of being picked up," shouted one of the two women members, a dried-up, spinsterish creature with prominent ribs and vertebrae.

"Slim," said Hawkins. "As you know, no communication is possible with other ships, or with planet stations when the Interstellar Drive is operating. When we snapped out of the Drive and came in for our landing we sent out a distress call—but we couldn't say where we were. Furthermore, we don't know that the call was received—"

"Miss Taylor," said Boyle huffily. "Mr. Hawkins. I would remind you that I am the duly elected president of this council. There will be time for a general discussion later.

"As most of you may already have assumed, the age of this planet, biologically speaking, corresponds roughly with that of Earth during the Carboniferous Era. As we already know, no species yet exists to challenge our supremacy. By the time such a species does emerge—something analogous to the giant lizards of Earth's Triassic Era—we should be well established—"

"*We* shall be dead!" called one of the men.

"*We* shall be dead," agreed the doctor, "but our descendants will be very much alive. We have to decide how to give them as good a start as possible. Language we shall bequeath to them—"

"Never mind the language, Doc," called the other woman member. She was a small blonde, slim, with a hard face. "It's just this question of descendants that I'm here to look after. I represent the women of childbearing age—there are, as you must know, fifteen of us here. So far the girls have been very, very careful. We have reason to be. Can you, as a medical man, guarantee—bearing in mind that you have no drugs, no instruments—safe deliveries? Can you guarantee that our children will have a good chance of survival?"

Boyle dropped his pomposity like a worn-out garment.

"I'll be frank," he said. "I have not, as you, Miss Hart, have pointed out, either drugs or instruments. But I can assure you, Miss Hart, that your chances of a safe delivery are far better than they would have been on Earth during, say, the Eighteenth Century. And I'll tell you why. On this planet, so far as we know (and we have been here long enough now to find out the hard way), there exist no microorganisms harmful to Man. Did such organisms exist, the bodies of those of us still surviving would be, by this time, mere masses of suppuration. Most of us, of course, would have died of septicemia long ago. And that, I think, answers *both* your questions."

"I haven't finished yet," she said. "Here's another point.

There are fifty-three of us here, men and women. There are ten married couples—so we'll count them out. That leaves thirty-three people, of whom twenty are men. Twenty men to thirteen (aren't we girls always unlucky?) women. All of us aren't young—but we're all of us women. What sort of marriage set-up do we have? Monogamy? Polyandry?"

"Monogamy, of course," said a tall, thin man sharply. He was the only one of those present who wore clothing—if so it could be called. The disintegrating fronds lashed around his waist with a strand of vine did little to serve any useful purpose.

"All right, then," said the girl. "Monogamy. I'd rather prefer it that way myself. But I warn you that if that's the way we play it there's going to be trouble. And in any murder involving passion and jealousy the woman is as liable to be a victim as either of the men—and I don't want *that*."

"What do you propose, then, Miss Hart?" asked Boyle.

"Just this, Doc. When it comes to our matings we leave love out of it. If two men want to marry the same woman, then let them fight it out. The best man gets the girl—and keeps her."

"Natural selection . . ." murmured the surgeon. "I'm in favor—but we must put it to the vote."

At the crest of the low hill was a shallow depression, a natural arena. Round the rim sat the castaways—all but four of them. One of the four was Doctor Boyle—he had discovered that his duties as president embraced those of a referee; it had been held that he was best competent to judge when one of the contestants was liable to suffer permanent damage. Another of the four was the girl Mary Hart. She had found a serrated twig with which to comb her long hair, she had contrived a wreath of yellow flowers with which to crown the victor. Was it, wondered Hawkins as he sat with the other council members, a hankering after an Earthly wedding ceremony, or was it a harking back to something older and darker?

"A pity that these blasted molds got our watches," said the fat man on Hawkins' right. "If we had any means of telling the time we could have rounds, make a proper prizefight of it."

Hawkins nodded. He looked at the four in the centre of the arena—at the strutting, barbaric woman, at the pompous old man, at the two dark-bearded young men with their glistening white bodies. He knew them both—Fennet had been a Senior Cadet of the ill-fated *Lode Star;* Clemens, at least seven years Fennet's senior, was a passenger, had been a prospector on the frontier worlds.

"If we had anything to bet with," said the fat man happily, "I'd lay it on Clemens. That cadet of yours hasn't a snowball's chance in hell. He's been brought up to fight clean —Clemens has been brought up to fight dirty."

"Fennet's in better condition," said Hawkins. "He's been taking exercise, while Clemens has just been lying around sleeping and eating. Look at the paunch on him!"

"There's nothing wrong with good, healthy flesh and muscle," said the fat man, patting his own paunch.

"No gouging, no biting!" called the doctor. "And may the best man win!"

He stepped back smartly away from the contestants, stood with the Hart woman.

There was an air of embarrassment about the pair of them as they stood there, each with his fists hanging at his sides. Each seemed to be regretting that matters had come to such a pass.

"Go *on!*" screamed Mary Hart at last. "Don't you want me? You'll live to a ripe old age here—and it'll be lonely with no woman!"

"They can always wait around until your daughters grow up, Mary!" shouted one of her friends.

"If I ever have any daughters!" she called. "I shan't at this rate!"

"Go on!" shouted the crowd. "Go on!"

Fennet made a start. He stepped forward almost diffidently, dabbed with his right fist at Clemens' unprotected face. It wasn't a hard blow, but it must have been painful. Clemens put his hand up to his nose, brought it away and stared at the bright blood staining it. He growled, lumbered forward with arms open to hug and crush. The cadet danced back, scoring twice more with his right.

"Why doesn't he *hit* him?" demanded the fat man.

"And break every bone in his fist? They aren't wearing gloves, you know," said Hawkins.

Fennet decided to make a stand. He stood firm, his feet slightly apart, and brought his right into play once more. This time he left his opponent's face alone, went for his belly instead. Hawkins was surprised to see that the prospector was taking the blows with apparent equanimity—he must be, he decided, much tougher in actuality than in appearance.

The cadet sidestepped smartly . . . and slipped on the wet grass. Clemens fell heavily on to his opponent; Hawkins could hear the *whoosh* as the air was forced from the lad's lungs. The prospector's thick arms encircled Fennet's body—and Fennet's knee came up viciously to Clemens' groin. The prospector squealed, but hung on grimly. One of his hands was around Fennet's throat now, and the other one, its fingers viciously hooked, was clawing for the cadet's eyes.

"No gouging!" Boyle was screaming. "No gouging!"

He dropped down to his knees, caught Clemens' thick wrist with both his hands.

Something made Hawkins look up then. It may have been a sound, although this is doubtful; the spectators were behaving like boxing fans at a prizefight. They could hardly be blamed—this was the first piece of real excitement that had come their way since the loss of the ship. It may have been a sound that made Hawkins look up, it may have been the sixth sense possessed by all good spacemen. What he saw made him cry out.

Hovering above the arena was a helicopter. There was something about the design of it, a subtle oddness, that told Hawkins that this was no Earthly machine. Suddenly, from its smooth, shining belly, dropped a net, seemingly of dull metal. It enveloped the struggling figures on the ground, trapped the doctor and Mary Hart.

Hawkins shouted again—a wordless cry. He jumped to his feet, ran to the assistance of his ensnared companions. The net seemed to be alive. It twisted itself around his wrists, bound his ankles. Others of the castaways rushed to aid Hawkins.

"Keep away!" he shouted. "Scatter!"

The low drone of the helicopter's rotors rose in pitch. The machine lifted. In an incredibly short space of time the arena was to the First Mate's eyes no more than a pale green saucer in which little white ants scurried aimlessly. Then the flying machine was above and through the base of the low clouds, and there was nothing to be seen but drifting whiteness.

When, at last, it made its descent Hawkins was not surprised to see the silvery tower of a great spaceship standing among the low trees on a level plateau.

The world to which they were taken would have been a marked improvement on the world they had left had it not been for the mistaken kindness of their captors. The cage in which the three men were housed duplicated, with remarkable fidelity, the climatic conditions of the planet upon which *Lode Star* had been lost. It was glassed in, and from Sprinklers in its roof fell a steady drizzle of warm water. A couple of dispirited tree ferns provided little shelter from the depressing precipitation. Twice a day a hatch at the back of the cage, which was made of a sort of concrete, opened, and slabs of a fungus remarkably similar to that on which they had been subsisting were thrown in. There was a hole in the floor of the cage; this the prisoners rightly assumed was for sanitary purposes.

On either side of them were other cages. In one of them was Mary Hart—alone. She could gesture to them, wave to them, and that was all. The cage on the other side held a beast built on the same general lines as a lobster, but with a strong hint of squid. Across the broad roadway they could see other cages, but could not see what they housed.

Hawkins, Boyle and Fennet sat on the damp floor and stared through the thick glass and the bars at the beings outside who stared at them.

"If only they were humanoid," sighed the doctor. "If only they were the same shape as we are we might make a start towards convincing them that we, too, are intelligent beings."

"They aren't the same shape," said Hawkins. "And we, were the situations reversed, would take some convincing that three six-legged beer barrels were men and brothers. . . . Try Pythagoras' Theorem again," he said to the cadet.

Without enthusiasm the youth broke fronds from the nearest tree fern. He broke them into smaller pieces. Then on the mossy floor laid them out in the design of a right-angled triangle with squares constructed on all three sides. The natives—a large one, one slightly smaller and a little one—regarded him incuriously with their flat, dull eyes. The large one put the tip of a tentacle into a pocket—the things wore clothing—and pulled out a brightly colored packet, handed it to the little one. The little one tore off the wrapping, started stuffing pieces of some bright blue confection into the slot on its upper side that, obviously, served it as a mouth.

"I wish they were allowed to feed the animals," sighed Hawkins. "I'm sick of that damned fungus."

"Let's recapitulate," said the doctor. "After all, we've nothing else to do. We were taken from our camp by the helicopter—six of us. We were taken to the survey ship—a vessel that seemed in no way superior to our own interstellar ships. You assure us, Hawkins, that the ship used the Ehrenhaft Drive or something so near to it as to be its twin brother. . . ."

"Correct," agreed Hawkins.

"On the ship we're kept in separate cages. There's no ill treatment, we're fed and watered at frequent intervals. We land on this strange planet, but we see nothing of it. We're hustled out of cages like so many cattle into a covered van. We know that we're being driven *somewhere*, that's all. The van stops, the door opens and a couple of these animated beer barrels poke in poles with smaller editions of those fancy nets on the end of them. They catch Clemens and Miss Taylor, drag them out. We never see them again. The rest of us spend the night and the following day and night in individual cages. The next day we're taken to this . . . zoo . . ."

"Do you think they were vivisected?" asked Fennet. "I never liked Clemens, but . . ."

"I'm afraid they were," said Boyle. "Our captors must have learned of the difference between the sexes by it. Unluckily there's no way of determining intelligence by vivisection—"

"The filthy brutes!" shouted the cadet.

"Easy, son," counseled Hawkins. "You can't blame them, you know. We've vivisected animals a lot more like us than we are to these things."

"The problem," the doctor went on, "is to convince these things—as you call them, Hawkins—that we are rational beings like themselves. How would they define a rational being? How would *we* define a rational being?"

"Somebody who knows Pythagoras' Theorem," said the cadet sulkily.

"I read somewhere," said Hawkins, "that the history of Man is the history of the fire-making, tool-using animal . . ."

"Then make fire," suggested the doctor. "Make us some tools, and use them."

"Don't be silly. You know that there's not an artifact among the bunch of us. No false teeth even—not even a metal filling. Even so . . ." He paused. "When I was a youngster there was, among the cadets in the interstellar ships, a revival of the old arts and crafts. We considered ourselves in a direct line of descent from the old windjammer sailormen, so we learned how to splice rope and wire, how to make sen-

nit and fancy knots and all the rest of it. Then one of us hit
on the idea of basketmaking. We were in a passenger ship,
and we used to make our baskets secretly, daub them with
violent colors and then sell them to passengers as genuine
souvenirs from the Lost Planet of Arcturus VI. There was a
most distressing scene when the Old Man and the Mate found
out. . . ."

"What are you driving at?" asked the doctor.

"Just this. We will demonstrate our manual dexterity by
the weaving of baskets—I'll teach you how."

"It might work. . ." said Boyle slowly. "It might just work.
. . . On the other hand, don't forget that certain birds and
animals do the same sort of thing. On Earth there's the beaver,
who builds quite cunning dams. There's the bower bird,
who makes a bower for his mate as part of the courtship
ritual . . ."

The Head Keeper must have known of creatures whose
courting habits resembled those of the Terran bower bird.
After three days of feverish basketmaking, which consumed
all the bedding and stripped the tree ferns, Mary Hart was
taken from her cage and put in with the three men. After she
had got over her hysterical pleasure at having somebody to
talk to again she was rather indignant.

It was good, thought Hawkins drowsily, to have Mary with
them. A few more days of solitary confinement must surely
have driven the girl crazy. Even so, having Mary in the same
cage had its drawbacks. He had to keep a watchful eye on
young Fennet. He even had to keep a watchful eye on Boyle
—the old goat!

Mary screamed.

Hawkins jerked into complete wakefulness. He could see
the pale form of Mary—on this world it was never completely dark at night—and, on the other side of the cage,
the forms of Fennet and Boyle. He got hastily to his feet,
stumbled to the girl's side.

"What is it?" he asked.

"I . . . I don't know. . . . Something small, with sharp
claws . . . It ran over me. . . ."

"Oh," said Hawkins, "that was only Joe."

"Joe?" she demanded.

"I don't know exactly what he—or she—is," said the
man.

"I think he's definitely *he*," said the doctor.

"What is Joe?" she asked again.

"He must be the local equivalent to a mouse," said the doctor, "although he looks nothing like one. He comes up through the floor somewhere to look for scraps of food. We're trying to tame him—"

"You encourage the brute?" she screamed. "I demand that you do something about him—at once! Poison him, or trap him. Now!"

"Tomorrow," said Hawkins.

"Now!" she screamed.

"Tomorrow," said Hawkins firmly.

The capture of Joe proved to be easy. Two flat baskets, hinged like the valves of an oyster shell, made the trap. There was bait inside—a large piece of the fungus. There was a cunningly arranged upright that would fall at the least tug at the bait. Hawkins, lying sleepless on his damp bed, heard the tiny click and thud that told him that the trap had been sprung. He heard Joe's indignant chitterings, heard the tiny claws scrabbling at the stout basketwork.

Mary Hart was asleep. He shook her.

"We've caught him," he said.

"Then kill him," she answered drowsily.

But Joe was not killed. The three men were rather attached to him. With the coming of daylight they transferred him to a cage that Hawkins had fashioned. Even the girl relented when she saw the harmless ball of multi-colored fur bouncing indignantly up and down in its prison. She insisted on feeding the little animal, exclaimed gleefully when the thin tentacles reached out and took the fragment of fungus from her fingers.

For three days they made much of their pet. On the fourth day beings whom they took to be keepers entered the cage with their nets, immobilized the occupants, and carried off Joe and Hawkins.

"I'm afraid it's hopeless," Boyle said. "He's gone the same way . . ."

"They'll have him stuffed and mounted in some museum," said Fennet glumly.

"No," said the girl. "They couldn't!"

"They could," said the doctor.

Abruptly the hatch at the back of the cage opened.

Before the three humans could retreat to the scant protection supplied by a corner a voice called, "It's all right, come on out!"

Hawkins walked into the cage. He was shaved, and the beginnings of a healthy tan had darkened the pallor of his skin. He was wearing a pair of trunks fashioned from some bright red material.

"Come on out," he said again. "Our hosts have apologized very sincerely, and they have more suitable accommodation prepared for us. Then, as soon as they have a ship ready, we're to go to pick up the other survivors."

"Not so fast," said Boyle. "Put us in the picture, will you? What made them realize that we were rational beings?"

Hawkins' face darkened.

"Only rational beings," he said, "put other beings in cages."

Star-Crossed Lover

by William W. Stuart

So HELP me, I'm not really a fiend, a monstrous murderer or a Bluebird. I am not, truly, even a mad scientist bucking for a billing to top Frankenstein's. My knowledge of science ends with the Sunday magazine section of the paper. As for the bodies of all those women the front pages claim I butchered and buried somewhat carelessly out by the garage, all that is just—well, just an illusion of sorts.

Equally illusory, I am hoping, is my reservation for a sure seat, next performance, in the electric chair which now seems so certain after the merest formality of a trial.

Actually I am, or was, nothing but a very normal, average —upper middle average, that is—sort of a guy. I have always been friendly, sociable, kindly, lovable to a fault. So how did lovable, kindly old I happen to get into such a bloody mess?

I simply helped a little old lady cross the street. That's all.

All right, I admit I was old for Boy Scout work. But the poor old bat did look mighty confused and baffled, standing there on the corner of York and Grand Avenue, looking vaguely around.

So, "What the hell," I said to myself; and, to her, "Can I help you, Madam?" I had to cross the street anyway. Traffic being what it was, I figured I'd feel a little safer with her for company. It was silly, of course, to think that a poor old lady on my arm would ever inhibit the Grand Avenue throughway traffic but I tried it. Good job I did, too.

It was an early fall afternoon, a bit before rush hour. I had knocked off work early. It was too nice a day for work and besides the managing editor had fired me again. I had nothing better to do, so I thought I'd wander over to Maxim's for a drink or two. Then, on the corner, I found the old lady.

She was a pretty sad-looking old lady. Matter of fact she

was—just standing there, not even trying—the worst-looking old lady I ever saw. She looked, to put it kindly, like a three-day corpse that had made it the hard way after a century of poor health. First I thought, hell, I'll give the old bag of misery a boost, shove her under a bus or something. It would be the decent, kindly thing to do.

I spoke, tentatively. She half-turned and looked up at me from her witch's crouch. The eyes in the beak-nosed, ravaged ruin of a face were big, luminous, a glowing green. They clearly belonged elsewhere and there was a lost, appealing look in them. There was a demand there, too.

"I—uh—that is, would you care to cross with me, Madam?" I asked her.

She took my arm. There was a moment's lull in the wake of a screaming prowl car. I muttered a word of prayer and we were off the curb. The old hag was surprisingly quick. It looked as though we were going to make it. Then, three-quarters across, I came down with a rubber heel in an oil slick just as a roaring, grinding cement-mixer truck was coming down on me like an avalanche. My feet went up. I gave the old witch a shove clear and shut my eyes for fear the coming sight of smeared blood and guts—my own—would make me sick.

And then, instead of a prone, cringing heap on the pavement sweating out the ten-to-one odds against all those wheels missing me, I was airborne. Cable-strong arms caught and lifted me. We were racing down field, elusive, unstoppable, all the way—touchdown.

So there we were, safe on the sidewalk. Traffic on the freeway, gaping at us, was chaos as the frail, doddering little old lady put me down. Me, I was never any extra large size. But still, a touch under six feet, maybe a little too friendly with beer and rich desserts—say, 210 pounds—I had considered myself a little big for convenient carrying about.

This was something new in little old ladies.

I stared down at her. She wasn't even breathing hard. In fact I couldn't tell if she was breathing at all. "Madam," I said, "my sincere thanks and admiration. I wonder now. If you're not late for practice with the Bears or something, perhaps we could go someplace and talk?" I couldn't guess what, but there was for sure some sort of a story here. If I could get something hot for the Sunday magazine, I'd have my job back.

The old crone looked up at me with those oddly out of place, compelling eyes of hers. "You will listen to me? You will help?"

"Madam, help you don't need. But listen, yes. This is my great talent. I will be happy to listen to you."

I thought a quiet booth and a couple of cold ones in Maxim's would be nice. No. She wondered in a different, quavering old voice, if greater privacy might not be better. "What I have to tell you, young man, may be difficult for you to grasp. It may be necessary to show you some things."

"Uh." She wasn't the type of doll I favored taking home for a sociable evening but it wouldn't have seemed mannerly to say no to the look of appeal in her eyes. "All right."

We went on over to the parking lot and I drove her to the very comfortable home out in Oakdale that Uncle John and Aunt Belle turned over to me when they rolled off to see the world from their house trailer a year and a half back. Of course they dropped anchor in Petersburg and haven't budged since, but I guess it gives them the footloose feeling they were looking for. And I have the house, which is quite a pleasant little place.

I think Aunt Belle figured giving me the house would off-set my own dubious attributes so that some nice girl might just possibly marry and make something of me. But I kept a picture on my bureau of Uncle John, standing by the sink in his apron, and was still holding out.

Well, the old bat didn't clue me in on anything on the drive out there in my car. We chatted along the way, mostly her asking the questions, me answering. She was just a visitor to the town, she said. She wanted to find out all about it —with ten thousand nonsensical questions.

I parked in the drive and we went in. While she settled down on the sofa I went to the bar, my addition to the home furnishings, to fix a drink; wondered if there might still be any tea knocking around; thought better of that and mixed two drinks. Then I turned back toward her.

"Now," I said, "tell me."

"Well," announced that ravaged wreck of an old woman, "the fact is that I am from another world."

"Oh, hell," I said, "how did you come in? By saucer or by broom?" It was a mean remark, I suppose. Not kindly. Even so, the way she took it seemed all out of proportion. The old bat's face suddenly went slack. She slumped over side-ways on the sofa, those big, green eyes open, staring, empty.

There was no need to go check for a pulse or heartbeat. She was plainly, revoltingly dead.

"Ugh!" I said and tossed off one of the two drinks I was holding. It seemed the thing to do.

"Do not be alarmed," said an apparent voice. "I am really perfectly all right. I have simply left that poor vehicle I was using. I had thought, wrongly it now seems, that communication with you chemically powered life forms might be easier if I too were concealed within one such structure."

The voice actually wasn't so much a voice as a voice impression. It came from a point in the air above the body on the sofa. And it did make an impression. It came through in a rush of meanings, too loud somehow, almost overpowering.

I looked toward the point of origin. That's what it was, as near as anything, a tiny pinpoint of intense, green-gold light. It was too intense; I had to turn my eyes away. My head started to ache. I felt and knew that, whatever species this might be, my visitor was a female of it. She was, at the moment, horribly overbearing. She was communicating effectively, enthusiastically, but unclearly and it wasn't easy. Not on me, anyway. My mind was swamped with a mass of concepts, jabber and ideas, like all the womens clubs of the world talking at once.

I groaned and staggered back against the bar. "All right," I yelled, "all right, I believe you. You come from another world. You are an amazing, wonderful girl and I am proud to entertain you. But please—go back to being an old woman, or something I can handle."

The ravaged old crone's eyes glowed again. She blinked and sat up. "Please don't shout so. I can hear you," she remarked primly.

I drained the other drink and put both glasses back on the bar. "Ugh. Uh, that's better. But who—where—what—?"

"Please do stop and think a minute," the old witch told me. "If you will simply use that electro-chemical mental equipment of yours, you will find that I have already given you the answers to those questions about who and what I am and where I come from."

"Nonsense." But then it came to me that she had. I just hadn't taken time to sort any of it out.

I tried sorting. Much of it remained fuzzy, I suppose because some aspects were so far outside the range of anything known to me. She was, the way I got it, a life form based on something approximating atomic energy. She came from a dwarf star out someplace, I couldn't quite place it, out Orion way I think. Sure, the entire concept was beyond me and completely alien. And yet, oddly, in a lot of ways it was like old home week. This was a kind of life totally different from ours in all structure and development; and yet their kind of thought, their relationship to their world and their social organization, seemed weirdly familiar. They had work, recreation, social organization. They reproduced by some sort of polarity business I didn't get then and still don't; but it required mating and it certainly seemed a fair approximation of sex.

They had arts based on forms and shaped patterns of energy. I don't get it. She said it compared to our literature, music and painting and I take her word for it. "Only," as she later explained a touch wistfully, "terribly, terribly decadent in the present era."

There was their problem. Their social structure and individuals alike seemed, at last, to be losing all vitality. The birth rate dropped. Culture declined. They had, fairly recently by their standards, discovered the possibility of freeing themselves from their sun and travelling through space. But, while they found planets with chemical life forms like us not uncommon in space, they had found no form comparable to their own. Outside contacts, they had thought, might stimulate and revitalize their society. But, of course, where there is life there is politics. They had developed many and bitter differences of opinion regarding the feasibility or value of any attempt to communicate with chemical life forms. There was a party for, a party against and several favoring an agonizing reappraisal of the position whatever it might turn out to be. Nothing was done. And that, in due course, had brought me my lone lady visitor.

The "communication" party decided to take action in spite of the absence of official sanction. They worked cautiously, in secret. Specially selected representatives with certain exceptional kinds and degrees of sensitivity were made ready. Necessary energy supplies for distant space travel were carefully hoarded. Chances of anything coming of it were considered slim but . . . there was the horrible old hag sitting on my sofa, looking hopefully up at me out of great, youthfully glowing green eyes.

Anyway, that's the way the thing shaped up in my mind. And it seemed plenty hard to believe.

"Must I come out and show you again?"

"No," I said quickly. "Oh, no, please don't. I'm convinced."

"Or will be," she remarked cryptically. "Good. This now proves that at least one level of communication between us is possible. This is promising. It could mark the beginning of a relationship which may be most stimulating for both life forms."

Well, it was startling at least, I would have to admit that. "Speaking of forms," I said, "You sure picked an ugly one there. Why?"

"Oh? But I am only now beginning to understand your standards of attraction. I took this structure—" she pointed one gnarled, knotty hand at herself—"because in my own form no one seemed willing to listen or accept me logically. They only yelled that I was an A-bomb or a short circuit or lightning, or else simply pretended they didn't see me at all. So I took this body, making only a few small internal repairs and improvements. But then, until you came along, no one would stop long enough to listen to me."

"Hum. Where'd you get it?"

"I picked it up at one of your places for them to die. What you call the cold room at the County Hospital. There was, I admit, some confusion."

That I could believe.

"You are not nearly as different from us in mental processes and customs as I should have thought. Such an intriguing life form, with such amusing complications. Just strange enough to be exciting. Come over here and sit by me."

She beckoned coyly, like a flirtatious girl, and winked one youthfully glowing eye at me. The effect, in that ruin of a face, was appalling. I stayed where I was.

"Oh," she said in a hurt tone, "you don't like me? And you seemed so attractively receptive at first. How can we communicate completely on your plane if you are to be so aloof?" She stopped and seemed to concentrate a moment. I felt as if something gave my thoughts a brisk stirring with a long swizzle stick.

"Damn it," I snapped, "quit that, you hear me? You've got to stop messing around in my mind. It's an outrageous invasion of—"

"All right, all right," she said. "I won't do it again, I

promise. Unless—well, never mind." A typically feminine-type promise. "But now I see that it is simply this body that offends you. Except for this, you are quite ready to love me."

That was putting it a little strongly. I had to admit though, that she was a pretty interesting proposition.

"It is odd to attach such importance to form. A chemical life characteristic, I suppose. I do note that your own structure has its—well. There is no reason for this present form of mine being a problem between us. I shall simply change it."

"Oh?" Like changing a dress, she made it sound. It wasn't quite that easy.

"You must make it clear to me what sort of body you prefer. Oh, I see. That tall, widely curved one with the red hair. Yes, I see the image . . . my . . . and so lightly clad. Very well. I will have this body for you."

She was reading my mind again, the back corner section where I was keeping a few brightly descriptive memos on Venus de Lite, that luscious, languorous, long-legged new stripper-exotic dancer downtown at the Roma. "That," I told her, not without a touch of wistful regret, "is a live body. You cannot take live bodies. And stop reading my mind."

"I'm sorry. I won't do it again." She kept saying that; and doing it just the same. "I shall not have to take the original body. I can simply duplicate it."

"How could you do that?"

"It should not be difficult. The elements in the structure are common enough here and in readily modified forms. The body organization is complex, true, and not particularly efficient in many respects. However, the patterns can be readily traced and duplicated. It is a simple question of the application of energy to chemical matter. So now you must take me to observe this body which has such attraction for you."

That, as it turned out, was the toughest part. I did what I could, trying to fix the horrible old witch up in an outfit from one of Aunt Belle's old trunks and a few rather elementary cosmetics. The end result was that, instead of looking like a plain old witch, she seemed a scandalously depraved, probably drunken old witch. The Roma, in a long history dating back to prohibition days, has seen all kinds and conditions. But I don't doubt we were one of the damnedest looking couples on record.

"This—uh—this is my Grandma," I told the few, nastily

grinning acquaintances I couldn't duck on our way into the joint. "Grandma is just up on a little visit from Lower Dogpatch. Excuse us, would you? Grandma needs a double shot quick."

That seemed unarguable. We finally settled at a small table off by the swinging doors to the kitchen and sat there through one floor show. "All right," said my old witch, as Venus closed the set with her final frenzy in the blue spotlight, "I have the pattern. There are a number of differences there from the picture in your mind. The age, the chemicals applied."

Venus went off to vigorous applause. The club lights came up and the M.C. stumbled out to favor us with his version of The Gent's Room Joe Miller. I considered. The more beautiful looking the doll, I suppose, the greater the probable degree of illusion. "Where you find discrepancies," I told my old witch, "be guided by my imagination. Right?"

"All rightie," she remarked brightly, patting my hand on the table as she favored me with what I would estimate as one of history's lewdest winks. I noted a mutter of contempt from surrounding tables. "Shall I go ahead? Perhaps you'd better close your eyes," she said, "I—"

"No, not here!" I grabbed her arm and dragged her to her feet. Neighbor tables gave us their full attention and the muttering took on an ominous tone. "Come on. For pity's sake, let's get on home." I wasn't exactly convinced this proposition was going to work out; but a crowded nightclub was no place for her to try it.

"Graverobber!" was one of the indignant remarks that caught my ear as I dragged the harridan out. She giggled. The female, species immaterial, seems to have a sense of humor ranging from the Pollyanna-like to the graveyard ghoulish—missing nearly every point between.

She was quiet and thoughtful on the ride back home. So was I, pondering the doubtful status of my reputation around town and my sanity.

In the house, she was brisk and businesslike. She got me to help her stack a bunch of canned goods and junk from the refrigerator on the kitchen table—"Just for convenience." She remarked domestically, "It would have saved your fuel and power if I had made the change at the other place. I must draw heavily on the power that runs into this house. I must, you understand, conserve my own supply."

"Perfectly all right. Be my guest." The whole thing had a sort of dream quality to it by then. You know how it is in dreams sometimes? The action and story lines are fantastic. You know the whole thing must be nonsense. You could, by an effort of will, wake up and end it. And yet you go along with the thing just to see how the foolishness will turn out. That is the way I felt then.

"Oh yes, one more detail," said my witch. "What about the eyes? I found nothing about the color of the eyes in your largely imaginary mental picture of the cheap floozy in that second-rate saloon."

Already she was not only speaking the language but thinking the thoughts like a native female. The eyes. Hmm. I guess my mental film strips of Venus had kind of skipped past facial closeups. "Why don't you just keep the same eyes you have now?" I suggested.

"Good," she said. "They are my own design. Here goes. Close your eyes; there may be some glare."

I closed my eyes. For a moment there was nothing. Then, for about a second, say, there was an intense, flaring glare that shone reddish through my closed lids. Then it was dark.

"All righty," said a sweet-soft voice, ending in a little, half-breathless giggle. "Now you can look."

I looked.

Trouble was, it was still dark. No lights. All I could see by the faint light of a half moon filtering in the kitchen window was a dim figure standing by the table.

Fact was, I found later, a sudden power surge on the main line outside the house blew a transformer and blacked out the whole blinking suburb.

I snapped out my lighter and flicked it on. Well now, indeed! There, half shy, half not so shy and wearing the same negligible costume as in her final number at the Roma, was Venus, constructed just exactly the way she should have been.

"The way I built me," she said, and giggled, "to your very explicit order. So now what are you going to—"

I wouldn't say that I am notably more impetuous than the next man. That was just an impetuous situation. I let the lighter go and grabbed her. "Ah," I remember her saying softly, "now we can truly begin to communicate."

I can say with every reasonable assurance that we did so most effectively. Alien she was, but she was also a lovely girl, my own dream girl. Or girls. What man of any imagination at all is a totally monogamous dreamer? Anyway, she was unarguably lovely, loving, uniquely adaptable, generally sweet. And if, once her frequently unfathomable mind was made up, she had the determination of seven dedicated devils—well, she was female and probably no worse than some billion local girls. My little atom-powered space girl had a lot more built-in compensating factors.

But that's as it developed. That night, naturally, was largely devoted to communication. Luckily, having been fired, I didn't need to worry about getting up to go to work.

Along about eleven or so the next morning she bounced out of bed, bright, beautiful and lively. I dragged on down to the kitchen with her to see if we could put together a breakfast from whatever staples she hadn't found it necessary to incorporate into new construction. By the kitchen table I stumbled over the most ravaged, deadest looking corpse I ever hope to see. It was, of course, the unlamented body of the original witch, lying just where it had dropped the evening before.

"Look, hon, what about this?"

She shrugged quite charmingly, in spite of the tentlike dimensions of Aunt Belle's nightgown. "What about it?"

"Well, why didn't you use the—uh—material there, instead of all the groceries?"

Another shrug. "I wanted something fresh."

She had a point. I couldn't argue. I never could, when she turned those big green eyes of hers on me, full power. "Yeah," I said. "Only what are we going to do with it?"

"What do your kind do with old bodies here?"

"Mostly we bury them."

"All right then."

That was unassailable feminine logic. All right. So I'd bury it.

That night, by the eerie light of the waning moon, I went at it with Uncle John's pick and shovel and buried the old witch's body next to Aunt Belle's rose bushes by the garage. My bright, new-incarnation girl lounged around and chatted sociably. Everything still had quite a dreamlike quality; the corpse was a final, nightmare touch. But even so, I was beginning to wonder a bit about things; such things as, specifically, where we went from there.

"Star-doll-baby—" well, hell, there are times when a man

has to use terms like that to communicate with the female—
"you aren't going to vanish all of a sudden and leave me
now, are you? Ugh!" That was a heavy shovel and thick
clay. "What are our plans?"

"Sil-ly. I understand your custom now. We are going to be
married, of course. Then we shall see. There is no hurry. I
have, by your standards, plenty of time. I must assimilate and
learn to understand you and your fascinating life-form. We
shall live together and be man and wife. As I have said, your
species and mine may derive much benefit from this inter-
mingling."

That, if I understood her correctly, sounded fine to me. It
was the best proposal I'd had yet. And surely it would have
been poor hospitality to a lonely little girl some light-years
away from home for me to have refused. "This is terribly
sudden," I told her. "Uf! That ought to be enough of a hole
for as wizened up a little old body as that . . . yes, darling,
I will marry you. Who's going to earn us a living?"

I climbed out of the hole and kissed her and, in time, we
did manage to get the old woman buried.

The next day we applied for our license. Three days later
we were married—so far as I know, an interstellar first.
The job or money problem, as it turned out, was no problem. Her first thought was the direct, female approach to
the problem. She could simply make it out of old newspapers whenever we needed some, as she had the body. She
made some to show me.

"Well now," I told her, "it does seem the simplest way, I
admit. But the government is pretty jealous of its ability to
print money. It likes to think that nobody else can do the
job just right."

I was afraid this might be one of her stubborn points but
it wasn't. Government restrictions, bureaucracy and red tape
were things she had no trouble understanding. "It is the same
way back home with power and energy rations," she told me.
"You have no idea the difficulty we had in building up the
capital supply necessary for my trip here. So I suppose we
must find another way. Don't you already have some of this
money? Or couldn't you manage to borrow some?"

I had $37.62 in my checking account, but the house was
in my name. I borrowed five grand. I invested. I was probably the most successful investor since old King Midas developed his touch. If I sank a buck in land, oil would turn

up within the week, and if it turned out to be a geologically inexplicable tiny pocket the next week—that would be after I had unloaded. Stocks, commodities, it made no difference. The money rolled in. We had the touch. Paid our taxes, too, but she had a way with tax loopholes that gave the district collector a nervous breakdown.

We traveled, but we kept the old house. We always came back to it for sentimental reasons. We spent a lot of time in libraries, museums. We went to shows and concerts. Anything that was going, we went to it. She had a contagious interest that she communicated to—not to say forced on—me; and if some of the operas and symphonies we caught seemed to my elemental musical taste to run a little long and loud, I had my compensations. And a lot more than most; our adjustments were not all one-sided.

Example: We made a tour of Europe. Now, I always was a fine, loving husband to her. Completely faithful. But—well, there was a dark-haired, laughing, button-cute little chick who sang Spanish songs in English with an Italian accent in a little place on the Riviera. I didn't make a pass. I didn't even speak to her. But I have to admit that, as a strictly idle fancy, she did cross my mind once or twice.

"Hah!" my tall, statuesque, beautiful red-haired wife snorted at me one evening after we were back home. She was sitting listening to hi-fi, some of the very long-hair music that she called "the second most fascinating development of your kind." I was just sitting, maybe dozing a bit.

"So!" She gave it full-force, wifely indignation. "You sit there and you smile on me—and all the time you are thinking of this cheap, female, singing bullfighter you have seen two times. You have two timed me in your mind!"

Already she was talking with just the accent that chick had used.

"Now look here," I protested, "you promised not to go prowling through my mind. A man is entitled to a little privacy!"

"How can you think so of this other woman? You don't —" sob—"love me any more!"

Women! That's the way trying to argue with them goes. You are always on the defensive.

"Aw, now, Star-hon-baby," I said, "honestly, it was just a passing thought. I only—"

"I know what sort of thought it was! Very well." She got up and stalked off to the kitchen. I didn't get what she was up to, not even when I heard her banging temperishly about out there.

When there was a sudden flash and the lights blinked out, the idea hit me. I was scared. What if she had gone back, left me? I dashed to the kitchen. Just through the swinging door, I tripped over a body and fell into the kitchen table. Had she—? Then I heard a charming, slightly accented little giggle.

I didn't bother with my lighter. I reached out, caught her, pulled my sweet little dark-haired baby to me and kissed her. "Honey-doll, believe me—I do love you. No matter who you are, I love you!"

I meant every word of it, too. That was a brand of accommodation you will never get from any local girl.

The next night I had to dig a new grave out by the garage —a bigger one this time, for a big, beautiful, long-legged, red-haired body. Funny thing. Contrary to general belief, none of this ever seemed to do anything for the roses by the garage. They had done poorly ever since Aunt Belle left and they kept on doing poorly. Well, no matter. Six months later it was the little brunette's turn to go and we went back to red hair. When I say my wife was all women to me, I mean it.

The last model was medium height, Titian shade hair, not spectacular but cute, very companionable, very lovable, beautifully built, built to last. She was some builder, my wife, and she did a lot of fine construction work for me.

One night, back along about the third week of our marriage, I got to feeling lousy—sniffles, headache, no appetite.

It was no dramatic plague; just a typical, nasty case of flu. I used to get them every fall and winter. I mixed myself a couple of hot lemon and's, and explained it to my (tall, red headed) wife. "Oh, yes," she said. "I see."

I had an idea she took another quick prowl through my mind but I felt too sick to complain. "I'm going to bed," I told her. I went.

Oddly enough, instead of putting in a restless night, I slept like a log. When I woke up the next morning, I felt great. In fact, as I burst into a spontaneous and very tuneful chorus of *Body and Soul* in the shower, it came to me that I had never in my life felt so well. When I looked in the mirror to shave, it seemed to me I was even looking better.

Later that day I was up on the roof putting up a TV aerial. I hadn't ever bothered with TV, but she wanted to learn all about even that. I put up the aerial. Then I fell off the roof. I dropped twelve feet, landing on my left arm and shoulder on hard-packed lawn. Then I got up and dusted myself off. No damage. I was all right.

"Clumsy," she said to me from the porch.

"No," I said. "Damn it, there was this loose shingle up there. It slipped right out from under me and—anyway, you might at least be a little sympathetic. It's a wonder I didn't break my arm. In fact, I can't understand why I didn't."

"Nothing broke because of the improvements I made in you last night."

"What?"

"Darling," she said, "I made a few improvements. Of course, you were very attractive, lover. Perfectly charming. But structurally, really, you were a most imperfect mechanism. So now that I have made a study of these bodies your people use, I . . . rebuilt you."

"Oh? Oh! Now, look here! Who in hell said you could?"

It did, at the time, seem pretty damned officious. I was sore. However, I had to admit that the changes she made worked out rather well. A strong, light metallic alloy seems to make much better bones than can be made of calcium. General immunity to disease was desirable, I couldn't deny. My re-wired nervous system and modified muscular structure were as pleasant to work with as they were efficient. I was a new man.

Of course, every woman always wants to make a finer specimen of whatever slob she marries. Only I had the luck to get the one who knew how to do the job properly—from the inside out, rather than by simply peck, peck, pecking away at the outside.

It was all as near perfect as a marriage can be. I have no complaints now—and very few even then. She had built me to last a couple of centuries. I was ready and willing to string along with her all the way.

But it never does work out that way, does it?

What happened to us, as it does to most, was that at the end of the third year she got pregnant. A very ordinary female trait, you may say, and not ordinarily surprising. No. Except that she was no ordinary female.

We were in bed one night—our last as it turned out —when she told me.

"Darling," she said, and kissed me. "I have something to tell you."

"Haw?" I was sort of sleepy.

"I've been hoping and hoping it would happen, but I wasn't sure it could."

"Ha? Whatsat?"

"Darling, we—are going to become parents."

"What?" I was awake then. "We're going to have a baby? Why, that's great. Wonderful! Do you think he'll take after me?" As I thought it over, it seemed something of a problem. What would the heredity be? In fact, *how* could it be?

"Never mind, darling," she said quietly—sadly, I like to think, as I look back on it. "That's woman's work, you know. Just leave the details to me."

I kissed her. We were very loving and tender. I went to sleep, and dreamed all night long that I was Siamese twins in a fratricidal finish fight over my model wife.

I woke up by daylight to a horrible, icy, lost and separated feeling, as though part of me had really died. I reached out my hand for reassurance—and I yelled.

That sweet, soft-curved body in the bed next to me was cold and dead.

"Please! don't be frightened. It's all right. Really, it's all right." That was a voice that wasn't a voice again, as back in the beginning. It was familiar and at the same time new. It *wasn't* all right! I looked up, over the bed. There were not one but two tiny, blinding-bright pinpoints of light.

"What? Who?"

"Father," they said, "we are your children."

They were certainly not my idea of it.

"No. Oh, no! Star-baby, where are you?"

"Here. We were she. Now she plus you has become us. She has divided and now we are two, the children of you and she."

"Nonsense. Quit the double talk and give it to me straight!" Double talk it was. But if it was nonsense, it was an unhappy sort of nonsense I couldn't get around.

Coming slightly out of shock, I tried arguing and got nowhere. I never won any arguments from their mother either. I was convinced in spite of myself that this was the simple, brutal truth. It was the way of reproduction of her form of life. My alien wife had divided, to become two half-alien offspring.

I felt lousy. I didn't *want* two bright, pin-point kids. I wanted my wife. "But look, why couldn't one of you—"

"Why, father!" I got it in a tone of shocked horror. "Such a thing would be positively incestuous. No. We must go now. This is what mother-we came here for—to mix and to re-vitalize her-our people by the addition of a fresh, new stream of life force."

"You mean me?" It was flattering to think my stock would invigorate the population of a sun, but it was no cure for the loneliness in which I was lost. "You are going back across space—and leave me here alone?"

"Yes, father. We must leave at once."

"Oh, now, wait just one radiating little minute! You say I'm your father. Well, I forbid—"

Weary patience. "Now, father, please."

"But—will you come back sometime?"

"Certainly. With the success of her-our mission, we hope the factions back home will unite in a policy of further inter-change. We and others of our family will come. Soon, we hope. It could even prove possible to find a way of con-verting you to our own form, so that later you may return with us."

"But look—"

But that was it. A few more words and, "Goodby, father," they said, putting a reasonable amount of regret into it—even though I know damned well they were itching to get going. "And do take care of yourself."

They were gone. I was alone. No big, lush and lovely wife; no button-cute little brunette wife; no gay, lively, companion-able, loving Titian-haired wife. No wife at all.

I had never been so alone. Nothing but me. What was I to do?

Well, there was only one possible thing to do, and I did it. I got drunk. I hung one on. It was a beauty. Sometime in the course of the following night I held a tearful wake out by the garage and I buried my wife's last body. That, I recog-nize, was thoughtless. I could and should have called doctors and undertakes to tell me there was no life left in the body, and then let them do the digging for me in a more formal, costly manner. But, for one thing, I was drunk. For another, I guess I'd just sort of gotten into the habit of doing it the other way.

Much too early the next day—like about 2:30 in the afternoon—the doorbell rang. I was totally despondent, nursing my sorrow and a fat hangover with a cold beer and some of my Star-baby's more heavily long-hair, hi-fi selections.

I let the bell ring for a while. Then I let somebody pound on the door for a bit. But that got to be hard on my headache so I went to the door.

There was Mrs. Schmerler, from next door, who used to be a real biddy-buddy of my Aunt Belle's. There were a couple of hard-eyed cops with her, too. They all pushed right on in.

"Celebrating something, Mac?" inquired cop number one, while Mrs. Schmerler and the other glared suspiciously about.

"No," I said, too miserable to think. "Not celebrating, mourning. Just lost my wife, and kids, too."

"He never had any children!" said Mrs. Schmerler. "Only women. And a great deal too many of the cheap tarts. What his poor, dear Aunt Belle, as saintly a woman as ever lived, would say . . . Why don't you ask him what he was digging for—digging and yowling *Star dust*—out there by his garage last night? And not the first time, neither!"

The sudden realization of what could be turned up out there by the garage—and how that would look to the unsympathetic and non-credulous eyes of the law—hit me. I opened and closed my mouth three or four times like an unwell goldfish. Nothing came out except a miasma of alcohol. Mrs. Schmerler gaped at me with delighted shock, indignation and horror. It was the great moment of her life.

The cops stepped in—not aggressively, more big-brotherly —and took a good, firm grip on my arm.

I won't go into the rest of all that. They got a squad and they dug. They took me in. I wouldn't talk. They locked me up. Cell block bookies quoted 50-1, no takers, I would make the death cell. The way I felt, I didn't care. The newspapers went wild. Things had been slow since the election. All my old pals from my working days on the paper were making a buck with special "Even then there was something frighteningly different about him" feature stories.

The next day, as my hangover faded and I got to thinking things over, my outlook changed. It was no time for me to give up. I would get a lawyer.

I walked over to rattle my cell door for a bit. "Hey! Hey there, guard. Come here a minute, huh?"

He came. "So? Is our Bluebeard softening up? Want to make a statement?"

"Uh-uh. Not me. I just want to ask a question. Those bodies, are they going to autopsy them?"

"Not yet. Today."

"Well, look—"

I had a little trouble persuading him, but I got him to take down all the data I could remember on the first one, the old hag. There would be records on her at the County Hospital. They'd never make any charge worse than body-snatching stick on that one.

The others? I chuckled. I was imagining the medical officers' expressions when they ran into those stainless-steel bones, plastic circulatory system, metallic wiring and the assorted other little innovations that my wife—my *late* wife—had installed in her body-building exercises. That would give them something to think about.

So—that's my story; all of it up to now. I'm still here in my cool little cell, and I am damned lonesome. But I am not scared. I figure I have about four different kinds of insurance.

In the first place, the way I am built now, with all the improvements in structure and durability she put into me, I doubt they could electrocute me. I'd probably just short the equipment out. A thing like that would make me quite a scientific curiosity, no doubt; but not, at least, a dead one.

Second, there are my investments and the way the money has piled up. You know and I know perfectly well that they just don't ever send a million bucks plus to any electric chair.

Besides, third place, while I have no doubt I can be convicted of something, I don't see how it could be murder. I wouldn't be surprised to see me get sent to the loony bin. I won't much mind that. I have nothing to do but wait anyway.

And, in the fourth place, which is what I am waiting for, there are my children—hers and mine. They are coming back. Soon, I hope. Not alone, I hope. "Tell them back there," was the last thing I said before they left, "tell them I want a girl just like the girl that married your dear old dad."

I admit it's a poor thing for a man to have to send his kids to do his courting for him—but at least mine are pretty exceptional children. Much better informed than most, too. They should bring me back a new bride. They've got to.

Somehow I kind of have a feeling now that a blonde—maybe a tall, willowy, statuesquely stacked type—might be nice for a while. After that, I don't know. I'll have to think it over. The waiting is what is going to be tough.

Kids aren't really undependable today. Are they?

Immortality . . .
For Some

by J. T. McIntosh

HE WAS on the run again. This time there was no exhilaration in it, only a dull expectation of defeat. You couldn't hide in society from society forever.

His greatest advantage had always been that the police, smugly certain that there couldn't possibly be any crime they didn't know about and hadn't already solved, were always slow to investigate things they decided were none of their business.

Another big advantage had been that so far he had always been alone. This time he wasn't alone. As he sat on the beach under the blazing Florida sun, he waved occasionally to a girl in a silver swimsuit who was bathing in the shallows.

If the police weren't looking for him, he was still safe. But this time the police would be looking for him, and that meant that at any moment a heavy hand would drop on his shoulder and his freedom and his life would be over.

Thinking back, he couldn't put his finger on any mistake he had made, any avoidable mistake. Of course, if he hadn't gone to the Blue Moon night club, things would have been different. Lacking second sight, however, he could hardly have known that. It might have been better if he had given Marita a false name. But then, giving a false name could be even more dangerous. You couldn't stop people who knew you under one name meeting people who knew you under another.

A bronzed young Adonis ran into the water, straight for the girl in the silver swimsuit. Ignoring him, she blew a kiss up the beach, and the self-confidence of the Adonis faltered. He swam out past her.

The man on the beach waved back. She was in love with him, obviously. He wondered if she knew he wasn't in love with her—if she was going to be hurt.

Barely a dozen feet from him the air crackled. Sometimes that happened when you were being peeped by transmitterless TV. Feeling an impulse to jump up and run, he fought it down. If it *was* TTV, the more unconcerned you could be the better. What you had to remember was that when the air popped, that was like seeing a cop. Naturally you'd soon land in trouble if every time you saw a cop you took to your heels.

All the crackle meant was that someone had looked at him. That might be the end, it might be the beginning, or it might be an abortive, unimportant episode in the course of a search for somebody else.

Two women passed him, walking along the beach. Neither of them could afford to wear swimsuits, but both were wearing them. One said:

"See that girl in the silver bathing costume? That's the type I mean."

"What type?" the other asked.

"Too naive to be true. Baby blue eyes. Curves she pretends she doesn't know about. I bet she's forgotten more about men than you and I ever knew."

It was amazing, the man on the beach thought, how shrewd women could be about women. That one had sounded just like Susan Sonnenburg.

Susan Sonnenburg . . . in a way it was her fault he was on the run again. Although Susan had ceased to exist more than a week ago, Susan had unwittingly set things in train which had resulted in the present situation. Why hadn't she minded her business?

"Right to the front door, please," said Susan Sonnenburg firmly, as the cab dipped to land a block away from the Musicosmos Building.

"Sorry, lady, I got no VIP license," said the cab pilot. "If I touched down on the Musicosmos frontage, the air would be blue with cops before you could get the door open."

"No, it wouldn't. I have a card."

"O.K., let's see it."

"I'm not going to rummage for half an hour in my bag. Kindly take my word for it."

"I ain't taking no chances, lady. You can walk from here."

"I most certainly can *not* walk from here, and I don't intend to try. At my age I get quite enough exercise changing my mind."

The pilot grinned. "Say, if you rate a card, I should know your name. Who are you, lady?"

"I said I had a card," said Susan. "You very rudely doubt my word. Why should you believe me if I tell you I'm Martha Washington?"

The pilot suddenly thought of something and looked down at her hands. Obstinately, perversely, she put them behind her.

But his face had lighted up. "You are Susan Sonnenburg, the pianist," he said. "I got your record of that Chopin sonata, the one in D Flat."

"B Flat Minor," said Susan.

"Have it your way. Five flats anyway. You play the funeral march too fast. But sure, you got a card. I'll land you right away."

The cab hopped the block to the Musicosmos Building and dropped gently toward the reserved landing lot.

"I don't play it too fast," Susan retorted. "You just listen too slowly."

"And the movement before that," said the pilot, "the one with the chromatic chords running up, you take like a funeral march. When it comes to the bit that ought to go faster, you keep it the same speed."

"You ought to hear me play Minuet in G," said Susan acidly. "I often get some of it nearly right."

The pilot touched the button that opened the door. When Susan opened her purse he shook his head. "This one's on me, Miss Sonnenburg. When I said you played the second movement too slow and the third too fast, I didn't mean I didn't like it."

"Well, there's no need to rave enthusiastically about my performance like a lyric poet," said Susan sarcastically and hobbled inside, leaning on her stick.

The Musicosmos Building swelled to heaven like a hymn of praise. Music made money these days, even serious music. Some people said the change had come when the schools started to teach children not to be scared of thinking, not to be afraid of being different, not even to be ashamed of secret cravings for taste and culture. Others said that when detection and punishment not only caught up with crime but got 'way ahead of it, what was there to do but make strictly legal love, read books, watch TV and even listen to Beethoven and Brahms? A third group, the supreme optimists, said, Who knows—maybe the human race is maturing at last?

Sixty years after Borodin died his music was made into a hit musical consisting mainly of lush blondes, brunettes and redheads wearing diaphanous pants' and jewels. Two hundred years after Borodin died his second symphony, in its original form, topped the hit parade. It all went to prove something.

Old Benny touched his cap to Susan as she entered the building. He was even older than she was, nobody knew how old.

"They're ready for you in Studio Seven," he mumbled, shook his head for no obvious reason, and gave her his arm. Susan took it gratefully.

She had had a bad fall eight months before, and although it had been easy enough to pin the broken bones, she'd been hardly as good as new since. Curiously enough, as science made things easier for the average person, things became tougher and tougher for the semi-cripple. In the Nineteenth Century if you were old and tottery—and rich—you'd have servants to help you around and wrap you up and even carry you if necessary. Now there wasn't a personal servant left in the United States, and you had to walk farther—because of the parking problem—climb more stairs—since there were no pedestrians on traffic lanes any more—and cope with more high steps—cabs, buses, escalators—than any Nineteenth Century lady of advanced years had ever had to do.

It was for that reason that Susan had always appreciated the shambling but gentle helpfulness of Old Benny. As this was the last time she would need it, she stopped suddenly, unable to let the occasion pass without some word of thanks.

"Benny," she said. "I'm an old woman, and crotchety, and dried up. Why have you always been so nice to me?"

The abrupt question was too much for him. His vacant, friendly face registered bewilderment and conflict. He seemed to feel something was demanded of him but had no idea what.

"Never mind," said Susan with unusual gentleness. "I want to tell you I've appreciated your kindness, anyway."

"Kindness?" said Benny, still bewildered.

"Like now. Like getting cabs for me and making the pilots bring them right to the front door. Like fixing a room for me that day I felt sick. Like cutting a bit off my stick when I said it was too long. Like bringing me sandwiches at a long rehearsal. Like—"

"It's my job, Miss," said Benny, embarrassed. "I'm care-taker, odd-job man. Most of the day I don't have nothin' to do. So I—"

"So you help anybody who needs help. I know. I guess I'd have gone on for years taking you for granted, Benny, only today something made me realize how much you'd done for me, in a lot of little ways."

She hesitated, for what she wanted to tell him was rather like telling a hungry man she had just had dinner and now she had to go to a banquet. But she couldn't just disappear without a word, without saying good-by. Old, inarticulate, not too bright and awkward as he was, she liked Old Benny.

"Today is the last time I'll be here, Benny," she said quietly, her usual sarcasm absent. "I'm making my last recording today, then going for Rebirth."

The sudden blaze in his dim eyes startled her. But all he said was: "Yes, Miss Sonnenburg."

"I once hurt your feelings by offering you a tip," she said. "I'm not going to do it again. I know you don't do things for any reward. But have you ever heard of an honorarium?"

"Orrorrarian?"

"Sometimes when someone's done something over and above his duty, or his job, or his obligations, people want to express their gratitude somehow. So they give him something and call it an honorarium. That isn't like a tip. Anybody can accept an honorarium."

"What does an orrorrarian look like?" Benny asked doubt-fully.

"All I can give you is money. But you can take it and buy anything you like, and whatever you buy will remind you of me. Thanks, Benny—and good-by."

She left him outside Studio Seven, three crumpled notes in his hand. Painstakingly he smoothed them out.

Two hundred and fifty dollars.

They weren't ready for her in Studio Seven after all. Collini, the conductor, hadn't finished shaping the *tuttis*.

Most recordings were like jigsaw puzzles since the advent of wave matching. Although some old-fashioned conductors and performers still adhered to the old hit-or-miss methods, what usually happened these days was that a master was prepared, a blueprint for a particular performance, a sort of picture of the desired orchestral sound. This visual master could easily be transferred direct into sound, but, if it were, it would be of interest only to music students. It would be entirely too mechanical for anyone else.

When the master was complete, the orchestra would record the music and an automatic process of comparison would be carried out. The machines would ignore the nuances of expression and phrasing which they didn't understand, but would point out the factual, measurable differences which they did—where the second trumpet played an E natural instead of an E flat, where the second violins swamped the firsts, where somebody in the woodwind squeaked during a rest. The engineers, conductor, soloist if any, and supervisor would go over these points carefully, deciding what didn't matter, what they preferred as played to what was on the master, and what would have to be done again.

This system didn't produce music of any greater artistic worth, it merely produced much more immaculate music much quicker.

Collini hadn't quite completed his orchestral master, so Susan withdrew to a rest room off the studio while he did so. To her disgust, Weygand followed her.

"So this is the last Susan Sonnenburg recording session," Weygand sighed sententiously.

"When you make a statement like that, Mr. Weygand," said Susan, "one cannot but agree with you."

He was a fussy, coventional little man. Indeed, his job was to be conventional. He was one of the directors of Musicosmos, and what he liked, nearly everybody would like.

"The Mozart G Major, Köchel 453," Weygand mused. "One could have wished the last work you recorded could have been something grander and nobler—Beethoven's 'Emperor,' for example. But then, we have the 'Emperor' you recorded fourteen years ago."

"As you say."

"Aren't you a little sad—a little regretful?" Weygand asked. "After all, you probably won't be a pianist again. You may not even be a musician. You may not be famous."

If she shocked him, he might go away. "On the other hand, I won't have to go to bed alone any more."

Weygand had a literal mind. "Yes, you will, for years yet. At least four years."

Susan resigned herself to the conversation. If she was honest with herself, which she usually was, she was forced to admit that the only real reason for her dislike of Weygand was the practical musician's contempt for the theoretical musician. Plus the fact that you always knew what he was going to say before he said it.

"I've done most things a pianist can do in music," she said. "I wouldn't want to do them all over again."

"Wouldn't you?" said Weygand wistfully.

"Maybe this time I'll be a jazz trumpeter or a blues singer."

Weygand sniffed. "That wouldn't be right. You're a great artiste, Miss Sonnenburg."

"I've got a fair rating on the mechanical side. Perhaps I'll turn out to be a physicist or a doctor this time."

"A scientist!" said Weygand, horrified.

"Oh, it's all right," Susan reassured him blandly. "According to my rating, I wouldn't be a very good one. That makes it all right, doesn't it?"

Weygand was struck speechless—a consummation devoutly to be wished. She enjoyed the silence until suddenly she thought of something Weygand could and would do for her. "Mr. Weygand," she said, "you know Old Benny?"

"The caretaker? Of course."

"Would you do something for me? Would you have him tested?"

"What do you mean, tested?"

She could hardly say: For Rebirth. The idea was too fantastic. Rebirth was the prerogative of the Top Ten—the top ten per cent of the population on the VTC scale (value to the community).

Ten per cent was a pretty wide band, really. Susan, of course, was well up in the top one per cent on the VTC scale. Everybody she knew, all her friends would qualify. Any college graduate, any executive, any artist, writer, musician, technician, doctor, nurse—indeed, practically anybody who had achieved moderate success in anything—was almost sure to qualify for Rebirth.

Everybody Susan knew, except Benny.

She couldn't explain to Weygand, of all people, the feeling she had. The feeling, the intuition, the hunch that there was more in Old Benny than met the eye. She was well-aware that she was biased—she liked Benny, and he might die at any moment, strong and healthy though he appeared to be for his age. It was natural for her to want Rebirth for him for no more reason than that he was a good Joe.

Yet she was sure that there was more to it than that. The VTC scale included intelligence, a wide variety of talents, and among many other attributes a thing called affinity, sometimes called empathy. In a word, this meant that though Rebirth eliminated all psychosis anyway, a good Joe was always more likely to qualify, other things being equal, than the kind of fellow who tore the wings off flies.

Benny would rate high on affinity, if nothing else.

"You know what a test is," she said irritably. She didn't want to say the VTC test. That was for Rebirth.

"The musical capacity tests?"

"Sure, they'll do," she said. The MC tests were for an entirely different purpose, but they included a sketchy intelligence test and an even sketchier personality rating. If Benny turned out to have any talent or capacity or intelligence or potential, the tests would show it, and sending him for a VTC rating would be a matter of routine.

"Anything you say, Miss Sonnenburg," said Weygand. "You trying to prove something about Benny?"

Susan dodged the question. "You'll do it?"

"Of course."

One of the engineers tapped on the door and opened it. "Ready for you now, Miss Sonnenburg," he said.

It was no ordinary session. Everybody knew that immediately it was over, Susan was going straight to the Rebirth Institution. Although that wasn't death, although only relatives and female ones at that cried when somebody went there, although everybody who rated Rebirth was cordially thankful and everybody who didn't wished passionately that he did, in some ways it was just as final as death. Susan Sonnenburg the pianist would be just as dead as if she dropped away from the piano keyboard now with heart failure. She wouldn't be told that she had ever been Susan Sonnenburg unless the psychologists decided it wouldn't do her any harm to know, and the psychologists were known to have a bias against such disclosures.

They had to be pretty careful over the wave matching, for there could be no re-takes, not of Susan's part anyway. Curiously, when everybody was ready for a long and hard session, everybody hit top form at once and hardly anything had to be done again.

When Susan saw that her solo part was safely taped, she turned and went out through the rest room so casually that Collini and Weygand and everybody else assumed she was merely going to the washroom. But she went right on out of the building, avoiding even Benny.

Susan didn't like farewells.

The cab pilot who took her to the Rebirth Institute was surprisingly casual, too. "Sure, you're the pianist," he said. "Guess I'd better be specially careful. You don't want to get killed on your way to Rebirth."

"As you say," Susan agreed.

"I'm coming here myself in about sixty years. You wouldn't think a cab pilot would rate Rebirth, would you?"

"So you'd better be even more careful. We don't both want to lose our chance of immortality, do we?"

They didn't. As Susan hobbled into the big square building which was the Rebirth Institute she sighed gratefully at the thought that the next time she had to walk she'd be able to run if she liked.

Weygand picked up the phone. "Yes, this is Weygand of Musicosmos. Rebirth Institute? Yes, of course . . . Benjamin Rice? He could be on the staff here, but the name doesn't ring a bell. Susan Sonnenburg named him as what?"

"We usually question people who were personal friends of our subjects," the quiet, anonymous voice said. "Their own information about themselves is too subjective, of course. Miss Sonneburg said this Benjamin Rice, Musicosmos, could help us."

"Let's see, it's been three days since she went for Rebirth," said Weygand. "How's she coming?"

The anonymous voice seemed faintly surprised by the question. "As expected, Mr. Weygand. A routine case. No complications. Now, this Benjamin Rice—"

"Wait a minute. Could that be Old Benny? Look, I'll make inquiries and send over Rice, whoever he is, just as soon as I can. O.K.?"

"Thank you, Mr. Weygand."

On the house phone Weygand called Personnel. "Who's Benjamin Rice?" he asked.

Checking took less than a minute. "One of the caretakers, Mr. Weygand. Do you want his file?"

"No, that's all, thanks."

He rang Benny's tiny office. "Benny? This is Weygand.

The Rebirth Institute just called. Miss Sonnenburg left your name there. Seems they want to ask you some questions. Now don't get worried, there's nothing wrong. Just routine. Will you go over there right away? And Benny—"

He had just remembered, guiltily, that he had promised Susan to have an MC test run on Benny. He hadn't forgotten; he had merely not remembered.

"It doesn't matter," he said, and hung up. He'd call Walter Jennings of the testing bureau and Jennings would send for Benny when he was ready. In fact, just to make sure the matter didn't slip his mind, Weygand picked up the house phone and called Jennings right away.

Benny took his coat from a hook and put it on slowly, thoughtfully. Something crawled inside of him at the thought of going to the Rebirth Institute. However, there was no help for it. He left a note in bold block letters on his table, OUT ON BUSINESS, and walked out.

Benny Rice was over a hundred years old, and sometimes in the Musicosmos Building he looked it. But as he walked to the Rebirth Institute—it didn't occur to him to take a bus or cab, although the distance was two miles and either Musicosmos or the Institute would certainly have paid for the ride—he gradually straightened, his eyes brightened, his chest expanded, until by the time he had walked a mile he could have passed for fifty. Since the normal expectation of life these days was about one hundred seven, a man of fifty was quite young.

Physically, Benny was a remarkable specimen, so remarkable that to avoid notice at Musicosmos, where they knew exactly how old he was, he habitually moved a little more slowly and much more awkwardly than he might have done. Outside Musicosmos he was always prepared to pretend to be fifty if he could get away with it. He usually could. With luck, he had another forty years of life remaining to him.

The Institute from the outside was a cold, white, bare, impersonal building. Inside, the difference was startling. The furnishing and design suggested a luxury hotel rather than a hospital or a nursing home.

"Benjamin Rice?" said the smart blond receptionist. "That's right, Dr. Martin wants to see you. He's out in the gardens. Sammy here will take you to him."

Sammy was a redhaired youth who didn't talk. This puzzled Benny, for Sammy looked friendly and chatty. "What's the matter, son?" he asked, as they emerged into the gardens behind the Institute. "Cat got your tongue?"

Sammy gave him a look so alive with intelligence and mischief that Benny expected a smart retort. But what Sammy said was: "Da-da."

Benny understood then, and grimaced at his own dumbness. Sammy, of course, was one of the Reborn. He had all the intelligence he would ever have; he just hadn't learned to talk yet.

The receptionist was probably another Reborn. Naturally, if the Institute had to keep people in their care for nearly four years, they'd put them to work.

Dr. Martin looked no more than twenty, but he couldn't be a Reborn. Rebirth wasn't run like an exclusive social club. Although necessarily the Reborn had to be kept together to mature and re-acquire the basic information which every intelligent citizen was assumed to possess, as soon as possible they were dispersed far and wide and mingled with the rest of society again. Martin wouldn't be a Reborn because no young Reborn doctor would be encouraged or allowed to hide himself from the world in the Rebirth Institute. It would be like going back to the womb.

He looked up with a grin. "Benjamin Rice?"

"Everybody calls me Benny."

"Sure. O.K., Sammy, you can go back to the desk."

They were standing on a huge lawn on which scores of deck chairs were arranged in neat rows. Although there were no nurses and no supervisor except Martin, the scene looked normal enough at first, like any lawn in any rest-cure sanatorium. But then one noticed that all the occupants of the deck chairs were about fourteen, that they were all in the deep sleep of heavy sedation, and that they all, boys and girls, wore plain white smocks. The white smocks, like baby doll pajamas except that there was no attempt in cut or trimming to make them look attractive, were strangest of all, for it was obvious that no ordinary boys or girls of fourteen would consent to wear them if they had any choice in the matter.

Clear-skinned and healthy though they looked, these overgrown infants had minds as empty as a scarecrow's pocket. The boys didn't even know they were boys, nor the girls that they were girls.

"You work at Musicosmos, Benny?"

"I'm the caretaker."

Martin seemed puzzled. "How did you get on with Miss Sonnenburg?"

"Swell, doctor. She was a fine lady. I was sorry when she came here."

"Sorry? You wouldn't want her to die, would you?"

"She was a fine lady," said Benny vaguely.

Martin was more puzzled than ever. Susan had filled in Benny's name on the reference sheets as a friend who could be consulted if necessary on her personality, behavior, and temperament. Martin had assumed that Benjamin Rice would be a colleague of Susan's, a musician, writer, artist or something of that sort.

"Tell me about her," Martin said encouragingly.

"She was always nice to me. She said I was nice to her, but I don't know what she meant. Of course she couldn't get around so well, not since she fell that time, and I helped her around, little things like that. They said she was a great pianist, but I wouldn't know about that. All I know is, she was a fine lady."

Martin was silent. It was obvious that Benny wasn't going to be able to tell him anything useful. Presumably Susan Sonnenburg had entered Benny's name as a joke, just as under "Other Activities" she had put down *tiddleywinks*.

It would be easy enough to find plenty of other people who had known Susan Sonnenburg well. The interesting thing was that Susan had elected to put down Benny's name. Was it just a pointless and rather tasteless joke, or was there something back of this?

"How long did you know Miss Sonnenburg?" he asked idly.

"Just a year. No, a little less. I went to Musicosmos last September."

So that was that. Martin discarded the idea that Sonnenburg and this old man had once been lovers, long ago. It was a pretty fantastic idea anyway.

Martin stood up. He'd have to find someone else to give some impressions of Sonnenburg for the case book. Benny was a nice old fellow, but not very bright.

"Would you like to see Miss Sonnenburg now?" he asked.

Benny took an involuntary step back. "No," he exclaimed vehemently.

That was interesting. Could they have been lovers, long ago?

"She isn't Sonnenburg any more. But if you liked her,

Benny, I think you should see her now. She's different, of course. Still, I think when you've seen her you won't feel so bad about it. There's a lot of happiness ahead of her."

Unresisting, Benny was led across the lawn. Martin stopped beside a deck chair and pointed. Benny caught his breath.

The girl in the chair, in a deep, drugged sleep, was about fourteen, like all the others on the lawn. Her smooth, pretty face was vaguely reminiscent of Susan's. It was full of intelligence and absolutely empty of experience. But for the intelligence in it and the hint of a sense of humor, it was the face of a beautiful idiot.

Rebirth was a convenient name for something which was nothing of the kind. People weren't reborn, they were wiped clean and rapidly refurbished in a culture tank. The clocks of their lives were set back eighty years. They got new cells for old, youth for age. To pay for it they had to give up all they had ever known.

The girl who slightly resembled Susan wore a plain smock which made no concessions to sex. Her body, although barely nubile, was at least as beautiful as her face. She looked like a newlyborn child who somehow had the body of an adolescent, which was pretty near the truth.

Betty Rogers—Martin was careful not to mention her new name to Benny—had all the talent, capacity and intelligence of Susan Sonnenburg. Whether she would turn out to have the same personality was anybody's guess. In a particular case, no one could say how much of the personality grew from heredity and how much out of environment. Betty and Susan had the same heredity, but environment was going to treat them very differently. Probably Betty would be happier than Susan and would accomplish less. But it was quite possible that Betty would accomplish even more.

"I thought she'd be a baby," Benny said hoarsely.

Martin shook his head. "We could do that, but it's unnecessary and even undesirable. We've improved on nature. In nature a child takes twenty years to grow up mentally and physically. We can teach them enough in four years. At eighteen, she'll be in no way inferior to a girl who's had a normal birth and childhood. We don't take them back the other side of puberty because we have enough time as it is and this way we avoid a lot of emotional problems. It's almost certain—"

His voice trailed away. He'd been talking as if Benny had

turned out as he expected. The old man's bewilderment showed he was wasting his time.

Martin led him back across the lawn. "Thanks for coming, Benny," he said. "You've been a great help. I just want to talk to a few people like you who knew Miss Sonnenburg well. Now, maybe you can tell me who I should see next?"

"You should see Mr. Collini," said Benny, proud to be consulted. "He's a conductor. Miss Sonnenburg worked with him a lot."

"Thanks, Benny. I'll do that."

On the way back to the Musicosmos Building, Benny slouched and looked his years.

Susan Sonnenburg was gone. The beautiful half-child half-woman he had seen was not Susan Sonnenburg and would never be Susan Sonnenburg.

But strangely enough, that hardly affected Benny and was not responsible for his depression. After all, Susan had been at an age where death at any moment was a possibility, approaching an age when death was a certainty. (Only five years younger than he was.) She was not more dead now than she would have been if she had actually died. By reckoning, she must be less.

When Benny got back to his single room that evening, he took out the two hundred fifty dollars Susan had given him, untouched so far. "Buy something that will remind you of me," she had said.

He didn't want to be reminded of her. There was no point in remembering her. The sensible thing was to put the money with the rest and forget where it came from.

He took a large envelope from behind the old-fashioned dressing table and looked in it. Two thousand dollars. He didn't want or need more. Closing the envelope, he put it back. The money Susan had given him was still on the table.

Susan Sonnenburg was gone, finished. He would get rid of the money she had given him as quickly and completely as possible. Scatter it to the winds. Keep nothing of it, not as much as a book of matches from a night club.

Night club. He hadn't been in one for twenty years. He wouldn't end his life heartbroken if he never entered one again. Still, when you were trying to get rid of money without actually burning it—

From a cupboard he produced evening clothes which were cheap but well-cut, so well-cut that when he put them on they entirely ceased to look cheap. They also made him look younger—not in years as much as in spirit. A man of seventy dancing a jig looks much younger than a man of sixty in a bathchair. People might still estimate Benny's age pretty accurately. Nevertheless, he would look less out of place with girls of twenty than many men half his age.

He was not unaware of this.

Whistling contentedly, if not particularly tunefully, as he dressed, he thought without regret about Susan. It was easy to get sentimental when people died or went for Rebirth, but the truth was that neither Susan nor anybody else for the last twenty years had ever come close to being a friend of his. He couldn't allow that. He might allow women to fall in love with him, if they could and would; he couldn't allow anyone, man or woman, to become a friend.

But Susan could have been a friend.

Ready for the pleasures of the evening, he had a good meal at a restaurant nearby, lingering over it. It wasn't a big meal, but it was a well-chosen one, washed down by a bottle of Yugoslav Riesling.

Then he went to the Blue Moon. Before going to the bar he paused to watch the floor show for a few minutes. A magician with some electronic tricks in keeping with the Blue Moon's cover charge was getting far less attention than he deserved. Some of his gadgets were radio-controlled. When he blindfolded himself he used radar. And all his animals were beautifully designed robots. Someone should have told him to be old-fashioned and put a few girls in the act.

There were two girls at the bar as Benny approached it, one in pink whose lines were uncertain and one in red who showed how the other's ought to have gone.

"Hi," said the girl in pink.

Benny's smile for the pink girl was much brighter and friendlier than the look he gave the girl in red. Yet he made the situation clear in the nicest possible way, and the pink girl sighed philosophically.

"This is Marita," she said. "Buy me a drink and I'll blow."

Marita didn't look like what she was, any more than the top members of her profession throughout history had looked like what they were. Apart from fitting her like suntan, her gown was decent, and she looked intelligent.

When he arrived at the Musicosmos Building next day, nothing remained of the money Susan had given him except a slight hangover and a feeling of lassitude natural enough in a man of his age.

Jennings dropped a file on Weygand's desk. "I did that test you asked me to do—on Benny Rice. Want to look at the results?"

"Not unless there's anything interesting in them. Is there?"

"Depends what you call interesting."

Jennings was a tall, untidy man who spent most of his life looking tired and disinterested, grinding along like a motor working on low voltage. Now and then, however, something would excite him. Immediately he would get the right voltage from somewhere and would sparkle like champagne.

His disillusionment arose out of the fact that few people understood or cared about his subject. He spent half his life explaining that his tests were meant to isolate *potential*. If somebody had an astronomical M.Q. of 185, that didn't mean he'd be a great composer, or recording star, or conductor. It merely meant he had an M.Q. of 185. Other things being favorable, he might amount to something musically. Other things being exactly right, he must amount to something, if he started soon enough and on the right lines. Other things being in any way unfavorable, he'd make a good bus driver or clerk.

"Well, is he a musical moron?" Weygand asked.

"Not quite that. A musical moron would have an M.Q. of 70-80. Benny's 42—that makes him a musical imbecile."

Weygand sighed. "Thanks, Jennings."

"What was the idea, anyway?"

"Susan Sonnenburg wanted him tested. Feminine intuition, I guess."

Jennings momentarily lost his harassed look and genuine enthusiasm came over him. "If Susan Sonnenburg requested it, I know what she was thinking about. Rebirth. She'd sensed that Benny wasn't as dumb as he looks. And she was right."

"You mean he's a Rebirth prospect? With an M.Q. like that?"

The harassed, tortured look settled back on Jennings' face. "President Fuller has an M.Q. of 61," he said. "That doesn't stop him being almost off the top end of the VTC scale."

Weygand's eyebrows indicated mild, not particularly interested surprise. "My M.Q. is the same as my VTC rating."

"And you're in a musical administration job."

"So what?"

An expression of agony crossed Jennings' face. Sometimes he wondered why he bothered.

"Want me to run a VTC test on Benny?"

"If he had a high rating, it would have been discovered long ago, wouldn't it?"

"Oh, sure."

"Then forget it. I've done all Susan asked me to do."

But Jennings didn't forget it. As he returned to his own department, he was mentally revising his assessment of Benny. Told nothing of the background, he had assumed the test had been requested because somebody thought Benny had musical ability. Well, he hadn't—to put it mildly.

Jennings had known Susan Sonnenburg quite well—in one respect, better than anyone else. He knew her test ratings. M.Q. 141 ("Only 141?" Weygand had said once. "That just shows what your tests are worth, Jennings. She's the greatest pianist in the world." Jennings had tried to explain how an M.Q. of 141 or even less could be enough for someone of Susan's intelligence and tenacity. You needed more than potential to achieve success in anything). I.Q., 155. Mechanical ability, 139. VTC, 198.

Damn it, there was nothing wrong with the tests if only you used them with a grain of sense. Those three figures of Susan's told a clear story—I.Q. 155, mechanical ability 139, VTC 198. Obviously she rated pretty high on intuition. There still wasn't any way to test intuition directly, but like radium in pitchblende it could be inferred. If 141, 139 and 155 averaged out at 198, there was some radium around somewhere.

Jennings, a mathematician and a scientist, was prepared to back Susan's hunch about Benny. Not that he cared about Benny as a person. What interested him was the operation of the testing system.

Back in his office he phoned a request to the Federal Rebirth Institute for Benny's registered VTC rating. In fifteen minutes it came back: 31.

When he saw that he caught his breath. His eyes glowed as he switched on his own auxiliary power supply and became a human bulldozer. There was something here that had to be investigated, something that wasn't right.

The VTC rating of 31 was impossible. Benny was a musical imbecile, true. The rest of the tests hadn't shown him up as any kind of genius, either. But a VTC rating of 31 meant someone was unemployable—far below the capacity of a caretaker. There was something strange here. Something strange and exciting.

Jennings sent for Benny again. He came at once. "You wanted me, Mr. Jennings?"

"Yes, sit down there, Benny. I guess you wondered what that test this morning was for. The truth is, Susan Sonnenburg requested it. She didn't say why, but my guess is she thought you'd rate Rebirth."

"I don't," said Benny simply. "And I'd rather not go into it again, if you don't mind, Mr. Jennings."

"Just for curiosity," Jennings said, "I found out your official VTC rating, Benny. It's 31. Now that's impossible. Take my word for it, it's all wrong. Tell me, do you remember anything about that test?"

"Not much. It was seventy years ago."

Jennings leaped to his feet. "If you really rated 31, Benny, you wouldn't remember it was seventy years ago. You wouldn't be able to calculate it was seventy years ago. Understand?"

"If you say so, Mr. Jennings."

"What else do you remember about the test seventy years ago? Was there anything special about it? Were you sick, or anything?"

"I don't remember, Mr. Jennings."

"Would you like to do that test again?"

"No, Mr. Jennings."

The blunt, unequivocal answer threw Jennings for a moment. "But, Benny, that rating's all wrong. It must be. I can't promise anything, of course, except that you must be a lot higher than that. How much higher I don't know."

The top ten per cent were those above 120. It was highly unlikely that Benny was anywhere near 120, and Jennings had no desire to raise the old man's hopes, even with Susan Sonnenburg's hunch to go on. But the test had to be carried out.

"Look, Mr. Jennings," said Benny appealingly. "All my life I've known Rebirth wasn't for me. I've grown old knowing other people could look forward to it, but not me. Long ago I came to accept that. I've taken it for granted for so long I don't want Rebirth—can you understand that?"

"Well, you don't have to have it. People aren't forced to go for Rebirth, you know—unless their rating is so high that society just can't afford to lose them. Benny, I want you to take the test just to set the record straight. Your VTC rating isn't really 31, and never was. Suppose it's 70 . . . 100 . . . even 110. Wouldn't you like to know that—just so you won't go on thinking you're a no-good never-was?"

Benny shrugged. "If you like, Mr. Jennings. Anything you say."

Later that day Jennings had the result. He stared at it incredulously. VTC, 30.

He didn't know what to say to Benny. Now that it had happened, now that there was no conceivable doubt, possible explanations suggested themselves to him.

Just as Susan Sonnenburg could total more than the sum of her parts, Benny could total less. I.Q. 98. M.Q. 42. Mechanical ability, 116. Mathematical ability, 126—an incredibly high rating for a caretaker, that. Self-assertion, 41—just as incredibly low, that one. Memory, 110.

Nothing on the card lower than 41, rising through 126, and the VTC rating was 30. It could have been criminal, psychotic, antisocial tendencies that brought the figure down, but it wasn't. The antisocial tendency figure was neutral.

Jennings solved the problem of what to say to Benny by not seeing him at all. He merely sent down a note saying the new test confirmed the old one.

Then he tried to do what Weygand had told him to do—forget Benny.

Benny's single-room apartment was twenty minutes' walk from the Musicosmos Building. As he walked home, he was wondering whether to leave Musicosmos. He was cool, unalarmed. Unworried, he weighed the two sides of the question.

On the one hand, once people started getting interested in you they usually went on until they found out altogether too much. On the other hand, if you stood your ground for once and brazened it out, all curiosity about you might be stilled forever and you'd be safe as you'd never been before. People didn't look where they'd looked already. You wouldn't know about that—you'd always run out when things got too hot.

Just as he was deciding that this time he'd stay put as long as he could, he became aware that he was being followed.

His steps didn't falter. Who would follow him? Only someone who did not know too much about him. Anyone who knew more would be aware that he was simply walking home from Musicosmos, as he did every day, and that there wasn't the slightest need to follow him.

Maybe he'd made a mistake in that VTC test.

Why had they tested him, anyway? He had thought it was merely something to do with Susan Sonnenburg, that she'd arranged a test under the impression that she was doing him a good turn. But if so, who was following him now? Susan was in the Rebirth Institute, and had long since ceased to know or care anything about Benny Rice.

Deliberately passing the newsstand where he usually bought a paper, Benny acted as if he'd suddenly remembered it and went back for it. That gave him a chance to get a good look at the man tailing him. He was between thirty and forty and the most nondescript individual Benny had ever seen. Even looking straight at him Benny could hardly decide on any feature that might help to identify the man later. Catching Benny's gaze, he stared back so indifferently that for a moment Benny thought he had been mistaken.

But he hadn't been mistaken, he realized. This man was a master at his job. He was so good that Benny wondered if he'd been allowed to realize that someone was following him, simply to see what he would do.

No longer unworried, Benny made his plans in a flash. He had to go to his room, for his money was there, his escape money. But the last thing the detective following him would expect was that he would bounce out the moment he went in.

Gone forever was the possibility of staying put and brazening it out. When top-grade detectives followed you around, it was too late to rely on the pretense that you were a dumb ancient caretaker, VTC 30. When top-grade detectives followed you around, you just weren't a dumb ancient caretaker, VTC 30, and you'd never manage to convince anybody that you were. It didn't matter who was employing the detective or why; once anybody got that far his goose was cooked.

The detective wasn't police, for the police would peep you with TTV. His best chance was to be far, far away before the cops became interested.

He was on the run again.

When Benny Rice didn't appear at Musicosmos the next morning, the matter wasn't sufficiently important for anyone to pay much attention. Certainly his nonappearance wasn't reported to anybody as important as Weygand or Jennings.

It was only when a woman came round making inquiries that the blank-eyed porter who took Benny's place at the door linked the events of the last few days and called Jennings in the testing Department.

"There's a woman here asking about Benny, Mr. Jennings," he said. "You've had him up there a lot lately. I wondered if maybe—"

"What do you mean, asking about Benny? Isn't he there?"

"No, he ain't here. Ain't been in all morning. I thought you—"

"What's the woman like? Old?"

"No, young." The porter, who had not been young for a long time, left it at that.

"Send her up."

Jennings was surprised to meet a girl in her twenties who was obviously a professional beauty of one kind or another. She introduced herself as Marita Herbert.

"Sorry to trouble you, Mr. Jennings," she said. "I'm interested in Benny Rice. I want to find him, that's all."

"Why?"

Her smile didn't go, but it froze a little. "Frankly, Mr. Jennings, I don't see that that's any concern of yours."

Jennings shrugged. "If you want me to help you find Benny, you'll have to tell me something. I'm not in the slightest interested in your affairs, Miss Herbert. But I'm still very interested in Benny."

"Still?"

"Why do you want to find him?"

She shrugged ruefully, almost irritably. "I met him the other night. He's three times my age, but he did things to me. I want to see him again. I have to. I even had a detective find him for me."

Jennings swallowed. "You're in love with him?" he asked incredulously.

"Not that. Not exactly. Can't I want to see him again without being in love with him?"

"You said you had a detective trace him. Didn't you know where he lived?"

"I only knew his name. The detective I hired found he worked here. They tell me he's a caretaker, but that can't be right."

"Why not, Miss Herbert?"

"Well, the other night he was spending money like water."

"Perhaps he won it on a horse."

"Maybe, but— Well, he's nice. Understanding. Clever, but not clever the way a professor is clever. Good at guessing. Educated. And he has taste."

Startled, Jennings said: "Many such men are caretakers."

"Are you kidding? Maybe you think I'm dumb, and wouldn't know class when I see it? Look, Mr. Jennings, I want to see Benny Rice again because . . . well, in just a few hours he made me see things differently. He gave me back my self-respect, understand? I need him like some people need to go to church. Do you have the faintest idea what I'm talking about?"

Jennings thought of Benny's VTC rating: 30. He had given up too soon. Of course that figure was incredible, just as he had told Benny before the test. He wanted to think.

"Leave your name and address, Miss Herbert. We'll let you know about Benny once we've done some checking. We'll send somebody to his apartment."

She shrugged. "You can save yourself the trouble. He isn't there. Seems I know a heck of a lot more about him than you do."

"What do you know, Miss Herbert?"

"I've told you. He isn't at his apartment. Silver, the detective I hired, phoned me last night to tell me he'd just followed Benny to his apartment. Seems that while he was doing this, Benny was walking out. And nobody's seen him since. That bright private eye of mine says he has some clues, but I'm not counting on it."

When she had gone, Jennings' eyes were alive again.

Somehow or other Benny had faked that VTC test. He must have, because the Benny Jennings knew bore little or no resemblance to the Benny whom Marita Herbert had met.

In one way Benny had done an extraordinary job—any ordinary attempt to fool the test would show up like a sore thumb. In another way he had been astonishingly dense. Why should anyone who had the brains to fool the test and the testers be such an idiot as to get himself a rating of 30? If Benny merely wanted to hide, not to be noticed, he should have scored around 90 at least, perhaps 100. There could be nothing less remarkable than being average. Instead, he'd twice achieved a false rating which must puzzle everybody.

Benny had never given any evidence of intelligence in the presence of Jennings, as he must have done with Marita and possibly with Susan Sonnenburg. Nevertheless, he had never managed to be dumb enough to fit a VTC 30 rating.

Why should anyone pretend to be a useless moron when he wasn't? Jennings could think of only one answer.

The police were polite but unimpressed. However, Sergeant Basch came to see Jennings. He was a bright young man who looked as if he had no intention of being a sergeant for long.

"I understand this man Rice has disappeared?" Basch said.

"He went to his apartment last night as usual, but didn't stay longer than five minutes. He hasn't been seen since."

"I didn't quite get what you meant about this test, Mr. Jennings. Why are you convinced that Rice faked it?"

"Like all personality tests," said Jennings, "this one is empirical. It's constantly being checked against facts, against other data and other results. And in the light of these it's modified. This has been going on for a long time. We can even invert the test, sort of, and instead of saying 'This man's VTC is so-and-so, therefore he ought to be capable of such-and-such,' we can say 'This man does such-and-such, therefore his VTC must be so-and-so.' Now Benny Rice hasn't exactly been running Musicosmos, but even what he's been doing here would need a rating of about 80."

"But the test shows 30."

"Yes."

"And therefore?"

"Therefore there's something funny about the test. Not the test itself or the way it was carried out, but the way Benny did it."

"I see. So you think—?"

"That he has his own reasons for pretending to be useless and of no account. The obvious possibility is that he committed some kind of crime."

Basch shook his head. "There are no unsolved crimes, Mr. Jennings. You know that. Any criminals around, we know about."

"That's if you established the crimes as crimes."

Basch was quite definite. "With transmitterless TV, crime has just about stopped," he said. "Not crimes of passion, of course. Not crime on impulse. But crime for profit, yes. There just isn't any profit."

"I don't think you've seen the significant point in this affair, sergeant. Benny is over a hundred. And if he faked the test he had yesterday, *he also faked the one he had seventy years ago.*"

"Maybe I'm just a dumb cop. I still don't get it."

"If Benny had to cover up seventy years ago, the crime, if any, must have occurred before that."

Basch snapped his fingers. "Of course. You mean it was so long ago we didn't have TTV?"

"Not exactly, but certainly before the present position was established—when everybody knows that crime doesn't pay, and doesn't try to buck the odds."

Basch grinned boyishly. "If this old guy has got away with something for more than seventy years, I say good luck to him."

"That's not the point, is it? Don't you want to find out the truth? I do. I can't understand how Benny got round those tests."

"Surely if you gave me the test, and I wanted a low rating for some reason, all I'd have to do would be answer most of the questions wrong?"

"No. It's not a straight yes-no questionnaire. The questions dovetail, and often in checking afterwards I have to take several answers together. Inconsistency shows up, and a deliberate attempt to fool the test would fail."

"But you've just said—"

"There's one way it could be done. I could do it, because I know the test—remember the answers."

"Is that possible?"

"Yes, because you don't so much remember a lot of individual, meaningless answers as a pattern. You know the kind of relationships you're supposed to be able to see, and the kind that are supposed to be beyond you. You know when to answer correctly, when to leave a blank space and when to write gibberish."

"That would take a pretty clever man, wouldn't it?"

"Yes."

There was something significant in his glance, and once more light dawned on Basch. "You mean this Rice character rates Rebirth, but can't collect because he's pretending to be a moron?"

"Exactly."

Basch became serious. "If you're right—if there was a crime—it must be pretty serious. Nothing less than murder. Well, we'll soon find out."

"How?"

"Check back over Rice's life and see if anybody around him ever died. Then check all the deaths to make sure they were what they seemed to be."

"Can you establish that now?"

"Oh, sure."

"How?"

"In about a million ways. Suppose you shot me here and now. All the glass, metal, wood and plastic in the room would shiver and record the shot in their molecular structure. In ten years' time it could be established that a shot was fired, and the date could be fixed within a month. Likewise, the fumes would settle, dust would cover that, and even when the place was cleaned there'd be strata, just like in rock, and a careful examination might uncover the gas deposit. Might—wouldn't swear to that. Likewise, if I fell on the floor, that would make its record— 'Course, for every fact we want about the incident we want, we find a thousand we don't want about other incidents, other occasions—"

"You mean, once you have reason to look in a place, you find out everything that ever happened there?"

"Something like that. 'Course, we have to interpret what we find."

"And you're going to check back on Benny?"

"Well, that's what you wanted, isn't it?"

Jennings wasn't so sure now. He had nothing against Old Benny, and there was something inhuman about a method of detection which could find out what had happened in a room years ago, even if all the people who had been present were dead—

Marita climbed the stairs to her flat slowly, wondering if she was a fool. She hadn't been at the Blue Moon since the night she met Benny there. But who was she fooling?

If you were an unsuccessful call-girl, it was easy to decide to be virtuous and turn your back on it. But, if you made a far better living at it than you could possibly make at anything else, it wasn't so easy.

On the door was a note from Mrs. Gersteiner:

Man calling himself J. S. has called twice.

J. S. was John Silver, the detective she had hired to find Benny Rice. Perhaps he had something to report. But she wasn't so sure now that she wanted to find Benny Rice. There was something decidedly peculiar about Benny.

She went into the bathroom and turned the tap. As she undressed she found it hard to resist the impulse to call Silver.

In the bath she soaped herself luxuriously. And suddenly she realized that she felt cleaner than she had for years.

As she realized once again what Benny meant to her she jumped out of the bath, scattering water in all directions like a dog shaking itself dry, and ran through to the phone.

The shiny cream phone slipped in her soapy hands, but she got Silver.

"Miss Herbert? I got news for you. I'll come over right away."

"Can't you tell me over the phone?"

"That depends. You want me to say it over the phone?"

She hesitated. "No. Come up here."

She dropped the phone in its cradle. Going back to the bathroom, she showered and dried herself.

When the buzzer went, she hadn't even begun to dress. Silver must be the world's fastest mover. She slipped a dress over her shoulders and pushed her feet into mules.

Silver came in looking her up and down appreciatively. "This job I like," he said.

"Spill it," said Marita briefly.

Letting his eyes play over her like a fire hose, Silver spoke absently but to the point. "Rice had his mind made up when he went to his apartment. That was obvious afterwards. If he was to shake me and everybody else, he'd have to go fast and far. So I assumed he'd gone straight to the airfield and took the first flight to anywhere."

"Benny wouldn't do anything as obvious as that."

"Wouldn't he? Lady, there are times when being subtle just gives people a chance to put a rope around your neck. The only answer to TTV is not being around when the cops start to get interested in you."

"The police aren't involved in this."

"No? Looked to me as if this guy Rice thought they might be. Otherwise why run like a scalded cat?"

"Did you have something to say?" Marita inquired.

"Sure. He took the first flight to anywhere. Florida, first stop Washington. I guessed he'd jump ship at Washington and had a man check. He did. He got on a flight for—wait for it—Florida."

"Huh?"

"Oh, he's no fool. If you're on a flight to Florida and jump ship, the last place anybody will expect you to go is Florida. Only if you're being tailed at the time, it's no good."

"So Benny Rice is in Florida?"

"He's living just outside Miami. I know where, but I haven't had anybody watch him."

"Why not?"

"He's not going anywhere. Either he was traced to Miami, in which case he can be traced from there, or he wasn't, and he'd be crazy to move."

Silver's aggressive assurance irritated Marita. He spoke and acted as if he had a private line to God. Nevertheless, she had to ask.

"Why would he be crazy to move?"

"When the cops are looking for somebody, they check transport. Airfields, seaports, bus and train depots. Anybody who keeps running gets caught. You're smart, you find a hole and pull it in after you."

"Suppose Benny Rice thinks one step further than you?"

"Then he isn't in Miami. Say, lady, what's an old guy like that to you?"

He had moved close as if merely for emphasis. Without appearing to move fast his hands were on her waist.

Marita shook herself impatiently, without managing to break his grasp. "Get out," she said dispassionately. "Behave yourself or get out."

"Who are you fooling, lady? Think I'd work for anybody without finding out about her?"

"I hired you to do a certain job. Apart from that, as far as I'm concerned, you're dead."

"I could come alive."

Marita broke loose and in the same movement clawed a tiny gun from a drawer in the table. "Out," she said. She had shown neither fear, interest nor disgust.

Silver could still grin. "You owe me a lot of money. You don't have to pay it."

"I prefer to."

His grin faded. "O.K. But what's wrong with me? Am I losing my fatal fascination?"

"I don't know. I never saw you with any."

Surprise and disbelief grew in his eyes. "You're in love with the old guy," he murmured. "Well, can you beat that?"

"What's that address?" Marita asked.

Marita waved again and started to wade toward him. Her silver swimsuit gleamed in the afternoon sun.

Benny watched her with the cool pleasure of his years. He

could hardly be a hot lover at his time of life. He could take pleasure in the perfection of her proportions; however, he could have taken just as much pleasure in her beauty if she had been some other man's wife or mistress.

Water glistened on her golden skin as she dropped on the sand beside him. "Why don't you swim, Benny?"

"I think I've been peeped," he murmured.

She seized his arms and held tight as though by her own determination she could ward off the rest of the world. "They'll never find us," she said.

"On the contrary," said Benny mildly, "they're sure to find us if you stay with me, Marita. If you really want to help me, please leave me."

"No. Never."

Benny sighed. The certainty of defeat was on him, or he would have tried something. You could always get rid of a woman—couldn't you?

"Marita," he said gently, sympathetically. "I don't love you, you know."

"No," she said bitterly. "You're the only man I ever wanted to love me so, naturally you wouldn't."

"You're too young to think like that, Marita. I'm four times your age, and I think a lot more of the world than you do."

"Benny, why don't you tell me? Can't I help you? Can't I do anything?"

"Yes. You can go home. Then maybe I'll have a chance."

"Why do you talk like that? What harm am I doing?"

"That detective of yours knew I was in Miami. When they start looking for me they'll find him. They'll find out that you went to Miami. They'll look for you and find me."

"But we left Miami."

"Yes. But we're still so near that if they start searching in Miami and really mean to find us, they'll find us. And if we take a trip on a plane, ship, bus or train, they'll find us."

"Benny, what did you do? What'll it mean if you're caught?"

"Death," he said simply.

She caught her breath. She wanted to cry, but it had been so long since she cried she had forgotten how.

"I still love life," he said. "I'm old, but I'm sound. If they left me alone, I could have another twenty years, easily. Maybe thirty. I could live longer than the whole life of your life, Marita—if they let me. But I must be getting old, old in spirit, or I'd fight. I'd give you the slip and find myself another hole to hide in."

"You won't?" she said sharply. "Promise you won't?"

He shook his head. "I won't promise, Marita. I should go on fighting—and once I can collect what moral courage I have left, I will go on fighting. I'll beat them yet—"

A hand fell on his shoulder. Marita screamed, and through her scream a voice said: "Benjamin Rice, I charge you with the murder of Ralph Charles Coleman."

Benny looked up and smiled.

"Allow me to tell you, Mr. Rice," said the lawyer frostily, "that that attitude cuts no ice. I have been retained to defend you. I shall do so to the best of my ability, whatever insults you heap on me."

"I expect you will," said Benny, "since you're prepared to accept in payment for your services the earnings of a prostitute."

Kensel breathed deeply. "Considering what Miss Herbert is doing for you," he said, "that remark reveals the lowest possible moral character."

"It reveals the truth."

Kensel swallowed. "Rice, can't you realize that girl . . . that girl *loves* you—" He had managed to say it, though the effort made his face pink with embarrassment.

"Apparently I'm not to be allowed to forget it," Benny said.

He was fighting now. It was too late to run; he had nothing but his wits left. First, he had to try to get rid of this man.

"Marita Herbert is one of the finest women I know," said Kensel. "It passes my comprehension how she could be so deceived in a man like you. But since she feels as she does, I am prepared to try to believe there is some good in you."

"That's big of you," said Benny. "I don't want you, Kensel. I'm going to plead guilty."

"You're not allowed to plead guilty."

"I'm going to conduct my own defense, then."

"That's your privilege."

"So why don't you get out?"

"For Miss Herbert's sake I am going to do my best for you. I hope you go to the gas chamber, but I am going to do my best to see that you don't."

He was, too. Benny was silent, planning a new tack. This one was no good. Marita had done a good job on Kensel. If she hadn't won him over to Benny's side, she'd won him over to hers.

"Since I was goaded into speaking plainly just now," said the lawyer, his pink cheeks even pinker, "I may as well say one thing more. Your crime in murdering a man like Ralph Charles Coleman twenty years ago—as I have no doubt you did—is such a particularly beastly one that I wish I were prosecuting you. You knew what you were doing. For a mere three thousand dollars, you silenced óne of the great voices of the century."

"He was an old bore," said Benny reflectively.

"The greatest authority on malaria in the world . . . the man responsible for more saving of life than all—"

"They'll never convict me, and you know it," said Benny.

"On the contrary, there's a better than even chance that they will. Although the police were quite satisfied at the time that Coleman shot himself, the recent examination of the room shows quite clearly that he fell and lay still and was shot *afterwards*. There can't be any doubt about that, and you can't explain it."

"Why should I explain it?"

"Because, if you don't, you'll be convicted. How can a man commit suicide if he falls first and *then* gets shot?"

Benny shrugged. "He got up, shot himself and fell down again."

"No. The evidence in Coleman's study, which hasn't been used since, is absolutely clear. There was only one fall. And afterwards he was shot. He was shot as he lay on the ground. He couldn't have done that himself."

No, he couldn't, Benny thought. He didn't. I did it. Funny how they haven't found out a dozen other queer and significant things about that day twenty years ago, yet they're absolutely sure of that.

These marvelous police methods couldn't be so marvelous after all. Twenty years ago the police had been convinced of one lie. Now they were convinced of another. In another twenty years, maybe they'd find out the truth.

The jailer spoke from the cell door. "Miss Herbert to see you, Rice."

"You can go," said Benny to the lawyer. He couldn't bring himself to be cruel to Marita, and if Kensel saw them together he might see through Benny's act.

"She wants me to stay. She wants to talk to you with me present."

Marita came in like a ray of sunlight. Another defense broke down in Benny. Let it go. He wasn't getting anywhere with his efforts to get rid of Kensel, anyway.

Benny took her hands and smiled. Beside him, Kensel choked at the sudden change in him.

"Three-quarters of the press is on our side," Marita said eagerly. "They say you're over a hundred and harmless. There's no suggestion that you committed any crime in the last twenty years. They say— Benny, I still can't believe it. I don't believe you ever killed anybody. You couldn't."

"But I did," said Benny gently. "Marita, I'm glad you're here. I've been trying to disgust Kensel so that he'll drop the case. But he won't. So let's try something else. Marita, you want what I want, don't you?"

"Yes."

"I want to die."

"No!" Marita whispered, while Kensel stared dazedly at this old leopard who had suddenly changed his spots. He was kind and gentle with Marita.

"You can't," Marita said with more conviction. "You don't. You love life. You still love life."

"Yes," Benny admitted, "if I'm allowed to live it my own way, in freedom. Marita, you know I'm not going to be acquitted. Once the police started tracing the history of Benny Rice, I was finished. They traced my life to the time I became caretaker to Coleman, and naturally, just in passing, they had another look into his suicide. Twenty years ago Coleman wrote letters and made phone calls that convinced people he was going to commit suicide. And while I was around I was able to direct the investigations so that the official conclusions came out the way I wanted them. But what can you do when the police can go back to the scene of the crime and from the vibrations damped by wood, metal and textiles twenty years ago, reconstruct what happened then?"

"*Some* of what happened twenty years before," said Kensel.

There was such significance in his tone that Marita stared at him, puzzled, and Benny with sudden foreboding.

"I had only seen you acting like a first-degree heel, or I'd have guessed long ago," the lawyer said. "You're Coleman, of course."

Benny had seen it coming and decided not to deny it. "Yes. And *now* do you see why I want to die? I'm Coleman. A great man, you said, Kensel. But murder's the same whether a useless old moron like Benny Rice kills Coleman or Coleman kills the useless old moron. It's the same crime —homicide. I've had twenty years as Benny Rice, and I'd do anything for twenty more. But if I'm to die, or worse still, go to prison, I'd rather stay Benny Rice."

Marita was frowning. "It's nothing to me who you are. I knew you as Benny Rice, and I don't care which you are."

"I know you don't, Marita. But I do. Kensel, will you get me the death penalty—knowing that's what I want?"

"I'd like to get you Rebirth," Kensel said quietly.

Marita jumped convulsively.

Benny laughed. "No, thank you. To get me Rebirth you'd have to get me off first, by showing there wasn't any murder twenty years ago. Then you'd have to show I was Coleman, not Rice. Then you'd have to—"

"Just a minute," said Kensel sharply. "I've just thought of something. If we can show you're Coleman, not Rice, the motive for murder disappears. You didn't kill Rice for your own three thousand dollars—a tiny fraction of your bank balance. You've got to show you're Coleman."

"On the contrary," Benny said, "I've got to stay Rice. Rice was a moron, by any reckoning. The charge against him can't be anything more than a brutal, simple crime. The case against Coleman—against me—is that I formulated a complicated plot, writing letters and phoning people falsifying all the records relating to myself, with the object of having the dead body of Rice taken for mine. It would also follow, since he was exactly the same age as me, and since I employed him weeks before, and since his face was changed to mine and mine to his, that there was a long-standing murder plot to kill a poor old derelict and substitute his body for mine, so that I could disappear."

Marita was looking lost and unhappy. In the last few minutes, somehow, she had lost Benny. The strange love affair between her and Benny had been unequal in many ways, but it had seemed to balance. The affair between her and Ralph Charles Coleman, who might have been a great man but who sounded an old bore, as Benny said, didn't balance at all.

Kensel was looking unhappy too. "Well, why *did* you do it?" he demanded.

Benny considered. "For two pins I'd tell you," he said.

But Kensel knew he was lying. Kensel knew he would never tell anybody.

Kensel was wrong. There came a moment in Benny's trial when the possibility that he was Coleman and not Benny Rice was mentioned. There came a moment when it looked as if he might get life imprisonment instead of death.

There came the moment when the judge asked if Benny had anything to say before he passed sentence.

The verdict was guilty; the sentence could only be imprisonment or death.

"Yes," said Benny. "Yes, I have."

There was a murmur in court. Throughout the trial he had remained as inarticulate as a man with his VTC rating might be expected to be. Now he spoke strongly and clearly and looked like his own son.

"The possibility that I might be Coleman and not Rice has been mentioned," Benny said. "Nothing came of it, because it was so manifestly ridiculous. Is it ridiculous now?"

The murmur in court grew to a roar. Everyone knew Rice's I.Q. and VTC. This wasn't Benny Rice speaking.

"I am going to tell you," said Ralph Charles Coleman, "why I killed Benny Rice.

"I did not want Rebirth.

"I wanted to live my life to the full and die when it was over. When a man goes for Rebirth, does he survive? No. He remembers nothing of his previous life, of his own personal history. He becomes another person.

"I didn't want to become another person. I wanted to live until I died. Many people are like me, feel as I do, but they are silenced by pride in being thought worthy of Rebirth, and fear of the eternal night. Rebirth is a postponement. Even if the thing they become remembers nothing of the thing they were, at least there is no ending—yet. They surrender their lives at seventy, at eighty, instead of risking death at any moment if they chose to try to live longer.

"At eighty I was subject to increasing pressure to accept Rebirth. I didn't want it. I wanted the twenty years I've had since then, the twenty or thirty more I could have. But Ralph Charles Coleman had no choice. He was too important, too valuable. The world couldn't afford to lose his valuable brain. The pressure was approaching a point where it would become compulsion.

"I had to escape. I was selfish. I didn't care about the

value to the world of Ralph Charles Coleman. I was concerned about my value to myself. I wanted to go on being myself.

"And the only way I could do so was to cease being myself.

"My plans worked well, as you'll agree. If only people had left poor harmless old Benny Rice alone, they'd have worked perfectly. Knowing I had no natural ability in music I went to Musicosmos as a caretaker. Completely lacking in talent, how could I give myself away? But unfortunately one woman liked me, another loved me. And things happened, and it was discovered that twenty years ago the man who died wasn't the man who fired the shot?"

He looked straight at the judge. There was complete silence in court.

And at that moment, of all moments, a picture of what had happened twenty years ago flashed through his mind.

Old Benny had died, and he had shot him, but he hadn't killed him. It was after Benny died of a seizure that the brilliant Ralph Charles Coleman conceived his fantastically complicated scheme to steal his own life from the Rebirth Institute. Only a doctor could have done it. Many things had had to be done—many things had been done. But the only part of it which had been found out, even now, was that the fall had preceded the shot.

Coleman could be acquitted. Even now he could be acquitted. He could have a fuller investigation made, and this time, not merely looking for evidence that a suicide was murder, the investigators would find that there had been neither, and that a dead man had been shot.

But that wouldn't be acquittal. That way led to Rebirth for Coleman.

"I have made this statement," he said, "because imprisonment would be worse to me than Rebirth. But I must suffer imprisonment, Rebirth or death. Society would not let me go free, to die my own death. I killed a man to escape Rebirth. The crime still keeps me safe from it. So since it must be imprisonment or death, may I ask for mercy?

"May I ask for death?"

There was silence for a long time. And then the judge granted his wish.

The wonder didn't quite last nine days. After the execution, the legal question whether Coleman could be convicted for the murder of Rice after being convicted, as Rice, of the murder of Coleman, became academic.

It was decided that the verdict was wrong.

And after that everybody wanted to forget about it.

Marita was married within three weeks to Kensel, much to everybody's surprise, including their own. He was a little old for her; but then, he was sixty years younger than Benny.

Everyone still thought of him as Benny. Indeed, one reason why the hubbub soon died was the nasty taste which was left behind by the case. Some felt that even a man like Ralph Charles Coleman should be allowed to live his own life if he wanted to, and not have Rebirth thrust upon him. Some felt a man shouldn't have to kill to avoid Rebirth. Nearly everybody, sympathetic or unsympathetic, felt that the whole business undermined the name and fame of a great man.

It was much better to think of him as Benny Rice.

At the Rebirth Institute Dr. Martin looked at the sleeping boy and recalled with wonder the shambling old idiot who had certainly had him fooled. Must have been a pretty good actor, the old boy.

Betty Rogers came and stood at his shoulder.

"He's new, isn't he?" she said—she could speak now. Also she had begun to care how she looked, and in a white nylon dress, she looked all right.

"Yes."

"What's his name?"

"Dick Herman." Or Benny Rice, or Ralph Charles Coleman, Martin thought. Poor Old Benny, who didn't want Rebirth but couldn't escape it.

"Why has he been asleep so much longer than everybody else?"

"We weren't sure he'd be allowed to stay. You see, Betty, we wanted him here, as we want all of you, but if people have done certain things, they're not allowed to stay. Dick was brought here, because we wanted him so much, and because somebody thought, being such a nice boy, he couldn't really have done what he was supposed to have done, after all."

And *that* was quite a nice allegory to explain how Old Benny had been brought from the gas chamber, unconscious but certainly not dead, and put through the Rebirth process still thinking that he'd died in the gas chamber—if you could put it like that.

"How could they think he had done something if he hadn't?" Betty asked.

The questions of a Reborn child were quite as difficult to answer as those of an ordinary one. But Martin accepted the challenge.

"He wanted everybody to think he had done it, because he didn't want to stay here."

The police had eventually decided that after Benny Rice died of natural causes, Coleman had evolved a brilliant scheme which won him twenty more years of life and nearly got him executed at the end of it. But there were red faces all round at the way Benny Rice had not merely been arrested but had been convicted of a murder when there hadn't really been a murder at all, and if there had been it would have been the other way round.

Martin wondered daringly whether the powers that be had simply decided that there hadn't been a murder because a man like Coleman couldn't be allowed to go to the gas chamber merely for putting a creature like Benny Rice out of its presumed misery. But such thoughts were dangerous.

"Why didn't he want to stay here?" Betty asked.

"He didn't know what it was like," said Martin patiently, "or he wouldn't have minded."

"How do you know? Didn't I want to stay here either?"

"You didn't mind coming here. Look, Dick's wakening up."

Betty bent over him like a child mother. "You'll like it here, Dick," she said soothingly.

Under his breath, Martin bet he would. He wouldn't mind marrying Betty Rogers himself in a year or two.

But then, the Rebirth Institute didn't actually fix marriages. Marriages were made in heaven.

With material supplied by the Rebirth Institute, of course.

"You can't talk yet," said Betty, "but we'll teach you to talk. Oh, Dr. Martin, look what a nice smile he has. I think I'm going to like him."

In heaven, something was made.

66-5-2